DEATH ON THE RIVIERA

JOHN BUDE

With an Introduction by
Martin Edwards

BRITISH LIBRARY

This edition published 2016 by
The British Library
96 Euston Road
London NW1 2DB

Originally published in 1952 by Macdonald & Co.

Cataloguing in Publication Data
A catalogue record for this book is
available from the British Library

ISBN 978 0 7123 5637 4

Typeset by Tetragon, London
Printed and bound by CPI Group
(UK) Ltd, Croydon CR0 4YY

CONTENTS

INTRODUCTION

Death on the Riviera combines a lively police hunt for a gang engaged on a currency racket with a neatly contrived murder mystery. John Bude teams his good-natured but determined series detective, Inspector Meredith of the C.I.D., with an eager young sidekick, Acting-Sergeant Freddy Strang, and sends them off to the South of France to work on a joint operation with the local police. The French investigators believe that the gang is being run by an Englishman, and evidence suggests that the counterfeit thousand franc notes now flooding the Riviera are the work of a skilled English engraver, "Chalky" Cobbett.

The book opens with a casual encounter between the detectives and a fellow Englishman, Bill Dillon, who is also heading for the Riviera. Soon their paths cross again. Bill is heading for the Villa Paloma in Menton, a lovely town on the Mediterranean, close to the Franco-Italian border. The owner of the villa is Nesta Hedderwick, a wealthy widow who divides her time between Britain and France, and who has acquired an assortment of house guests. They include her niece, Dilys, the mysterious Tony Shenton, his girlfriend Kitty Linden, and an artist called Paul Latour. Before long, it becomes evident that more than one of the occupants of the Villa Paloma has something to hide, and Bill's arrival there proves to be the catalyst for murder.

Death on the Riviera was first published in 1952, at a point when John Bude was at the height of his powers. He had been publishing crime novels for almost two decades, at a rate of slightly more than one book a year, and the assurance with which he blends the plot-lines in this book reflects his experience and confidence as a writer. The characters are well-defined, the atmosphere of life on the Riviera is nicely evoked, and the device employed by the killer to fool the police pleasingly ingenious. Above all, Bude focuses on telling a good story, and he keeps the action flowing from start to finish.

Setting mattered to Bude, and he began his career with mysteries located in attractive parts of England such as Cornwall, the Lake District, the Sussex Downs, and Cheltenham. After the Second World War, at a time of rationing and austerity, he recognized that readers hungered for a touch of the exotic, and *Death on the Riviera* was the result. But who exactly was John Bude?

Until recently, little had been written about this once-popular author. He merited an entry in the first edition of *Twentieth Century Crime and Mystery Writers*, published in 1980, but this was dropped from subsequent editions, as if to signal that his time had passed. Happily, publication of his first three detective stories in the British Library's series of Crime Classics has resulted in excellent sales, and rekindled interest in the author as well as his work. Thanks to information kindly supplied to me by his daughter, Jennifer, it is possible to fill in some gaps in public knowledge of this underestimated writer.

John Bude was a pen-name for Ernest Carpenter Elmore (1901-57), who turned to writing crime fiction after starting out under his own name with books such as the improbably titled *The Steel Grubs* (1928). His early mysteries were published by Skeffington, a small firm which catered mainly for the libraries; as a result, first editions are now very hard to find, and command high prices when they do come on to the market. After a brief spell with another library-oriented publisher, Hale, he moved to Cassell, and then to Macdonald, indicating that he was climbing the ladder in terms of sales potential. He did not manage to gain election to the prestigious Detection Club, which was presided over by Dorothy L. Sayers, and highly selective (and sometimes idiosyncratic) in its recruitment policy, but he was sufficiently well-regarded by his peers to be invited by John Creasey to become one of the founder members of the Crime Writers' Association in 1953. On one occasion he told Jennifer that he reckoned he earned "sixpence a word", and his earnings were sufficient to enable him to write full-time.

He had acquired a taste for travelling around Europe as a young man, and in later life he seized every available opportunity to take his wife, Betty, and Jennifer with him to the Continent, and in particular to France, a country he loved. Betty would drive them all the way to the Riviera (Bude himself never learned to drive) and their favourite destination—this will come as no surprise to readers of this novel—was Menton. On other occasions they stayed at Le Touquet (hence his *A Telegram from Le Touquet*, published in 1956), or in Paris; he was particularly fond of Montmartre, and enjoyed going to the opera and ballet.

Jennifer remembers her father making notes, and collecting local literature, as they travelled around. A sociable man, who enjoyed chatting with the people he met on his travels—even the most casual conversation may provide a spark of inspiration for a novelist—he was equally content to sit in cafes and watch the world go by, while letting his imagination roam. When he returned home, he would write every morning, and spend his afternoons getting exercise—typically, gardening, walking, or playing tennis. After an early supper, he would resume his writing until 9 p.m., when he listened to the news. He wrote his stories in hand before typing them, using four fingers and a thumb. Industrious as he was, he would take a day off if the weather was good, and go to the beach or indulge in a little tourism. Once he had delivered a novel to his publishers, he would take a holiday before starting a new book. There was every chance that the holiday itself would plant fresh ideas in his fertile mind—and result in a book such as *Death on the Riviera*.

Martin Edwards
www.martinedwardsbooks.com

CHAPTER I

ASSIGNMENT ON THE MIDI

I

BILL DILLON turned up the collar of his tweed overcoat and thrust his hands deeper into his pockets. Five a.m. of a frosty morning in late February, he thought, was a devil of a time to be dumped off a boat on to a confoundedly draughty quayside. There were about a dozen other cars lined up in the customs-yard awaiting the attention of the little group of officials, who were now sorting through their papers under a naked light-bulb near the passport office. The night-ferry, from whose maw the train had already been disgorged in the direction of Paris, loomed up, gently swaying, against the starlit sky. A few strings of street lamps and a score or so of lighted windows were all that was visible of the shattered and martyred town beyond the oil-dark waters of the harbour.

Bill lit a cigarette and began to pace up and down, his footsteps echoing on the *pavé,* his thoughts on the rove. He was thinking back to that night, nearly ten years ago, when he'd last set eyes on Dunkirk; so many splintered impressions that stabbed out in his memory like gun-flashes. The red, roaring inferno that was the town; the spangled web of tracer shells slung over the sea and beaches; the orange blossoming of bombs; the noise; the heat; the indifference to danger that stemmed from an exhaustion that had almost deadened fear. In the maelstrom of defeat he'd no longer been an individual. Just a worn, obedient cog in a relentless machine—Lance-Corporal Dillon of the 6th Southshires—one of the dust-specks that added up to the miracle of Dunkirk.

There was a shuffle of feet at his side, a discreet cough.

"Anything to declare, M'sieur?"

Bill came out of his reverie with a jerk.

"No—nothing."

The sleepy-eyed official stuck his head through the car door and flashed his torch around the interior. Then he opened the rear door of the saloon, flicked back the clasps of Bill's unlocked suitcase and dabbled around with an expert hand. He moved round and tried the handle of the boot.

"Please, M'sieur."

Bill pulled out a bunch of keys and unlocked the boot. It contained the usual paraphernalia—a couple of pairs of shoes that wouldn't go in his case; a rucksack; an old military gas-cape; a half-gallon can of oil; dusters; cleaning-rags; and foot-pump. The *douanier* eyed the collection, nodded, and carefully closed the lid. It was all very polite and very perfunctory.

"*Merci, M'sieur.*"

"O.K.?" asked Bill.

The Frenchman beamed broadly.

"*Oui, oui, M'sieur*—O.K.! O.K.!" He flicked a hand towards the invisible hinterland of France. "*En avant, M'sieur! Et bon voyage.*"

"Thanks," said Bill.

Inwardly he heaved a sigh of relief. It was not that he had anything to declare, but there was one object aboard the car that might have caused comment. And once interest had been aroused an explanation might have been demanded. And at that ungodly hour of the morning Bill felt disinclined to discuss technicalities with a man whose knowledge of English was obviously limited, and who, in any case, would fail to grasp the finer details of his exposition.

II

Once off the quayside Bill realized that the small hours of a bitter February morning was not the ideal time to weave one's way out of Dunkirk. Presumably there *had* been roads between the rubble heaps and undoubtedly, before the holocaust, they'd led somewhere. But now there was nothing but a maze of treacherous, pot-holed tracks meandering aimlessly between a network of railway-lines and flattened buildings.

After a bit, utterly flummoxed, Bill braked up and studied his map. The first sizeable place on his route was Cassel. But how the devil was he to break out of this shambles on to the appropriate road? So far he hadn't noticed a single sign-post. He remembered that road all right. The long hellish strip of *pavé* down which the disintegrated but undaunted B.E.F. had jerked its way towards salvation. Sitting in his pre-war but still serviceable Stanmobile Ten something of the desperate hopelessness of that nightmare returned to haunt him. The scars of memory never really healed, he thought.

There was a screech of brakes and a small black "sports" slithered to a stop beside him. A head thrust itself out from beneath the hood.

"*Pardon, M'sieur... à Cassel?*"

Bill, no linguist himself, was swift to recognize a fellow sufferer. He chuckled:

"Don't ask me! I'm heading for the same road. Not a damned signpost anywhere."

"English, eh? Got a map?"

"Sure," said Bill.

"Same here. Let's take a look at the darn thing in our headlamps."

Bill glanced at the man who joined him on the road—tall, athletic, aquiline features, something decisive in speech and movement that marked him down as a man of action. A reliable fellow in a tight corner, he thought. His companion, hatless, in belted raincoat, a muffler slung round his neck, was far younger though equally well-built. He seemed to treat the elder man with the respect that was due from a subordinate to a superior.

Barely had they gone into a huddle, however, when an early workman in a shabby overcoat and the ubiquitous blue beret, evidently intrigued by the set-up, jumped from his bicycle and crossed over to them.

"*Est ce que je vous aide, Messieurs?*"

Bill explained in halting French that they were anxious to get on to the road to Cassel.

"Ah! that is simple, M'sieur. Follow me. I will ride ahead. You keep me always in your headlights."

Ten minutes later the good-hearted fellow, who had been pedalling like a madman, slowed down and indicated with a violent wave of his arm the route they were to take. Bill leaned out and yelled his thanks, glancing back to see if the second car was following. A few hundred yards farther up the road it drew abreast and for a brief time the two cars ran level.

"O.K.?" shouted Bill.

"Yes, thanks."

"Where are you making for?"

"Paris!" came the answering yell. "And you?"

"Rheims first stop. After that down the Rhone valley to the Cote d'Azur."

"Well, I hope it keeps fine for you. Good hunting."

"Thanks. And the same to you."

With a lifting drone the little black "sports" suddenly drew ahead and a few seconds later vanished behind an enormous *camion* that was lumbering with infuriating complacency down the very centre of the highway.

III

Detective-Inspector Meredith of the C.I.D. turned to his companion and observed sardonically:

"For Pete's sake relax, m'lad. I'm not going to hit anything."

"It's this right-of the-road rule, sir. Can't get used to it."

"You will... after another eight hundred miles."

"By the way, sir—what was the idea of telling that bloke we were heading for Paris?"

"Professional discretion, Strang. We're over here on a job, remember. No point in advertising our destination."

"But damn it all, sir, he's also making for the Riviera. We'll probably run against him. Look a bit fishy, won't it?"

Meredith laughed.

"There's about fifty miles of that gilded coastline, Strang. Devil of a coincidence if we *did* meet again. In any case I doubt if he'd recognize us."

"Decent sort of bloke, sir. Useful in a Rugger scrum, eh? I wager I'd recognize *him* in a Derby Day crowd."

"You'd be out on your ear if you couldn't," retorted Meredith bluntly. "Don't forget, you've been trained to observe. I may be wrong but I've an idea that you've more than an average eye for faces. That's why the A.C. let you off the leash."

"Thanks, sir. But I wish the deuce you'd—"

Meredith broke in:

"You're wondering what it's all about, eh? O.K., Sergeant. I reckon it's time that I put you wise." Meredith took one hand from the driving-wheel, yanked a wallet from the inside pocket of his sports jacket and slapped it down on Strang's knee. "There's a photo in the first flap. Take it out and have a good look at it." His curiosity aroused, Strang did as he was told and studied the print closely. He recognized it at once as an official photograph from the Rogues' Gallery at the Yard—the regulation two profiles and a full-face. "Know who it is?"

"No, sir."

"Well, that uninspiring phiz belongs to a little runt of a chap called Tommy Cobbett—'Chalky' Cobbett to his friends, on account of his dead white complexion. One of the world's great artists, Strang."

"He's a painter, sir?"

"Not exactly. He's an engraver, m'lad—an engraver of notes."

"You mean he's a forger?"

"I do. And one of the finest we've ever come against. He was pulled in just before the War after flooding the West End with spurious fivers.

He got a six year stretch and came out about four years back. For a time he hung around his old haunts in the East End and, with our usual professional optimism, we thought he'd gone straight. Then eighteen months ago he vanished." Meredith clicked his fingers. "Phut! like that. Well, we knew darn well that 'Chalky' hadn't gone into purdah for nothing. We felt absolutely certain that somewhere or other he was 'working' again. But the point was where and for whom?"

"And now you've got the answer, eh, sir?"

"Six weeks back we had information from the police at Nice that a top-line currency racket was being worked along the Riviera towns. You know the set-up? English visitors anxious to exceed their hundred quid travel allowance. Obliging Wide Boys equally anxious to help 'em out. Normal rate of exchange about 980 francs to the pound. Black Market rate, say, 780. Profit to the Wide Boys about 200 francs for every pound changed. Easy money, Strang, even if you don't consider the profits spectacular."

"But 'Chalky' Cobbett," asked Strang still groping, "where does he come in? I don't get it."

Meredith chuckled.

"O.K. I'm coming to him. But there are a few other details I want you to cotton on to first. These currency blokes accept cheques on London banks, see? They're forced to because, as you know, you can only take five quid's worth of English notes out of the country. The Wide Boys have a grape-vine method of getting these cheques smuggled over to London and cashed as quickly as possible. So much for that. But the French police recently spotted a further complication in this racket. A flood of counterfeit thousand franc notes was appearing along the Riviera, and they soon traced some of these notes to our benighted countrymen who'd been diddling the Exchequer by their purchase of Black Market francs. In brief, the currency racketeers had been paying out their 780 francs to the pound in dud notes. Result, 980 francs to the pound profit, less overheads and, presumably, a rake-off for 'Chalky' Cobbett.

"But how the heck did the French cops know that 'Chalky' was responsible for the faked notes, sir?"

"They didn't. Nor did we at the start. As a matter of routine we got our forgery experts on to one of the specimen notes. And the experts recognized 'Chalky's' touch at once—microscopic details of craftsmanship that had turned up in all his previous work. That's why we're heading south on this cold and frosty morning, m'lad. We're going to snoop around and keep our eyes skinned and our ears wide open until we get a line on 'Chalky's' hide-out. We're over here at the request of the French police. So take a good look at that photo and keep on looking at it. I want you to get the details of 'Chalky's' dial fixed firmly in your mind, Strang. It's easier for me. I've seen 'Chalky' several times. Matter of fact I was responsible for pulling him in in '39."

Acting-Sergeant Freddy Strang carefully replaced the photo in his superior's wallet. So this was the mysterious assignment that had miraculously whipped him out of the London murk and was now speeding him south to the warmth and glitter of the Mediterranean. Damned decent of the Inspector to pick on him as his assistant. There wasn't another bloke in the C.I.D. he'd rather be working for. He said earnestly:

"I'll do my best not to let you down, sir."

"Sure of it, Sergeant. But I haven't quite filled in all the gaps. 'Chalky's' not our only concern. The French dicks have a very shrewd suspicion that the currency racket is being worked by an English gang or, at least, under English supervision. Point is these men may be known to us at the Yard. That's the second reason why we've been called in to help."

Freddy whistled.

"Quite a lot on our plate, eh, sir?"

Meredith nodded.

"Enough to keep you out of mischief anyway, young fellow. What's your particular weakness—wine, women or song?"

"Song, sir. It's the only vice I can run to on my present pay. Like to hear my rendering of 'Night and Day', sir? It was a smash-hit at the last Police Concert."

"God forbid!" breathed Meredith fervently.

CHAPTER II

THE VILLA PALOMA

I

NESTA HEDDERWICK, in a faded pink kimono, was sprawling in a wicker *chaise-longue* on the terrace of the Villa Paloma, sipping a tomato-juice. Behind her the walls of the villa, also a faded pink, were patterned with the fronded shadows of three enormous palm trees that rose from the exuberant vegetation of the steeply sloping garden. The sparkling air was sweet with the perfume of heliotrope and mimosa; the sky cloudless; the sea, glimpsed above the red roofs of the town below, an unbelievable sheet of blue.

But all this lavish beauty left Nesta unimpressed. It was too familiar, too unvarying. Her slightly bulbous eyes were fixed with unmitigated loathing on her glass of tomato-juice. She shuddered to think how many gallons of the vile stuff she'd decanted into her interior in the interests of her figure. But for the nagging accusations of her weighing-machine life might have been perfect. She'd money; one of the loveliest villas in Menton; a large and catholic collection of friends; splendid health; a sense of humour; and a virile capacity for enjoyment. Her husband, a successful but dyspeptic stockbroker, had died between the Wars of ptomaine poisoning. For the last twelve years Nesta had spent her time between Larkhill Manor in Gloucestershire and her villa in Menton. During these years of her widowhood she'd steadily and unhappily put on weight. She'd tried everything—from vibro-massage to eurhythmics; from skipping to Swedish drill; from Turkish baths to the most ghoulish forms of diet. With her faith unimpaired she'd lumbered excitedly from one cure to another. It was useless. As inexorably as a minute-hand the pointer of her bathroom scales crept round the dial. The moment was fast approaching—and Nesta was now quite prepared to admit it—when, abandoning all hope, she'd let Nature take the bit between her teeth. From then on, her figure could go to hell!

However, she was still vain enough to experience a stab of envy as her niece, Dilys, came through the french-windows to join her at the breakfast-table. For Dilys' slim, straight, brown-limbed figure was perfectly offset by the expensive simplicity of her frock. Nesta flipped a welcoming hand.

"Morning, darling. Sleep well?"

"Yes, thank you, auntie. I'm afraid I'm disgustingly late down."

"And you're not the only one!" snorted Nesta with a scowl. Then as Dilys began to sugar her grape-fruit she leaned forward and added confidentially: "You know, darling, she'll have to go! She will really. She's been with me far too long. She takes advantage of me. Don't you agree?"

Dilys sighed. Her aunt's companion, Miss Pilligrew, was an old bone of contention—a stringy rather pathetic little bone for whom Dilys felt profoundly sorry. In her opinion anybody who could have weathered the storm of her aunt's temperament for fifteen years was eligible for a gold medal. She said soothingly:

"Oh poor little Pilly—she does her best. I think she's rather a pet. You'd be absolutely lost without her."

"Personally," retorted Nesta, "I think she drinks!" Adding, with a sudden vicious turn of her head, "Ah! here you are at last. I've just been telling Dilys that you drink. Do you, Pilly?"

Miss Bertha Pilligrew granted her employer a wavering smile and sidled like a startled crab into her wicker-chair. She tittered with sycophant amusement:

"Ah, you will have your little joke, won't you, dear?" Adding brightly: "What a heavenly morning. It's very sinful of me to be down so late."

"It's very rude of you," corrected Nesta. "I wanted the *Tatler*. I particularly wanted the *Tatler*. And was Pilly at hand to fetch me the *Tatler*? You know damn well she wasn't! She was sleeping off the after effects of her overnight binge!" Miss Pilligrew's leathery hatchet face crinkled with delight at this malicious teasing. She tittered louder. Nesta went on: "Where's Tony? Has anybody seen Tony this morning?"

"I believe I heard him drive off in his car," ventured Dilys.

"Really! How long ago?"

"About half-past six according to my watch. I think the noise of the engine must have—"

Nesta broke in impatiently:

"Was Kitty with him?"

"She was not!" said a silky voice behind her. "Kitty on this occasion wasn't asked to go." A dark-eyed, raven-haired young woman with a provocative figure and considerable grace of movement strolled out on to the terrace. She was dressed in well-cut slacks, overtight silk jumper and scarlet wedge-heeled shoes. "'Morning, Mrs. Hedderwick. 'Morning, everybody. Am I late?"

"Abominably!" exclaimed Nesta. "Your own stupid fault if the coffee's cold." She snapped on her lighter and lit a cigarette which she'd already jabbed into a shagreen holder... "Pilly, go and fetch my *Tatler*. You've had quite enough breakfast."

"But... but, Nesta dear—"

"Don't argue. You eat too much."

"Yes, dear," murmured Miss Pilligrew, nobly bolting down her last mouthful of *croissant* and rising obediently. "I suppose you don't happen to know just where—?"

"No, I don't. It turned up with yesterday's mail. It's somewhere in the house. Don't be so darn helpless."

"No, dear."

The moment Miss Pilligrew had fluttered off, Nesta turned to Kitty.

"What's come over Tony? Odd, to say the least of it. Why this sudden passion for early rising?"

"Ask me another, Mrs. Hedderwick. It's the third time this week he's sneaked off before breakfast in the car."

"Umph! Secretive. I don't like it. Tony's a brute. He never tells me anything these days. You're a bad influence on him, Kitty."

Dilys smiled to herself. Poor Aunt Nesta. Tony Shenton was one of the many improvident young men upon whom, since her husband's death, she'd lavished her maternal solicitude. One of her "dear boys" as she collectively called them. Six months ago Tony had turned up from heaven knew where for a long week-end and stayed on ever since. With his slick charm and overwhelming bounce, Dilys detested him. He seemed to have usurped the place in her aunt's affections that should rightly have been hers. Since her parents had been tragically killed in an air-raid during the War, Aunt Nesta had become her legal guardian. Now that Dilys had left her finishing-school in Switzerland the Villa Paloma was, in effect, her home.

The strange thing was that nobody knew why Tony had been invited in the first place. When Dilys asked her aunt where she'd first met him, she shut up like a clam. But she made no effort to conceal her adoration for Tony. Dilys, still at the mercy of a conventional upbringing, considered their relationship unhealthy. She was shocked by their easy familiarity, their shameless, if playful caresses, their bantering endearments. Tony was twenty-eight. Her aunt at least thirty years his senior. On top of this, the contemptuous, casual way in which Tony accepted her aunt's unflagging generosity infuriated Dilys. Anybody would think by the way he treated Nesta that she was honoured in having him about the house; that in escorting her to the casino or an occasional ballet or theatre he was conferring a favour on her. Granted her aunt was blunt to the point of rudeness, difficult and unpredictable, but at heart she was kind and generous, and Dilys hated to see anybody taking advantage of her.

Three weeks ago Kitty Linden had turned up at the villa, evidently at Tony's invitation. Whether he'd first conferred with his hostess about this visit Dilys couldn't be sure. But one thing *was* certain—Aunt Nesta was riled. And not without reason; for, from the word "Go", Tony had made no bones about his attitude to Kitty. As far as

Dilys could make out he and Kitty had met during the War, when he was a Flying Officer and she a Corporal in the W.R.A.F. Apparently they'd met several times in the interim and kept up a desultory correspondence. Tony had told her the night before Kitty's arrival:

"She's had a tough time of late, poor kid. That's why I thought the change would do her good. Nothing like a spot of *dolce far niente* when one's nerves are shot to hell. Lovely girl. Believe me, she's got what it takes. Used to be on the stage."

During these last three weeks Dilys had developed a lively admiration for her aunt. It was absolutely wonderful the way she stifled her real feelings and treated Kitty like any other member of the villa circle. Gloriously direct, as she always was, but never by so much as a word or glance hinting at the jealousy that must have consumed her.

As for Kitty... well, a girl of her age and experience ought to have known better. The way she hurled herself at Tony was positively indecent. Dilys thought her a fool. If she ever fell in love *she* wouldn't behave like a lovelorn sixth-former with a hopeless pash on the music master!

II

It was at this stage in Dilys' reflections that Tony's crimson Vedette (a birthday present from Nesta) droned to a standstill in the garage-yard directly behind the villa. There stepped out of it a broad-shouldered, fair-haired young man, dressed in a pale blue singlet and butcher-blue shorts. At a casual glance, Tony Shenton had the appearance of one of those clean-living, clean-limbed young Englishmen who decorate the pages of women's magazines or preen themselves in muscular poses in advertisements for men's underwear. A more prolonged scrutiny would have given the lie to this illusion. Whatever Tony's constitution might have been at twenty-one, it was now very definitely on the down-grade. Good-living, hard drinking, late nights and lack of exercise had scribbled their signatures on his sun-tanned limbs and torso. His features, in repose, now clearly displayed the ravages of his dissipation. Yet Tony unquestionably had a way with him. When he exerted himself he could be both knowledgeable and amusing. His technique with wealthy, middle-aged women was a revelation. With Nesta Hedderwick it was faultless. No matter that his charm was synthetic, where Nesta was concerned it had rewarded him with a thumping big dividend.

By the time he'd garaged the car and strolled round on to the terrace Kitty was alone at the breakfast-table. On seeing him she glanced up and flashed him a little smile.

"Oh hullo, darling. Had a nice run?"

"Bang on, thanks."

"Had your breakfast?"

"No—I'm famished." He cast a predatory glance over the table. "Good lord! Two rolls, one small pat of butter and a small dish of marmalade. Just because Nesta's on a diet there's no reason why the rest of us should starve. What's the coffee like?"

"Lukewarm, darling."

"O.K. We'll look into this." He crossed to a bell-push by the french-windows, then crossed over and dropped with a sigh of exasperation into Nesta's *chaise-longue*. Patting the arm of the chair he added in a furry voice: "You don't look particularly matey on the other side of the table, sweetheart. Coming over?"

"I'm not so sure that I am," said Kitty slowly.

Tony jerked himself upright and stared at her in surprise.

"Hullo. What's biting *you?* Somebody been poisoning your sweet mind against me?"

"No, of course not."

"Then what the devil's wrong?"

"Tony?"

"Well?"

"Where did you sneak off to this morning? I think you might be honest with me. After all I—"

Lisette, the parlour-maid, appeared in the french-windows. Tony swung round with a whoop of satisfaction.

"Look here, Lisette, be an angel and make me a fresh pot of coffee, will you? This stuff's undrinkable. And what about a couple of fried eggs and some thin crisp toast? You know how I like it. Can do, *chérie?*"

"But of course, M'sieur."

"Splendid!"

The moment the girl had withdrawn, Kitty observed:

"Really, Tony, anybody would think you owned the place by the way you order the staff around. I wonder Nesta puts up with it."

Tony chuckled.

"Miraculous, isn't it? All done by kindness. But don't let's drag Nesta into this. You were just tearing a strip off me. You may as well finish the process."

"It's these early morning car drives—what's the big idea, darling?"

"Fishing," said Tony tersely.

"I don't believe it!"

"O.K. then—don't."

"You're sure... you're quite sure it isn't another woman?"

"Good God! before breakfast? Don't be crazy."

"Then why didn't you ask me to string along with you?"

"Because I never suspected you'd be interested in fishing. Women are usually bored stiff with this kind of thing."

"Quite. But I'm not that sort of woman. So the next time you sneak out all bright and early, darling, you'll take me with you. Promise?"

"Sorry, angel. Nothing doing."

"But, Tony—"

"Oh for crying aloud!" exclaimed Tony with a sudden flash of annoyance. "Don't let's natter about it. When a bloke goes fishing he likes to concentrate. And how the hell do you expect me to concentrate when you're around? Shall we leave it at that and keep the party sweet?"

"Oh very well, if that's the line you're going to take," said Kitty in surly tones. "I'm sorry if I'm such a millstone round your neck. I didn't realize..."

"Oh forget it! You're not. Now why not be sensible and give me a kiss?"

"I might," said Kitty, melting a little.

"There's no 'might' about it," concluded Tony forcefully. "You *will!*"

CHAPTER III

THE GIRL IN THE GALLERY

I

THE REMAINING GUEST at the Villa Paloma hadn't come down to breakfast because when Nesta had an artist living in the house she expected him to behave like one. Paul Latour certainly did his best to live up to the *fin de siècle* Bohemianism on which Nesta had erected her romantic ideas of the *genre*. He started off with one great advantage—with his tall, slightly stooping figure; his unruly dark hair and shaggy beard; his lean and hungry features—he looked the part. For the rest he took care to lay on a careful and wholly convincing act. He dressed sloppily in ginger corduroys, loose blue blouse, spotted neckerchief and sandals. He rose late, went to bed at dawn, made love to the maids, dropped ash on the carpets, poured scorn on the heads of the Philistines and corroded the reputation of his fellow artists with the acid of his vituperation.

It was Nesta Hedderwick's old friends Colonel and Mrs. Malloy who'd first introduced Paul into the villa circle. The Malloys lived a little farther along the coast at Beaulieu and came over once a week to play bridge—a game at which Nesta displayed more enthusiasm than skill. The Colonel had struck up a conversation with Paul in a café at Nice and, sensing that they'd many interests in common, invited him back to his house for dinner. Learning that Paul was more or less broke to the wide he hastily handed him on to Nesta, knowing only too well Nesta's predilection for romantic young men with more charm than money. As Malloy anticipated Nesta gobbled him up hook, line and sinker. She converted one of the attic rooms at the villa into a self-contained studio, gave him a small but adequate allowance and bored her more influential friends with garbled explanations of his peculiar genius. She hoped they'd buy his pictures. One or two did and furtively hid these masterpieces in the cellar.

For six months now Paul had been sitting pretty at the Villa Paloma. He was, so to speak, the second oldest inhabitant. Not quite so firmly established, perhaps, as Tony Shenton, but doing very nicely for himself. If he played his cards sensibly there was absolutely no reason why he shouldn't settle down indefinitely at the villa. Or at least until such times as he should find himself financially independent, with a villa of his own.

II

He was lounging that particular morning on the unmade divan-bed in a corner of the studio, viewing with distaste a large and impressive canvas set up on an easel in the centre of the room. For the last twenty minutes he'd been struggling to make up his mind just what the picture represented. Nesta's demands to see his latest masterpiece had been growing more and more urgent and he couldn't put her off any longer. And when Nesta looked at a picture the first thing she wanted to know was what it was *about*. In her opinion all the best pictures should tell a story, or, at least, bear a clear and appropriate label.

But, *mon Dieu!* a cod's head capping the naked torso of a woman, balanced on two cactus leaves and garnished with a *motif* of lemons and spaghetti... Paul shrugged hopelessly.

Then, coming to a sudden decision, he sprang up, snatched his beret from a wall-hook, slunk down the back-stairs, and slipped out into the road through a gate let into the garden wall. Five minutes later, about half-way down the Avenue de Verdun, he swung left into the Rue Partouneaux. Presently he climbed the steps between the narrow, twisting alleyways of the Old Town and ducked under a massive archway into a little courtyard shaded by a looped and trailing vine. Without knocking, he pushed open a rickety green door and ascended an equally rickety staircase that gave directly into the room above.

At first, after the glare outside, he could see little. Then, as his eyes grew accustomed to the gloom, he was aware of a troll-like figure squatting on an upturned box before a crudely constructed easel. On seeing Paul the midget creature sprang up and uttered a startled cry.

"M'sieur Latour!"

Paul smiled maliciously.

"You didn't expect to see me, eh, Jacques?"

"No, M'sieur. The picture is not ready for you. I told you next week. Before then it is impossible, You must understand I am not a machine—"

Paul cut in brusquely:

"*Eh bien!* you fool, there's no need to whine. I haven't come for the picture."

"No, M'sieur?"

"No, my friend. I'm here because I want to talk to you."

"You're not satisfied with my work—is that it, M'sieur?" The little fellow thumped his misshapen chest and burst out angrily: "There are limits to what even I can endure, M'sieur. You do not understand. The value of what I give to you—"

"Give to me!" Paul laughed sardonically. "Tell me, Jacques, how much did I pay you for your last incomparable *chef-d'œuvre?*"

"Two thousand francs, M'sieur."

"Exactly. Two thousand francs for a monstrosity of a canvas that isn't worth two sous. And who the devil would buy your stuff if I didn't? Answer me that."

The hunchback shrugged despairingly.

"*Hélas, M'sieur...* it is not easy these days to—"

"Quite. So if you want to retain my patronage no more monstrosities. Understand, idiot? No more of this abstract, surrealist nonsense. From now on I want pictures that a child could understand. No more cod's heads and spaghetti."

"No, M'sieur."

Paul gestured towards the canvas set precariously on the home-made easel.

"The new picture... what are you working on now?"

"It is a landscape, M'sieur." He stepped aside obsequiously. "You like it, perhaps?" He gesticulated. "The composition, M'sieur?"

Paul studied the half-finished painting with a critical eye.

"It's an improvement. I can recognize some cypress trees, a church and a stone wall."

"It is '*Le Monastère de l'Annonciade*', M'sieur."

"Good. I know where I am with a picture like this. But this other... this horror... what does it mean? What am I to tell people when they ask me what it's about? Can you tell me that, you bonehead?"

The hunchback considered the point for a moment, scratched his dark greasy hair and spat deftly through the open window into the courtyard below. Then abruptly his swarthy, hook-nosed features cracked into a grin.

"That is simple, M'sieur. Call it *Le Cauchemar*, the nightmare. For that is how it will doubtless appear to the ignorant and the stupid. Shall we say, perhaps, to your friends, M'sieur? But to those of us who see beyond, who have the vision..." Jacques Dufil shook his head sadly. "You will call for your new picture next week?"

"Next week," nodded Paul.

The hunchback raised three fingers in the air and gazed at Paul enquiringly. Paul scowled, shook his head and with an insulting gesture jerked two fingers in the little fellow's face.

With a fatalism born of much adversity, Jacques Dufil lifted his tortured shoulders and threw wide his hands. The obsequious smile was back on his twisted features, but as he thought of this nincompoop's ignorant remarks about his beautiful pictures there was black hatred in his heart!

III

Since Paul had gone to see the hunchback, Dilys got no answer when she knocked on the door of his studio. She'd planned a visit that morning to *L'Exposition de Peinture Méditerranéene* and, thinking his professional criticism might prove instructive, she wanted Paul to escort her. Dilys knew very little about painting, but being at heart a serious-minded young woman she was determined to seize every opportunity to widen her knowledge. Just because her aunt insisted on keeping her in idleness there was no reason why she shouldn't attempt to improve her mind.

The galleries, which looked out over the trim and exotic public gardens, were not particularly crowded. A few holidaymakers were trailing around with that sanctimonious look that is usually reserved for churches, museums and places of historic interest. An official was sitting on a Louis Quinze chair, viewing their progress round the place with the lynx-eyed apprehension of a private detective presiding over a valuable collection of wedding-presents. Dilys couldn't imagine why, because most of the canvases couldn't have been filched from the building without the aid of a hand-cart.

She bought a catalogue and, with typical conscientiousness, began to study the pictures in their proper numerical order. A few names were familiar to her—Matisse, Bonnard, Dufy and Utrillo, for example. These were the star performers, and before their work she stood earnestly and solemnly impressed. But what was she to make of the lesser lights? Was she to display amusement, scorn, horror or delight? It was all very difficult and she wished Paul could have been there to guide her safely through this aesthetic maze. In particular she would have valued his comments on a vast and vivid canvas labelled *Fiesta*, whereon a bevy of magenta-faced gargoyles were drinking and dancing in a grove of monstrous emerald cabbages against a savage purple sky. Arriving opposite this picture, she was suddenly aware of a tall, square-shouldered young man staring blankly at it over her left shoulder. And it was he who put into words, with admirable and virile brevity, her own instinctive reactions to the work.

"My God!"

Just that—clearly and vigorously articulated in what is usually referred to as "educated English". She swung round, delighted.

"Oh I'm so glad you agree with me! I'm always terrified of making up my mind about a picture in case it's by somebody I ought to like. I'm dreadfully ignorant of all this sort of thing."

"Same here. Mind you, I wouldn't have let fly like that if I'd known you were English."

"Oh, that's all right. Are *you* an artist?"

The young man flushed.

"Good lord, no! Do I look like one?"

Dilys eyed the broad-shouldered, tweed-jacketed, flannel-bagged six feet of manhood.

"Well, not exactly. But these days it's so difficult to tell. I know a dress-designer who looks like a professional boxer. Are you down here on holiday?"

"Er... more or less. Are you?"

"No. I live here with my aunt."

"Live here? Heavens! some people have all the luck. Wonderful spot, this. I just can't believe it's real."

"A lot of it isn't. Just paste and cardboard and tinsel, like most of my aunt's insufferable friends. Actually I find it rather boring. It gets that way after a time." Dilys accepted a proffered cigarette with a nod of thanks and went on with the devastating curiosity of an uninhibited and charming young woman of nineteen. "If you're not an artist what *is* your job in life? I hope you've got one."

"Oh yes. I'm a... er... I work in a sort of office."

"You mean you're a sort of clerk?"

"Well, yes... sort of," he said lamely.

Conscious of the inanity of this cross-talk they looked at each other and laughed.

"In London?" persisted Dilys.

"Er... yes. In London."

"*Pardon, Madame! Pardon, M'sieur!*" They swung round to face the agitated attendant. "*Je regrette, mais il est defense de fumer ici.*"

"Oh, sorry old boy," said the young man cheerfully, stubbing out his cigarette against his heel. "Bad show, eh? *Un mal spectacle. Comprenez-vous?*" He turned to Dilys. "He says he's sorry but we mustn't smoke in here. I learnt that bit off railway carriages." Then aware of his inexcusable assumption he slapped his thigh and added apologetically: "But good heavens! I was forgetting you lived here. You must speak French like a native."

"Just about," smiled Dilys. "An aborigine. Adequate, shall we say? but not idiomatic. Now what about taking a look at the rest of the pictures?"

"Yes—rather. Far more fun now I've met you."

They wandered on round the gallery, chattering like magpies, occasionally recalling where they were and pausing a moment to study one of the pictures. Within ten minutes they'd learnt quite a lot about each other. They agreed that it might be a sound idea to meet on the Casino terrace the next morning for an *apéritif.*

"Can't be absolutely sure about it," said the young man regretfully. "You see, I'm not exactly a free agent. I'm sort of stooging around here with another bloke. But you bet I'll make it if I can."

"Well, if you can't," pointed out Dilys after a moment's swift reflection, "you *could* telephone."

"Whacko! We simply can't afford to lose sight of each other after this morning. It's been—" He broke off and added anxiously: "I say—what's up? Anything wrong?"

"This painting—it's by a friend of mine," said Dilys, adding hastily: "Well, not exactly a friend. He's rather unbearable really. My aunt has very decently fitted him up with a studio at the villa."

The young man noted the number-disc on the frame and flicked over the pages of his catalogue.

"Yes, here we are. *Le Filou*... what the devil's a 'filou'?"

"A pickpocket, I think. Does it give the artist's name?"

"Yes... Jacques Dufil."

"Jacques Dufil!" echoed Dilys in amazement. "But it must be a mistake. It's so exactly like Paul's work. It's quite uncanny. They must have got the names mixed in the catalogue or something."

"I shouldn't let it worry you."

"I won't!" declared Dilys, glancing at her watch. "I've only got one worry on my mind at the moment. If I don't leave at once I'm going to be dreadfully late for lunch."

"Can I... er... see you home?"

Dilys hesitated.

"No—I think it would be more discreet if you didn't. So if you don't mind I think we'd better say 'Good-bye' here." Adding with a friendly smile: "Until tomorrow, I hope."

"Sure thing... until tomorrow." He thrust out a strong, sizeable hand and gripped hers so enthusiastically that she winced. "Slice of luck that I ducked in here to have a squint at these painter johnnies, Miss... By the way, what *is* your name?"

"Dilys Westmacott. And yours?"

The young man gulped.

"Mine? Oh, I'm... I'm plain John Smith. Pretty duff, I admit, but it's the best I can do for you."

Dilys threw him a suspicious glance.

"It sounds horribly like an alias. You're not pulling my leg, are you?"

"Heaven forbid!"

"Well... good-bye."

"Good-bye, Miss Westmacott."

As he watched her pass through the swing-doors into the brilliant sunshine, the young man experienced a pang of remorse. He hated having to deceive a charming girl like that, but what else could he do in the circumstances? What had Meredith been drumming into his head ever since they'd arrived in this playboys' paradise?

"No matter where you go or what you do, remember, m'lad, you're always on duty."

Exactly! And Acting-Sergeant Freddy Strang wasn't the sort of fellow to slip up on his instructions. No matter what happened he had to preserve his incognito!

CHAPTER IV

SECOND ENCOUNTER

I

THAT MORNING Inspector Meredith had driven over to police-headquarters at Nice for a pow-wow with his opposite number, Inspector Blampignon. They'd already met a couple of times since Meredith and Strang had settled in about a week earlier at their unpretentious hotel in Menton. Despite differences of language and temperament, the two men were already firm friends. Luckily Blampignon had a fair command of English and Meredith a smattering of schoolboy French. In consequence, after a certain initial embarrassment, they were soon able to chatter away pretty fluently.

Inspector Blampignon took life as it came, and accepted what *did* turn up with tremendous gusto. With his dark, humorous eyes, rotund figure, and easy rumbling laugh, he was a true Provençal. But behind that tolerant, comfortable personality was a quick intelligence and an astute practical mind. When the need arose Blampignon's plump and rather loose-limbed body could jerk, with surprising agility, into swift and decisive action.

As Meredith greeted him that morning in the cool, half-shuttered office on the second storey of the massive building, he sensed at once that Blampignon was worried. In a few moments the cause of this worry bobbed to the surface of their conversation. During the last few days information had come in about the resurgence of a well-tried racket that Blampignon and his colleagues had thought to be conclusively scotched. For a time it had proved to be one of the most profitable rackets along the Riviera. The details, as the Inspector pointed out, were simple. American cigarettes, which could be bought in Algiers and other North African ports for as little as sixpence a packet, were smuggled in fast motor-launches across the Mediterranean to suitable lonely spots along the coast-line and then sold on the Cote d'Azur at four shillings a packet. The profits on a single trip could run as high as ten million francs—about ten thousand pounds!

"*Hélas!*" sighed Blampignon. "So far all we find out is that the contraband is being put ashore somewhere between here and the Italian frontier."

"You mean these Yank cigarettes are being marketed only along this end of the coast?"

Blampignon nodded.

"It is like these counterfeit notes, *mon vieux.* They also are only making their appearance in the more easterly towns along the Midi. For that reason, of course, I settle you at Menton."

"I suppose there's no chance that the two rackets are being worked by the same gang?" asked Meredith.

"No—I think not. The currency racket demands a fixed headquarters on land—a place where they can set up their printing machine. But in this other game..." Blampignon threw wide his hands. "It is—how do you say?—fluid. And it does not do to join up something that is fluid with something that is fixed. You agree, M'sieur?" The inspector moved to his desk, opened a drawer and slapped a small wad of notes into Meredith's hand. "You see, *mon ami,* we have added to our little collection. Most of these notes we pick up in Monte Carlo. We have warned the... the..." Blampignon clicked his fingers irritably. "*Les boutiquiers* to be on the watch for such thousand franc notes."

"The shopkeepers, eh?" Meredith examined the notes minutely and nodded his admiration. "Beautiful work—we've got to admit it. Except for the two microscopic deviations spotted by your lab. wallahs at Lyons, the darn things might be genuine."

Blampignon chuckled and with a flamboyant gesture whipped a sheet of paper from his desk.

"Now here is the list of shopkeepers who hand over these notes to us. We question them one by one and in all cases it appears that they were passed over by English customers. But in two cases we have much luck. The shopkeeper sees in time the little errors we have warned him to watch out for. You follow, *mon ami?* He realize, *immédiatement,* that the note is fake. So he say to his customer 'Please to let me have your name and address, for the police desire to find out how these fake notes come to you.' Then I think to myself, this is a... a... *une besogne* for Meredith. He shall question these Englishmen, perhaps. That is why I ring you this morning and ask you to come over. It is possible you can do this?"

"My dear Blampignon," laughed Meredith, "it's what I'm here for. Let me have those addresses. I'll get over to Monte at once."

II

By midday Meredith had succeeded in interviewing the two Englishmen who, in all innocence, had tried to pass the spurious notes. At first both men had been disinclined to talk. After all, the purchase of francs on the Black Bourse was technically a criminal offence and they weren't at all sure how far Meredith was prepared to go. But a few broad hints soon reassured them. The French police were anxious to arrest the gang who were putting about the counterfeit notes. As Meredith pointed out with a withering look, they weren't concerned with a bunch of damfool, unpatriotic Englishmen who, in any case, had been very neatly diddled. Thereafter he got his information and at once Meredith realized that he'd picked up his first real clue.

Both Englishmen, who were unknown to each other and staying in different hotels, had bought their Black Market francs off the same man, and in both cases this man had struck up a conversation with them in one of the many cocktail bars in the town. He spoke English fluently but with a very strong foreign accent. Neither of the men believed him to be French. One suggested he was German; the other, Dutch. But their descriptions of the man tallied exactly—tall, stooping, iron-grey short-cropped hair, moon-like face, deep voice, urbane in manner and faultlessly dressed.

With this description jotted down in his notebook, Meredith rang Blampignon at Nice. Was this Dutchman or German known to the police? Had he, by any chance, ever been through their hands or, at any time, come under suspicion? Blampignon was desolate. There wasn't, he claimed, a single big-time racketeer along the coast with whom he wasn't familiar. It was a thumping big boast, of course, but it wasn't, perhaps, far short of the truth. In Blampignon's opinion this man was either a stooge, a hired nobody working for the Big Shots, or he'd only recently turned up on the Cote d'Azur from his own country.

"Good enough," said Meredith. "You leave it to me. I'll get over to Monte for the next day or two and drift around the likely bars. With a detailed description like this we ought to get on to the fellow. And with any luck—"

Blampignon broke in with a throaty chuckle:

"*Ah précisément!* How shall we say? The pilot-fish might lead us to the shark, eh?"

III

Twenty minutes later, after a brisk drive along the Moyenne Corniche, Meredith was back at the Hotel Louis where he'd arranged to meet Strang. As a change from hotel meals they often lunched out and they decided that morning to try their luck at *Le Poisson D'Or,* a nearby café that had been recommended by a fellow-guest at the Louis. It proved to be a casual, charming little place, with gaily-painted tables and chairs set out in a shady courtyard in the centre of which was an outsized aquarium stocked with goldfish. Meredith, who was beginning to find his way around the local menus, ordered a bottle of *Château de Cremât* and, later, over their *bouillabaisse,* brought the Sergeant up-to-date with the morning's events.

"For the next day or two, m'lad, we're going to hang around the more fashionable bars at Monte Carlo. Any objections?"

"No, sir, of course not," said Freddy, glumly realizing that his assignation with Miss Westmacott had abruptly gone up the spout. "All in the day's work, I guess." He added tentatively: "Do we... er... get our evenings off?"

"We do not!" snapped Meredith.

"No, sir... quite, sir," said Freddy hastily. "I only asked because—" He broke off and stared out across the sun-splashed courtyard as if he'd seen a ghost. "Well, of all the...!"

"What the devil's wrong with *you*?" demanded Meredith irritably.

"Take a look there, sir—the table under that orange tree. Do you see who I see?"

Meredith took a cautious glance, hastily concealed his surprise, and admitted with a chuckle:

"O.K., Sergeant—you win! You said we'd bump into him again and, by one of those crazy coincidences that are always cropping up in this benighted existence, we have. What's more he's just spotted *us*. Leave the talking to me, m'lad. He's coming over."

"Well, well, well!" exclaimed Bill Dillon breezily. "I never expected to see you chaps again. I thought you were making for Paris."

"We were... on business," said Meredith glibly. "But now, due to an unexpected turn of events, our business has brought us down here." He indicated an empty chair drawn up at the table. "Take a pew, Mr.—?"

"Dillon—Bill Dillon." He looked at Meredith enquiringly. "Funny thing, but I can't help feeling your face is familiar. It struck me that morning in Dunkirk. Are you the sort of chap who hits the headlines, by any chance?"

"Good heavens, no! Sales agent for an engineering firm—that's me. Meredith's the name. This is my assistant, Mr. Strang."

"Engineering!" exclaimed Dillon. "I'm in the same sort of line myself. What's your firm?"

"Er... Whitley-Pilbeams," said Meredith, mentioning the first name that came into his head. "Maybe you know 'em?"

"I'll say I do. Finest constructional engineers in the old country."

"Thanks," said Meredith drily. "And you... who do you—?"

Dillon broke in:

"Oh, since the War I've been working in the research department of the Hawland Aircraft Co. Not a bad job as jobs go. But not much chance of promotion. So I've just cut loose. Want to start up on my own when I get back. Garage or something. Don't much care as long as I'm my own master."

"And in the meantime you're treating yourself to a slap up holiday down here, eh?"

"That's about it," nodded Dillon. "Couldn't really afford it, of course. First time I've been abroad since I was demobbed in '46." He rose abruptly and thrust out a hand. "Glad to have met you chaps again. How long are you staying?"

"Well, that depends," said Meredith vaguely, "... on business. A couple of weeks—perhaps more, perhaps less."

"Maybe we'll be able to get together for a pint some evening. I'm staying at the Bandol. If ever you're at a loose end look me up."

"O.K.," nodded Meredith. "We will."

"Well, cheerio."

"Cheerio," said Meredith.

"Cheerio," said Strang, opening his mouth for the first time since Dillon had joined them.

IV

From *Le Poisson D'Or* Bill Dillon returned direct to the Bandol and went up to his room. There he lit his pipe and sat down at the table by the window to write a letter. For a whole week now he'd put off writing this letter, hoping he'd run into Kitty somewhere around the town. But although he'd kept a sharp look-out along the promenade and the more fashionable shopping streets so far he'd drawn a blank. On several occasions he'd even strolled up to the Villa Paloma and hung around in the vicinity on the offchance that Kitty would emerge.

It would, he felt, have been better that way—a casual, unexpected meeting... alone. That's why, even when he'd found out her address, he'd deliberately refrained from writing to her. But if it wasn't to work out like that then he'd darn well have to storm the stronghold and be damned to the consequences.

After all it was Kitty who was chiefly responsible for this Mediterranean jaunt. Admittedly the mountainous country behind the town had something to do with it. He needed those mountains, but not as much as he needed Kitty. A casual conversation with a mutual friend in London had enabled him to pin-point her present whereabouts. It was a lucky chance that, when Kitty had decided to walk out of his life, she'd decided at the same time to walk into Nesta Hedderwick's villa on the Riviera. Lucky because he knew Nesta Hedderwick; lucky because directly behind Menton reared the Alpes Maritimes. And since his future was inextricably bound up with Kitty and the presence of high mountains, he realized that in coming to Menton he'd very successfully brought off a right-and-left.

After a moment's reflection, he took up his pen and wrote:

Dear Mrs. Hedderwick,

I don't know if you remember me. I was one of the Airborne crowd stationed near Larkhill Manor who used to descend on you at week-ends during '44. I shan't forget in a hurry the grand time you gave us. Your hospitality was terrific and your patience inexhaustible! I expect you remember the crazy night when those Raff types showed up from Landsdown and we played an eight-aside rugger game with a cushion in your lounge-hall. At half-time you couldn't see across the room for feathers!

I remember you telling me that you had a villa at Menton and that after the War you intended to give up Larkhill and live permanently on the Riviera. You kindly suggested that if ever I came that way I should look you up. Well, I've just taken the chance to slip down here for a short holiday. I'm staying at the

*Bandol. So if your offer still holds good perhaps you could give
me a ring and let me know if and when it's convenient for me
to come along.*

I look forward to seeing you again after all these years.

Yours sincerely,
Bill Dillon.

*P.S.—I was the fair-haired, rather hefty three pipper who once
had the misfortune to spill a glass of sherry down your dress.*

V

The following morning, during breakfast on the sun-dappled terrace,
Nesta announced:

"I'm having a young man along to dinner this evening. I want you
all to be here. Such a nice boy. I met him at Larkhill during the War."
She jerked a glance at Miss Pilligrew who, indulging a little weakness
of hers, was furtively nibbling a lump of sugar. "You must impress on
cook to make a special effort. Understand, Pilly?"

"Yes, dear."

"I suggest *soupe au pistou* followed by *ratatouille.*"

"Yes, dear."

"Not that it matters to me, of course." Nesta gave a hollow laugh.
"I shall merely sit and watch other people enjoying the fruits of my
hospitality. *Mon Dieu!* What a life. It is a life, isn't it, Pilly?"

"Oh definitely, dear."

"Then we might have, say... *estocaficada.* And for sweet—"

Miss Pilligrew suggested timorously:

"What about *tourta de Blea,* dear?"

"Don't be stupid! You're so unhelpful, Pilly. I had in mind *robina*
fritters and—"

"Oh for crying aloud!" broke in Tony with a surly look. "Why all
this fuss? Is it somebody we're supposed to impress?"

"Don't be hateful, Tony. Of course it isn't. But he wrote such a charming letter and the least—"

"Do I know the fellow?"

"No, darling, I don't think so. His name's Mellon or Dillon or something of the kind."

"Dillon!" exclaimed Kitty, suddenly flushing beneath her tan.

"Yes—Captain Bill Dillon." Nesta sighed. "Such a handsome creature, with one of those nice bristly moustaches that—"

"Bill Dillon!" gasped Kitty. "But... but—"

"Don't tell me you *know* him!" cried Nesta, a shadow of disappointment passing over her heavily handsome features.

"No, of course I don't. But... but I once knew a Bill Dorman and it sort of struck a chord. You see how I mean, Mrs. Hedderwick? Dillon. Dorman. They're something alike and... for the moment..." With a little titter, Kitty swung on Tony. "Got a cigarette, Tony? Oh, thanks. Well, if you'll excuse me... I've got some letters to write. See you later, Tony."

A brief silence followed Kitty's hurried exit into the house. Nesta exchanged a meaning glance with everybody in turn and observed tartly:

"How very odd. She seemed quite upset. An unbalanced, neurotic type. She ought to see a psychiatrist. Don't you agree, Tony?"

"No, I don't!" said Tony shortly. "Kitty's had a tough time, poor kid." He gulped down the remainder of his coffee and got up abruptly. "Well, I'll be seeing you... I've got a job to do on the Vedette. I'll be out to lunch. Kitty and I are driving over to Monaco."

And with a brisk nod he stalked off through the garden to the garage-yard.

CHAPTER V

OMINOUS MEETING

I

CAUGHT UP in the useless existence prescribed for her by her aunt, Dilys was bored. Her encounter the previous day with the young man at the exhibition had suddenly forced her to see with devastating clarity the emptiness of her life. For a few hours she'd been buoyed up by the thought of the meeting they'd arranged on the Casino terrace. Then, just before dinner, she'd received a 'phone-call to say that the meeting was off. The young man was terribly sorry but it rather looked as if they wouldn't be able to get together at all for the next few days. It wasn't his fault but circumstances made it impossible.

Just that. No real explanation for the let down. Nothing but a vague suggestion that he would ring again in the near future. Dilys' high mood collapsed. She began to view the encounter at the galleries with a more calculating eye. Wasn't there, after all, something rather fishy about this Mr. John Smith? Anyway she refused to believe that Smith was his real name. He'd obviously blurted out the first thing that came into his head. But why? Because he wanted to conceal his real identity. And why had he wanted to conceal his identity? Well, most people adopted an alias because they had something to hide—more often than not, something criminal.

Dilys shivered. Could she believe *anything* he'd told her? Was he really a clerk in a London office? And this friend he spoke of—was it really a *man* friend?

By the time Dilys arrived at the breakfast-table, after a broken, restless night, she was prepared to erase Mr. John Smith from her memory. If he *did* have the audacity to ring up again, then she'd inform him, politely but firmly, that she no longer wished to meet him.

With all these unhappy reflections in her mind, it wasn't until she ran against Paul Latour on his belated way downstairs that Dilys remembered the picture.

"Oh hullo, Paul. You slipped out early yesterday. I wanted you to take me along to the exhibition and give me the benefits of your professional knowledge. As it was I had to go alone."

"Not a very good show, I hear. Too *recherché*. You agree?"

"Well, I'm not really qualified to say. But *I* found it... interesting. There was one picture in particular called... now what on earth was it? Oh, I know—*Le Filou*." Dilys watched closely for his reactions but Paul's features remained more than usually impassive. "It had a very distinctive style, Paul."

"Really? Who was the artist?"

"Well, quite frankly, I thought it was you."

Paul looked at her in astonishment.

"Me? *Me? Mon Dieu!* I'd sooner cut my throat than exhibit my work in the company of such mediocre nitwits!"

"But it was so exactly like your painting, Paul. Uncannily like it."

"But, *ma petite,* didn't you buy a catalogue?"

"Yes, of course—but I thought perhaps you were showing the picture under an assumed name."

"An assumed name? How do you mean? What name?"

"Oh Jacques somebody or other."

"Jacques?"

"Yes—I remember now. Jacques Dufil."

II

Bill Dillon stood before the wardrobe mirror in his hotel bedroom and took a final critical look at his appearance. Umph, not so bad. Lucky he'd had the good sense to pack his dinner-jacket even if it was a bit tight across the shoulders. No doubt that during these last two years he'd put on weight. No doubt either that all the violent and unaccustomed exercises of the last two days had developed his muscles.

Only that afternoon in an old bush shirt and khaki shorts, with a rucksack on his back, he'd been for his daily constitutional in the mountains. He'd driven up through Castillon and Sospey, parked the car near Col de Braus and struck out on foot to explore its rugged and precipitous environs. This was the third time he'd followed this particular route up from Menton for a scramble among the lower peaks of the nine thousand foot range. Up there the air had been clear as crystal, the sun scorching down from a cloudless sky, the heat reflected upward from the bare and shimmering rock. Certainly his complexion had suffered from the day's expedition. No getting away from it—at the moment his wasn't the sort of face that would look well at the dinner table. But Bill wasn't troubled. That afternoon up in the mountains he'd found the answer to a vital problem, a tantalizing uncertainty that for two years or more had nattered at his peace-of-mind.

He wound a silk muffler round his neck, locked the door of his room and went down to his car. Now that his visit to the Villa Paloma was imminent Bill's apprehension increased. All day, caught up in strenuous activity, he'd been able to forget this fateful meeting with Kitty. Now, as he drove through the cooling streets, with the strong sweet perfume of the mimosa in his nostrils, he wondered what the devil the outcome would be. Somehow he must edge Kitty aside and speak to her alone. It wouldn't be easy for, in her present mood, Kitty would probably do her damnedest to deny him this opportunity. He knew only too well how stubborn and wilful she could be. But the knowledge did nothing to ease the passionate longing that moved him when he thought of Kitty. No matter what had happened in the past, Bill knew that without her the future would be pretty well unbearable.

Yes, somehow during the course of the evening he must make a last desperate effort to win her back. An unreasonable hope, perhaps. But a man in love, thought Bill wryly, doesn't base his hopes on reason.

"My dear, dear boy!" boomed Nesta, grasping Bill's hands and shaking them frantically. "As if I *wouldn't* have known you!" She stepped back and viewed him with unblushing curiosity. "You've certainly broadened out since those gay days at Larkhill. Don't get enough exercise, of course. And where's your moustache? You used to have a moustache. One of those bristly little army affairs. So virile." Again the searching, slightly roguish contemplation. "You know, I always liked you, Bill. Not very subtle but no damn nonsense about you. Now come and meet the others. We're a rag-and-bobtail collection but I think we'll amuse you."

She led him through into the lounge and announced breezily:

"Hi! everybody. This is Bill!"

He saw Kitty at once, and his heart missed a beat. She was sitting on the arm of a settee, lovely and desirable as ever, with a cocktail glass in her hand and a small nervous smile playing about her lips. With the imperious gesture of a headmistress about to present a fourth-former to a visiting governor, Nesta beckoned her forward.

"And this is Kitty—Kitty Linden. She's down here on a visit." Adding with a baleful glance: "Just a *short* visit, eh, darling?"

Kitty, never quite sure how to take these devastating digs, smiled bleakly at Nesta and granted Bill a distant nod; then turned with sudden animation to Tony Shenton, who'd drifted up behind her. Bill was swift to notice how she slipped her arm through his—a familiar, possessive gesture that left no doubt in his mind as to the relationship between them. So there *had* been another man in the set-up—just as he'd always suspected. He wondered who the devil the fellow was and where Kitty had first met him. An outsized rotter by the look of him. Bill's jaw grew taut. He realized with a sudden stab of despair that this man's presence was just another knot in an already tangled situation.

Barely conscious of what he was saying, he was introduced to Dilys,

Miss Pilligrew and Latour. Then Nesta grabbed Tony by the necktie and jerked him forward like a recalcitrant horse. For the first time the two men found themselves face to face. And at that moment Bill suffered a shock. There was absolutely no question about it—somewhere, sometime, *he'd met this smooth-faced bounder before!*

IV

It was not until they'd moved out on to the moonlit terrace after dinner that Bill succeeded in detaching Kitty from the rest of the party. Tony had been called away to answer the telephone and the others were still seated at the coffee table. Seizing his chance Bill grabbed Kitty by the arm and more or less manhandled her behind a wisteria-covered pillar. He said urgently:

"I've got to see you alone sometime. We've got to have a proper talk about everything. We just can't go on like this."

Snatching away her arm she demanded furiously:

"Why did you have to come here? How did you find out that I was in Menton? Why can't you leave me alone?"

"You know well enough why I can't. Because I'm still in love with you, Kit. I've been nearly crazy with loneliness ever since you walked out on me. Don't you see—"

"For heaven's sake, keep your voice down!"

"When can we have a talk? It's no good drifting like this. We've got to have things out, once and for all. You see that, Kit?"

She said desperately:

"Oh, all right. If we must. When you leave, park the car at the foot of the hill. I'll try and sneak out to you for a few minutes."

"Good enough, darling. I'll be there." He tried to slip an arm about her waist but, with a fierce little shake of her head, she dodged aside. Bill shrugged miserably. "Oh, all right—if that's how you feel about it..."

"Now you two!" cried Nesta with coy innuendo. "What are you

whispering about? Kitty, how dare you buttonhole poor Captain Dillon. You're a brazen hussy!"

"Sorry, Mrs. Hedderwick. I was just showing him the view over the town. It looks heavenly in the moonlight."

As the couple rejoined the circle at the table, Nesta went on cooingly: "Bill darling, do you play bridge?"

"Well, I'm not a Culbertson, but—"

"Splendid! You must come along and make up a four. Next Friday, dear boy—that's the day after tomorrow. Friday at eight-thirty. Make a note of it in your diary."

"Well, I..." stammered Bill. "I'm not sure that..."

"Good! I knew you would. Colonel Malloy and his horrid little wife will be coming over from Beaulieu. We always make up a four on Fridays." Nesta turned a bolt-eyed glare on her long-suffering companion. "Bill can take *your* place, Pilly. You're dreadful. No finesse, dear, and far too talkative."

"Yes, dear," murmured Miss Pilligrew submissively.

"Now, Dilys, darling, come and sit next to Bill. I'm sure he's dying to talk to you. Where's Tony? And Paul? It's damned rude the way they just eat and fade away. But that's men all over. As long as they can satisfy their grosser appetites... no, not you, Bill. Your manners were always delightful. I'm so glad you took me at my word. We want to see an awful lot of you—don't we, Dilys?"

"Yes, auntie," mumbled Dilys uncomfortably.

"So from now on no standing on ceremony. Understand, dear boy? Just barge in whenever—" With a dramatic gesture Nesta clapped her hands to her head and uttered a wild little shriek. "Bill dear, what *am* I thinking about! I'm in my dotage. Why on earth didn't it occur to me at once? You must come and *stay* here. Of course you must! The Bandol's such a grubby little joint. And we'd simply—"

"But... but I can't do that," floundered Bill, glancing apprehensively at Kitty, thinking of the delicate and explosive situation that existed between them. "It's extremely kind of you but—"

"Now don't be so damned obstinate! You'll pack up and move in tomorrow. Promise, Bill."

Kitty muttered desperately:

"But perhaps Captain Dillon prefers staying at an hotel, Mrs. Hedderwick. Men often do."

Nesta quelled her with a contemptuous snort.

"Don't talk such poppycock, darling. Nobody in their senses would stay at the Bandol unless they had to. I hear the water's always lukewarm and the food absolutely ghastly. Of course he'd rather stay here. You would, wouldn't you, Bill?"

He glanced despairingly at Kitty and mumbled feebly:

"Well, I don't... I don't quite know what to..."

"Then that's settled!" shrilled Nesta, beaming delightedly at the little group about the table. "You hear that, everybody—Bill's coming! We'll expect you by lunch tomorrow. So glad I had the sense to—"

But Bill was no longer listening. Tony Shenton had reappeared on the terrace and suddenly Bill recalled where he'd first met the fellow. It was in 1943 at some aerodrome in Lincolnshire. He'd knocked up against him in the bar after dinner in the mess and exchanged a few words with him. Not many, for Shenton had been half-seas-over and more or less incapable of sustained conversation. Later that evening he'd learnt something of Flying-Officer Shenton's reputation, and what he'd learnt wasn't exactly edifying. Some question of a missing wallet that Shenton had inadvertently dragged from his pocket when searching for a packet of cigarettes. There'd been nearly forty pounds in the wallet, but for the sake of the squadron the affair had been hushed up.

And this was the fellow Kitty was going around with—a common pickpocket, a wastrel, a scrounger, a playboy! Good God! it was tragic. No doubt about it—unless he could break up this rotten affair before he left Menton then Kitty, poor kid, was heading blindfold for disaster!

V

But when, some twenty minutes after he'd driven away from the villa, she joined him in the parked car, he soon realized that Kitty was in no mood to listen to reason. She was furious with him for turning up again in her life. Furious with the mutual friend in London who sneaked of her whereabouts. Furious because, by a strange coincidence, he'd met Nesta in the past and had thus been able to wangle an invitation to the Villa Paloma. Over Tony Shenton she was brazen.

"I met him long before I met you. We've kept in touch for years. That shakes you, doesn't it? And if Tony asks me, I'm damn well going to marry him!"

"Marry him!" Bill was thunderstruck. "But, good lord, Kit, doesn't he realize? Haven't you had the decency to tell him?"

"Tell him what?"

"*That you're already married to me!*"

Kitty laughed maliciously.

"Oh, don't worry. I'll have to tell him sometime. Even *I* can see that. But I'm going to tell him in my own time—not yours."

"But, good heavens, Kit!"

"Well, what does it matter anyway? I'm not in love with you. I doubt if I ever was. Our marriage was about the grimmest mistake I ever made. Left high and dry in that pokey little Kensington flat all day while you were at the office... a thrilling sort of existence, wasn't it?" Kitty's laughter grew more shrill. "And I was supposed to be the good little wifey who sat twiddling her thumbs until her dear hubby came home tired and touchy from his work. Don't be so dim, Bill. If it hadn't been for Tony I'd have gone crackers."

"But, good lord, Kit—you don't mean that you and Tony—?"

"Oh, be your age! Don't tell me you didn't guess. That night after our final row, when I walked out on you for good... well, Tony had already fixed for me to join him down here. You're wasting your time, Bill. It's no good. I'm not coming back!"

"But, confound it all, you're my wife!" cried Bill vehemently. "Do you think I'm going to stand back and see you chuck yourself away on a rank outsider like Shenton?"

"I'd like to see you stop me. If Tony asks me to marry him you're going to give me my divorce."

"I'm damned if I am! I came across Shenton during the War and his reputation in the mess stank to high heaven."

"Oh well, if you must throw mud at him when he's not here to defend himself..."

Kitty opened the car-door and slid one silk-clad leg to the ground. With a muttered oath Bill dragged her back and, reaching across, slammed the door.

"Now look here, Kit—let's get this straight. I knew just what you were thinking about when Mrs. Hedderwick pushed out that invitation. That, in the circumstances, I was bound to turn it down. Well, I thought the same thing at first, even if I couldn't make up an excuse to put the old dear off. But since then I've changed my mind, and, whether you like it or not, I'm turning up at the villa tomorrow. And if Mrs. Hedderwick's agreeable, I'm damn well going to stay there for the remaining three weeks of my holiday. And there's absolutely nothing you can do about it. If you think I'm going to sneak out of your life with my tail between my legs just because you think you've fallen for Shenton in a big way then you're crazy! I'm giving you three weeks to find out your mistake and come to your senses. So now you know just where you stand."

"All right," retorted Kitty hotly. "Turn up at the villa. It won't worry me. It certainly won't break my heart to keep out of your way. But get this into your head. I'm not open to persuasion. You can say and do what you like but you won't make me change my mind. I'm going to marry Tony and you're going to make it possible. That's flat and final."

"What makes you so sure?"

"Well, if you must know I'm going to have a baby and it won't be *yours,* Bill. Now laugh that one off."

"Kit! it isn't true."

"Isn't it? Well, wait another couple of months and even *you'll* have to believe me."

For a moment Bill sat there, immobile, unspeaking; then, suddenly, desperately, he turned on Kitty and grasped her by the wrists. Even at that moment of disillusionment he felt no real enmity towards Kitty. She'd made a mess of her life—that was all. She'd been bored and lonely and he hadn't realized. And Shenton? How the devil was he to be blamed for this shabby set-up if he hadn't realized that Kitty was a married woman?

He said pleadingly:

"Kit darling—even now, I don't care... if only you'll come back to me. We'll forget all this rotten business. What do I care if this child isn't—"

"Let me go—do you hear? Let me get out of here!" With a sudden vicious gesture she snatched free her wrists and caught him a stinging slap on the cheek. "If you don't open that door and let me go I'll scream for help!"

"O.K." said Bill dully. "O.K."

He reached over and opened the door. She scrambled out and stood for an instant setting straight her hair, smoothing out her frock. Then, ignoring his "Good-night", she turned on her absurdly high-heels and clicked off up the hill. He watched her flicker through the dappled moonlight, and the fronded shadows of the palm trees, until she was out of sight. It was curious that even at that melancholy moment his heart was full of pity for her.

As he drove back slowly through the deserted streets to his hotel, he made up his mind just what his next move should be in this unhappy situation. He must tackle Shenton face to face and find out, once for all, what his intentions were towards Kitty. And if he were prepared to do the decent thing... Bill shrugged. Well, he knew when he was beaten. But, by God, Shenton must play fair, or else...

CHAPTER VI

MEREDITH IN MONTE CARLO

I

"LOOK HERE, SIR," protested Sergeant Freddy Strang, "duty's duty and all the rest of it, but if you force me to down another bottle of this darn Vichy water I'll be airborne!"

"Sorry, Sergeant," chuckled Meredith. "You've all my sympathy, but it wouldn't do to hang about in these places without ordering something. And if you think I'm going to let you spend your day knocking back double brandies and shoving 'em down on the expenses sheet, then you're a bigger optimist than I am."

"But three days of it, sir! I never want to swallow another mouthful of the poisonous stuff. And it isn't as if we've got anywhere. Not a sniff of the chap we're looking for. It's absolutely depressing."

"Well, that's how it runs. No good getting impatient. But I promise you this much. If we haven't pulled a rabbit out of the hat by ten pipemma this evening, then we'll call the hunt off."

"Sounds fair enough to me, sir," said Freddy, hastily raising a hand to his mouth to cover an indiscretion that had been plaguing him ever since this Monte Carlo roundabout had been set in motion. "Sorry, sir. Can't help it. Afraid it's getting a bit out of control."

Although Meredith had taken good care to conceal it from his subordinate, he too was feeling pretty down in the mouth. For nearly three days now they'd been haunting the more exclusive cocktail bars and cafés frequented by the foreign tourists. Blampignon had drawn up an appropriate list for his English *confrères*. In particular Meredith had kept a watchful eye on the Manhattan and Mirimar, the bars where this smooth-tongued foreigner had made contact with the two Englishmen. And from all these boring, fruitless hours he'd culled only a capful of further information. Discreet enquiries among the staffs of these various establishments elicited the fact that at six of them, including the Manhattan and Mirimar, this Dutchman or German was known to them by sight. For the most part Meredith and Strang had worked separately, coming together only at mealtimes to compare notes.

But at that moment—about six o'clock on the third day of their vigil—they were seated opposite each other at a little glass-topped table in a far corner of the *Bar Mirimar*. A few minutes earlier, in conversation with one of the many *garçons* attached to the place, Meredith had stumbled on a curious bit of evidence. According to this fellow, who luckily spoke English, he'd last seen the moon-faced gentleman come into the bar the previous Thursday. And thinking back, he was prepared to swear that the gentleman never patronized the Mirimar *except* on a Thursday—adding in explanation of this astonishing claim:

"You see, M'sieur, we are quick to remember faces. It is part of our job to do so. And this particular gentleman... he always order vodka. We do not often serve vodka in the Mirimar, so when he come in I think 'Ah, here is the gentleman who always drink vodka!' So I go up quick to him and say 'Vodka as usual, M'sieur?' And, *naturellement,* he is so flattered because I remember that he give me a most handsome tip. *Mais oui*—always Thursdays, M'sieur. I think you will find I am not wrong about that. And since it is Thursday today... perhaps later... you follow, M'sieur?"

Meredith followed perfectly. Recalling that the statements he'd taken from the two Englishmen were in his wallet, he took them out and hastily scanned them. He smiled to himself. Exactly! They too had met the fellow on a Thursday. So what? Didn't it suggest that he worked the Monte Carlo bars *only* on that particular day of the week?

II

It was about half an hour later when they saw him come in. There was no mistaking his identity. Every detail of his appearance tallied

exactly with the description given by the Englishmen. Meredith threw
a quick, meaning glance at Strang and muttered:

"O.K., m'lad. This is it. Stay here. I'll try and nab a bar-stool next
to him."

In this Meredith was unlucky. After ordering his customary glass
of vodka, the man glanced up and down the length of the bar and,
after a moment's hesitation, sidled on to an empty stool between a
snowy-haired, dandified old roué who was doddering, half-asleep, over
a half-empty bottle of Veuve Clicquot, and a brassy-haired, middle-
aged woman, whom Meredith judged to be English. Edging his way
cautiously through the crowd, the Inspector took up his position as
close to the group as he dared.

For five minutes or so nothing happened. Then suddenly the
moon-faced foreigner jogged his elbow against the Englishwoman's
arm just as she was about to take a sip from her cocktail glass. The
liquid slopped on to the bar-top. Instantly the fellow was all apolo-
gies. Whipping out a large silk handkerchief he began to dab up the
mess and, in a few seconds, the couple were engaged in animated
conversation. Too far away to catch what they were saying, Meredith
was perfectly content to bide his time. This, he realized, was merely
the opening gambit in the little game that was about to be played.

Presently the man ordered another round of drinks and the conversation became not only more animated but far more intimate.
Ten minutes later the Englishwoman, after visible protests from her
companion, returned the compliment. Thereafter their voices dropped
to a conspiratorial murmur and their heads came closer and closer
until they were almost touching.

Then, abruptly, the ill-assorted couple seemed to come to a decision. With a polished, practised gesture the man draped the woman's
sequin wrap about her plump, naked shoulders, helped her from the
bar-stool and ushered her obsequiously towards the revolving-doors.

In a flash Meredith swung round on Strang, still seated at the
corner table, and jerked his head towards the exit. Strang rose, joined

his superior and, without a word, they strolled across the bar and thus out into the broad moonlit square. The lamps were already gleaming among the exotic trees and flowering shrubs, where the beautifully-tended gardens sloped down to the fantastic towers and cupolas of the floodlit Casino. The warm, caressing air was redolent of the scent of heliotrope and, somewhere in the half-dusk under the palms, a fountain was plashing. But the romantic magic of the Mediterranean night left Meredith unmoved. His eyes were fixed on the couple, now a little way ahead, as they moved at a leisurely pace towards the Casino.

"Looks as if they're going to make a night of it, eh, Strang?"

"Wouldn't be surprised, sir. Probably going to try their luck at the tables."

"No—hang on!" exclaimed Meredith, puzzled. "They're not going into the Casino. They're heading for that car-park to the left of the main-entrance. Here, step lively, m'lad, else they'll give us the slip."

Quickening their pace the two officials were just in time to see their quarry clamber into the rear seat of an immensely dignified and old-fashioned Rolls Royce that was parked close to the pavement. Meredith turned excitedly to Strang.

"You parked our own car somewhere nearby, didn't you?" Strang nodded. "O.K. Then nip along and get the engine started. I want you to re-park on the far side of the road just opposite. That'll give us a chance to make a quick follow-up if this chap pulls away in a hurry. Get me?"

"Yes, sir. And then?"

"Sit tight in the driving-seat with the engine running."

No sooner had Strang dashed off when Meredith, with a studiedly casual air, strolled slowly past the Rolls and took up his position under a nearby lamp-post. Pulling a newspaper from his pocket, he began ostensibly to scan it. As Meredith had anticipated the light from the lamp cast a reflected glow into the interior of the car and he was able to see quite clearly all that was taking place in the back-seat. It was just as he'd expected. From a voluminous spangled handbag the woman pulled out a cheque-book. Coincident with this her companion whipped out a fountain-pen and almost thrust it into her outstretched fingers. Then, as the woman was filling in the cheque, the man took out a fat wad of notes and began hurriedly to count them. A few seconds later the exchange was made and, after a brief conversation, the man opened the car-door and with a short bow helped the woman to alight. A final flourish of his hat, another little bow, a quick furtive glance around and the man jumped into the driving-seat, slammed shut the door and started up the engine.

At that moment Meredith saw the little black "sports" come to a standstill on the far side of the road. A few seconds later he'd ousted the Sergeant from the wheel and the chase was on.

III

It was an exciting, not to say hair-raising, experience swinging round the outer bends of that tortuous road, with only a six-inch kerb between comparative safety and certain destruction. There were times, in fact, when the Corniche de Littoral, skirting some rocky promontory, seemed to hang poised over the sea. Meredith thanked his lucky stars that the Rolls hadn't followed one of the higher Corniche roads, for the fellow ahead handled the car with superb assurance and faultless judgment. More than once, hitting a straight and level stretch, the Rolls drew away. But always Meredith, tense and grim behind the wheel, was able to put on a spurt and bring the car once more into the rays of his headlamps.

"Hell's bells, sir!" breathed Freddy, who throughout the drive had been frantically pressing his foot against the floor-boards. "He's certainly cutting it out. Talk about the movies..."

"Do, if you want to," snapped Meredith. "I'm busy."

"Where d'you think he's making for, sir?"

"Nice, by the look of it. Or maybe Beaulieu. We're just coming to the outskirts of the place." Meredith peered ahead and suddenly jerked out: "By heaven, yes—he's slowing up. Looks as if he's turning off here to the right."

Jamming on his brakes Meredith succeeded in swinging the "sports" off the main-road into the long plane tree avenue where the Rolls had now come to a stop. Pulling up sharply, the inspector shut off the engine, switched off the headlights and rapped out:

"Come on, Strang—just an easy stroll. Light up a cigarette and talk like hell. Don't take the slightest notice of the chap as we pass the car. But, for Pete's sake, see if you can spot the name of the house."

"Good enough, sir. I'm with you."

At Freddy's instigation a discussion was started on the virtues of the English Test Team then touring Australia. As they drew level with the car they noticed that the driver had got out and was now opening the gates of a fair-sized villa set back a little way from the road. Clearly defined on the stuccoed pillars of the entrance was its name—Villa Valdeblore. Twenty yards further on Meredith drew up and glanced back. The Rolls was already disappearing through the open gates.

Ten minutes later Meredith was at the Beaulieu police-station trying out his schoolboy French on a bewildered and suspicious Duty Sergeant, who stubbornly refused to be impressed by the Inspector's official credentials. At the mention of Blampignon, however, the fellow's attitude softened somewhat and he agreed that Meredith should make use of the station 'phone to ring up Nice H.Q.

Inside another ten minutes, after Blampignon had exchanged a few terse sentences with the Sergeant, Meredith had the fellow eating out of his hand. Luckily Meredith could understand French far better than he could speak it so that he was able to grasp at least the salient points of the Sergeant's evidence.

Mais oui! the Villa Valdeblore—he knew it well. It was in the Avenue de la Palisse and was owned by a certain Colonel Malloy.

"A compatriot of yours, Inspector, and very much respected in the town. I think he bought the villa in 1946."

As far as the Sergeant knew he lived there with his wife. *Mais oui,* save for the domestic staff, *alone* with his wife. Was there not a Dutchman or German in the household? The Sergeant smiled.

"Ah, you are thinking, perhaps, of his chauffeur, Nikolai Bourmin. He is a White Russian. All this I learn because as an alien he has to report to us here at regular intervals. No—I know little of him. He behave himself. He does not get drunk or steal or commit a murder. That is all I care. Yes—it is about six months now since he first came to Beaulieu. I trust you have not discovered something about him that I should have found out for myself. If he is up to no good, it would not look well if I failed to comprehend it, Inspector. But I cannot believe that a man like Colonel Malloy would be easily deceived. It would not be like him to employ a rogue. If *you* think this Nikolai Bourmin to be a rascal..." The sergeant shrugged and added hopefully. "*Eh bien,* then perhaps you are wrong, M'sieur. You agree it is possible?"

Meredith could have expounded at length on the fallibility of assumptions that were not founded on proven facts, but playing for safety he said simply and conclusively:

"*Peut-être, mon ami.*"

Strang gazed at his superior in blank admiration.

IV

On their more leisurely drive back along the Littoral road to Menton Meredith fell silent. Aware that he'd dropped into one of his "broody moods", as Freddy called them, the Sergeant sensibly made no attempt to start up a conversation. As a matter of fact, Meredith was thinking fast and furious. He was analysing the evidence that had come his way during the course of that eventful evening.

So this fellow Bourmin was not the owner of the Rolls-Royce— he was merely chauffeur to this retired army bloke, Malloy. Now it was simple to explain away the fact that Bourmin only "worked" the Monte Carlo bars on a Thursday. It was, undoubtedly, his half-day off.

It seemed equally certain that on these occasions his employer allowed him to make use of the car. This argued, of course, a pretty friendly and trustworthy relationship between the two men. But accepting this premise was it reasonable to assume that Malloy himself was tied up with the racket? Umph—difficult to say without having had the opportunity to make a personal assessment of the man's character. The Beaulieu Sergeant spoke of him as being "highly respected in the town", but that was just a general opinion. Somehow or other they must get a more definite line on Malloy's past record and present behaviour.

For the moment it might be as well to make no move where the Russian was concerned. Strang could well take on the job of "tailing" the fellow on his Thursdays off in the hope that he might make contact with other members of the gang. As an alien, faced with the necessity of reporting regularly at the police-station, there was little chance of Bourmin slipping through their fingers even if his suspicions were aroused. Somehow the chauffeur had to collect the spurious notes as they came off the illicit printing-press. It was Bourmin, in fact, who might well lead them to "Chalky's" hide-out.

As for this Colonel Malloy, Meredith determined to get in touch with the Yard without delay. They, in turn, could make contact with the Records Department at the War Office and cable the relevant information concerning the fellow's *bona fides* and past history in the Service. If he appeared to be a sound egg then it might be a sensible move to take Colonel Malloy into his confidence. After all, as Bourmin's employer, he was excellently placed to keep watch on the chauffeur's activities. On the other hand Meredith couldn't dismiss the fact that Blampignon and his colleagues suspected the racket was being organized by an Englishman. And to pose as a retired Colonel of the British Army was just the sort of alias that would appeal to a criminal in a foreign country. There was something solid and reassuring, almost sacrosanct, about a retired Colonel; particularly when he was to be associated with a wife, a handsome villa, and a chauffeur-driven Rolls!

CHAPTER VII

CARDS ON THE TABLE

I

THE BRIDGE PARTY at the Villa Paloma that Friday evening had been, from Nesta Hedderwick's point-of-view, a great success. At the end of the evening's play, after a shaky start, she and Bill had taken about ten thousand francs off the Malloys. The Colonel and his wife, a brisk, talkative little woman with faded ginger hair, had accepted their defeat with the indifference and sangfroid of a couple to whom ten thousand francs was mere chicken-feed. They departed in an aura of vociferous good will and Armagnac brandy, leaving Nesta and Bill to enjoy a complacent post-mortem on the game.

Bill was in no hurry to go up to bed. Kitty and Tony had left directly after dinner for a flutter at the local casino, and since it was then long past midnight they'd probably show up at any minute. Dilys and Miss Pilligrew, placing a proper value on their sleep, had long since retired for the night. It wasn't Kitty that Bill was hoping to see. He felt pretty sure that when she *did* return to the villa and realized he was still in the lounge she'd go straight up to bed. It was Shenton he wanted to buttonhole. He was raring to have a private, straight-from-the-shoulder talk with ex-Flying Officer Tony Shenton.

Bill, in fact, was just having "one for the stairs" when he heard the Vedette swish up the drive *en route* for the garage at the rear of the villa. Nesta glanced at her watch.

"Twenty to one! Damned inconsiderate, Bill. This Linden girl's a puss. I suppose you realize she's crazy about Tony?"

Bill said bleakly:

"I... I rather suspected it."

"The child's a fool, of course. She's too infatuated to see it, but, if you ask me, he's already beginning to tire of her. He always does. Tony's women are here today and gone tomorrow. There's been a constant procession of disillusioned females in and out of this house ever since the heartless wretch came to live here. One fine day it's going to get him into trouble."

"Trouble? How do you mean, Mrs. Hedderwick?"

"Well, one of these rejected females is going to hit back and hit back hard. If Tony doesn't watch out some sweet wench is going to pop a pinch of arsenic in his—" The door opened and Tony stood there blinking owlishly in the bright light. Nesta's expression changed instantly. She said with a fond smile: "Well, Tony darling, did you break the bank? Had a lovely time? Where's Kitty?"

"Gone to bed." He nodded casually to Bill. "Oh, hullo, Dillon. What about a cognac?"

"I've already got a drink, thanks."

"Bang on. I'll join you."

Nesta eased her fourteen stone from the chair in which she'd been practically wedged and swayed, yawning, to her feet.

"Well, if you men are going to make a night of it, I'm off to catch up on my beauty sleep. Good-night, Bill. Don't let him drink too much." She held out her arms to Tony. "Goodnight, you wretch. Not too late up. You look tired."

With a dutiful air Tony kissed her on both cheeks and thrust her with playful familiarity towards the door. Nesta, almost cooing with gratitude for these little attentions, retaliated by tweaking the young man's ear. Tony winced.

"Hey! that hurt."

"Serve you right," bridled Nesta. "You've behaved abominably towards me of late. Ever since that Linden minx turned up you've ignored me completely. You're a brute, Tony. He is a brute, isn't he, Bill? A nasty, thoughtless, self-centred brute!"

"Oh, for Pete's sake—" began Tony irritably.

But Nesta had already stumped out, slamming the door conclusively behind her.

Bill said in subdued and level tones:

"I've been waiting for this chance, Shenton. You and I are going to have a talk."

"Are we? That's news to me, old boy. What about?"

"This affair of yours with Kitty Linden."

Tony, who'd been sprawling with his legs over the end of the settee, scrambled hurriedly to his feet. His pale face flushed blotchily. He shot out:

"What the heck's that got to do with you?"

"Quite a lot. I want to know just what you intend to do about Kitty."

"Oh, you do, do you?" sneered Tony, shakily setting down his half-empty glass of cognac. "Well, let's get this straight, Dillon. I'm not having you or anybody else poking their noses into my private affairs."

He moved a step closer to Bill, thrust out his jaw and menacingly clenched his fists. For an instant, thinking he was about to unleash a punch, Bill altered his stance and tensed himself, ready to defend himself if the fellow ran amok. He realized that if it did come to a show-down the odds were all in his favour. Although there was nothing to choose between them in the matter of height or build, after all his recent exercise in the mountains he was as fit as a fiddle. Shenton, on the other hand, was out of condition, flabby as a wet sponge. Bill said bluntly:

"You'd better give me a straight answer, Shenton."

"You think so?" Tony laughed sarcastically. "I suppose Nesta hasn't put you up to this by any chance? God knows she's a green-eyed old witch. But if that's the set-up you can call it a day. I'm not answerable to Nesta for my—"

"It's nothing to do with Mrs. Hedderwick," cut in Bill shortly.

"Then what the hell...? Don't tell me you've fallen for her yourself? Damn it! you've only met her once."

Bill said for the second time:

"I want to know what you intend to do about Kitty. I've a very good reason for asking."

"Oh," said Tony lightly, "what reason?"

"*She happens to be my wife!*"

He stared at Bill in blank astonishment. Then, reaching for his glass, he downed the remainder of his cognac in a single gulp and said with a sardonic chuckle:

"Are you crackers? Do you honestly expect me to swallow that one? Kitty your wife! Think again, old boy."

"Well, you needn't believe it if you don't want to, but it happens to be true. Kitty's had you on a string about this, Shenton. She guessed you'd get to hell out of her life if you knew she was married. So when you showed up in London about a couple of months back, she kept quiet about it and let you take her around until she'd angled an invitation to come down here. Smart of her, eh?"

"But what the—?"

"Hang on! I haven't finished yet. Kitty thinks she's in love with you. O.K.—if she is then there's nothing I can do about it. I've asked her to come back to me but she won't. She's quite determined about it. I don't think there's anything I can say or do that'll shift her. But before I return home there's one thing I *can* do… one thing I'm damn well *going* to do."

"Really—what's that?"

"See that Kitty gets a square deal."

"By me?" sneered Tony.

"By you!" exclaimed Bill savagely. "Kitty's going to have a baby. *Your* child, Shenton, not mine. There's no possible doubt about the kid's paternity so you can't wriggle out of that one. Now do you see what I'm driving at?"

"You mean…" stammered Tony, dumbfounded, "that I—?"

"You'll marry Kitty at once. Get me? God knows it's the last thing in the world I could wish for her—to be married to a bounder like you. But as she happens to be in love with you and anxious to marry you—"

"You'll divorce her, eh?"

"Just that."

"And if I refuse your very generous offer to take on a wife you've no further use for?"

Bill grabbed Tony by the wrist, jerked him forward, and raised his clenched fist.

"By God, I could knock you cold for that! Kitty's everything to me. I'd take her back tomorrow, child or no child, if she'd have me. And the sooner you get that into your damned head the better. I've been in love with Kitty ever since I first met her. I still am. I always shall be. But for her sake I'm asking you to do the right and decent thing and marry her."

"And if I don't?" asked Tony mockingly. "What then, eh?"

"Then, by heaven, I won't be answerable for the consequences! I'm warning you, Shenton. You may have played fast-and-loose with other women, but I'm damned if you will with Kitty. So if you've got any sense, you'll watch your step. That's all."

III

Kitty was sitting up in bed polishing her nails when the door stealthily opened and Tony came in. She was not particularly surprised. This was by no means the first time that Tony had slipped into her bedroom *en route* for his own. These lingering "Good-nights", in fact, were now an accepted ritual in their easy, slipshod relationship. It wasn't until Kitty noticed the set expression of his over-handsome features that she realized, with a quiver of apprehension, that something was wrong. This visit obviously had no connection with any form of amorous dalliance. Tony was in a mood and, by the look of it, a pretty ugly one.

She ventured nervously:

"Tony darling, what is it? Is there anything wrong?"

Shutting the door, quickly but cautiously behind him, he crossed to the bedside and rapped out with a scowl:

"I've just been having a talk with Dillon—that's all."

She caught her breath.

"Really? What about?"

Tony said witheringly:

"As if you didn't know!"

"But, darling," protested Kitty, with a little gesture of bewilderment, "why *should* I know? I wish you'd—"

He broke in sharply:

"Why the heck couldn't you have been straight with me about this?"

"I... I don't know what you mean, Tony. Honestly I don't."

"Oh for God's sake don't play the little innocent. Why didn't you tell me when we met again in London that you were married to that blighter Dillon?"

"But Tony darling—"

He went on with ever-mounting resentment:

"O.K., I'll tell you why you didn't. Because you knew darn well that I wouldn't have asked you down here if you *had* put me wise. You'd got your little story off pat enough, I'll admit. The lonely little bachelor girl, eh?—broke to the wide, without a friend in the world. And I fell for it like a lamb!"

"Tony! that's vile of you, and you know it is. I was going to tell you about Bill. Truly I was."

"Maybe—now that the situation's got too hot for you to hold."

She pleaded desperately:

"But darling, you must listen for a moment. I never really meant to deceive you about Bill. I was going to tell you when I first arrived down here. And then... well, everything seemed so marvellous between us that I just couldn't bring myself to... to..."

He broke in angrily:

"And you expect me to swallow that after all the other damned lies you've told me?"

"Why not? It's the truth."

"The truth!" Tony laughed sardonically. "Unfortunately for you Dillon was in a pretty talkative mood tonight. He's been telling me plenty. Pity you couldn't have followed his example, eh?"

"About what?" asked Kitty faintly.

He said with brutal directness:

"This brat you're going to have."

"Bill told you that?" gasped Kitty. "He told you I was going to have a baby?"

"Yes, and that's only half of it. You told him *I* was responsible, didn't you?"

"But Tony darling, it's true. I was only waiting until I was quite sure before I told you. It's *our* child, Tony. You realize that, don't you?"

"I see. And now you're planning for Dillon to divorce you, so that I can do the right thing and marry you myself. Oh for God's sake, don't trouble to deny it. Dillon's got the same bright idea. Well, you're crazy—both of you! I'm not falling for that one, so you may as well forget it."

"You mean, even if Bill's prepared to go through with a divorce, you *won't* marry me?"

"I'm not marrying you or anybody else. And that's flat."

"But Tony, you can't walk out on me now!" cried Kitty despairingly. "Not with our baby on the way."

"Oh, can't I! You watch!"

"But what shall I do? Where shall I go?"

"Ask me another. Why not go back to your high-minded husband. He's falling over himself to get you back into the fold."

"I'd rather die than go back to him!"

"O.K., if that's how you feel about it…" He shrugged. "But don't expect me to help you out of this mess. You walked into it with your eyes open. I didn't force you to come down here, so you can't blame me for what's happened. By heaven, you can't! If it hadn't been for your own damned carelessness you wouldn't have been in this jam."

"Tony! that's brutal of you."

Again he lifted his shoulders.

"Well, I'll give you a week to think out just what you're going to do. After that... you're out! Understand?"

And without giving her the chance to pursue the argument further, Tony turned on his heel, crossed quickly to the door and let himself out silently into the unlit corridor.

CHAPTER VIII

COLONEL MALLOY

I

ACTING-SERGEANT Freddy Strang was feeling thoroughly browned off. Twice the previous day he'd rung the Villa Paloma and asked to speak with Miss Westmacott and, on each occasion, he'd been told, evidently by some member of the domestic staff, that she was out. Freddy, in the hyper-sensitive stages of a first-class love affair, was naturally ready to believe the worst. No doubt about it—the girl, despite her extreme friendliness in the picture gallery, was now holding out on him. She'd instructed the maid to tell him a deliberate falsehood; perhaps smiling in the background as the snub winged to him like a barbed arrow over the wires. For the life of him Freddy couldn't imagine what he'd done to offend her. Of course it was vile luck having to scratch that meeting on the casino terrace on account of the job over at Monte. But, confound it all, he'd been terribly apologetic about it. Surely she must have realized that it was just about the last thing he *wanted* to do?

By the time he dropped off to sleep that Saturday night Freddy had successfully plunged himself into a state of acute melancholia.

He woke early to be greeted by the usual clean-washed, shimmering rectangle of sky beyond the open shutters of his window. Somewhere below his hotel room a woman was singing—a gay, lilting air that rose and fell like a jet of crystal water. A little farther off the laughter of children echoed in the silence of the early morning streets. Farther off still, beyond the red pantiled roofs of the Old Town, a thin sweet peal of bells was summoning the godly to matins.

In a flash Freddy was out of bed, his overnight depression already routed by the onrush of his reviving optimism. Good heavens! what if Miss Westmacott really *had* been out when he rang? What if he'd maligned her? Wasn't it little short of rank stupidity to throw up the sponge, so to speak, before the bell had rung for the end of the first round. Action! That's what the situation demanded. Immediate and decisive action.

With the aid of a street map Freddy had already pin-pointed the whereabouts of the Avenue St. Michel. Why shouldn't he walk up there before breakfast and take a look at the Villa Paloma? After all it would be interesting to see just where the girl lived. And besides—Freddy's mercurial spirits rose at the thought—wasn't it possible that Miss Westmacott might take the dog or something for an early morning constitutional? Quite by chance of course they might bump into each other. And thereafter... well, anything could happen!

Half-an-hour later Freddy was strolling nonchalantly past the gates of the Villa Paloma.

Already he'd plodded six times up the Avenue St. Michel and sauntered six times down it. Twice he'd stopped by the open latticed gates of the front drive to tie a shoelace that hadn't come undone. But behind the pink-washed walls and green-shuttered windows of the villa all was discouragingly quiet.

He was just pivoting at the bottom of the hill to make his seventh ascent when a crimson Vedette swung sharply into the avenue, climbed the hundred yards or so to the villa and swished in through the wide open gates. As the car flashed by Freddy hadn't failed to notice the fair-haired, well-built young man at the wheel. And any fair-haired, well-built young man who drove a crimson Vedette up to the Villa Paloma was, ipso facto, a potential enemy. He wondered if this was the artist bloke mentioned, albeit rather disparagingly, by Miss Westmacott—the fellow whose painting she thought she'd spotted in the gallery.

Quickening his pace Freddy once more drew level with the villa and glanced in through the gates. The Vedette was not drawn up in front of the house, which suggested that it had been driven direct to the garage that Freddy had already spotted to the rear of the place. A small latticed gate let into the garden wall a little higher up the road provided Freddy with the necessary peep-hole. Placing his eye to a crack in the lattice he was able to get a comprehensive view of the garage-yard.

The young man, in shorts and singlet, was standing beside the car with a fishing rod in one hand and a large basket-work creel in the other. Propping the rod, which had been dismantled and slipped into its case, against the side of the car, the young man proceeded to lift the lid of the creel. Although Freddy was no fisherman he was naturally curious to see what sort of catch the fellow had brought back from this early morning expedition.

It was then that Freddy suffered a decided jolt. From inside the creel the young man cautiously removed a large smooth boulder with a few black patches of tar on its rounded surface. What he intended to do with this peculiarly inedible catch Freddy never had the chance to find out, for at that moment a young and extremely winsome maid came out of the side door, portering a saucer of milk. She was followed by a small, smoke-grey kitten. At her appearance the young man hurriedly replaced the boulder in the creel and snapped down the lid. Then strolling over to the girl, who'd now set the saucer on the ground, he glanced quickly around and, with a familiar air, slipped an arm about her lissom waist and kissed her resoundingly.

Somewhat embarrassed by this sudden turn of events and realizing that nothing was to be gained by further eavesdropping, Freddy withdrew his eye from the lattice and turned to make off down the hill. And it was then that he suffered another unexpected jolt. Advancing slowly up the Avenue St. Michel, less than fifty yards away, was Miss Westmacott! She was in animated conversation with a young man whom Acting-Sergeant Strang, with his well-trained powers of observation, had no difficulty in recognizing. It was the chap they'd met in Dunkirk and again, only a few days ago, at *Le Poisson d'Or* in Menton!

II

For one ghastly moment Freddy thought they must have spotted him peering through the gate, but the girl's first words reassured him.

"Oh hullo! It's *you*. Where on earth did you spring from?"

Checking a salute just in time, Freddy put up a hand to raise his hat and then, adding further confusion to his already acute embarrassment, realized that he wasn't wearing one. He gulped out:

"Well, I didn't expect to bump into you, Miss Westmacott. Do you live around here?"

Dilys pointed to the villa.

"There," she said. "The one with the green shutters. Mr. Dillon and I have just been to early service." Adding as she turned to Bill: "By the way, Mr. Smith, I don't think you've met Mr. Dillon, have you?"

"Met!" cut in Bill promptly. "I'll say we have. We're always meeting. Can't get away from each other, eh, Strang?"

Freddy shuddered inwardly. Smith. Strang. He prayed Miss Westmacott wouldn't notice the discrepancy. But Dilys, already vaguely suspicious of the young man's *bona fides,* said instantly:

"Strang? But this isn't Mr. Strang. It's Mr. Smith—Mr. *John* Smith."

Bill laughed sarcastically.

"Well, it was Strang a few days ago—assistant travelling representative for Whitley-Pilbeam's."

"Whitley-Pilbeam's?" echoed Dilys faintly.

"Big constructional engineers in Middlesbrough," explained Bill promptly. "First rate firm, too. Wouldn't mind being with them myself."

"Middlesbrough!" Dilys turned and gazed at Freddy accusingly. "A travelling representative for an engineering firm? But... but I thought you told me—"

"I know," broke in Freddy miserably. "I'm frightfully sorry. I'm afraid I sort of led you up the garden path when we met at the exhibition."

"I see," said Dilys coldly.

"Mind you," floundered Freddy, "I didn't mean to lie to you... at least, not deliberately. I... I just couldn't help myself... if you see what I mean."

"Quite."

"I rang you twice yesterday but they told me you were out."

"Yes—Mr. Dillon drove me over to Nice to see the Primitives. He's staying with us at the moment. He's an old friend of my aunt's."

"Oh," said Freddy glumly.

Dilys turned to Bill, who throughout these exchanges had been wavering in the background with a sardonic smirk on his features.

"Well, I think we ought to be getting along. My aunt'll be furious if we're late for breakfast. So good-bye, Mr... er... Smith."

"Cheerio, Strang!" said Bill maliciously.

"Er... good-bye... cheerio," mumbled Freddy. "Glad to have met you..." He glanced despairingly at Dilys. "Perhaps sometime, Miss Westmacott, we might sort of... of—?"

"We might," concluded Dilys. "But I shouldn't really rely on it."

III

Back at the Hotel Louis he found Inspector Meredith sitting over his coffee and rolls in the dining-room. Meredith looked up sharply.

"Hullo, m'lad. What happened to you? I knocked on your door and got no reply."

"Been for a bit of a constitutional, sir," explained Freddy, adding with a ghoulish attempt at cheerfulness: "Lovely morning. Good to be alive, eh?"

"Well, I'm glad you've decided to show up, Sergeant. I've news for you." Meredith glanced round, lowered his voice and went on: "Blampignon's just been on the 'phone from Nice. It's this cigarette stunt I was telling you about. They've had information from the Algiers police that a fast cruiser-launch left there yesterday without proper clearance papers. Evidently there was a bit of a mist and the launch made a dash for it. Got clean away before the port authorities tumbled to it."

"And they think she's heading here, sir?"

"Exactly. Blampignon thinks they'll try and smuggle the stuff in tonight—somewhere between here and Nice. They're patrolling off-shore with half-a-dozen police launches and posting men at all points along the coast where they think the fellows might try and land the consignment."

For a moment, his interest stimulated by Meredith's terse recital, Freddy forgot the depressing scene that had just been enacted in the Avenue St. Michel.

"You mean they run the launch right in, sir, and unload off her direct?"

Meredith nodded his appreciation of the query.

"I asked Blampignon precisely the same question, Strang, and according to him they don't. The usual procedure is for two or three smaller boats to put out from various points along the coast and meet the launch a few miles out. The cargo's then split up—see? Result—if the police are lucky enough to nab one boat, the others get away. These smaller boats make for widely separated and prearranged rendezvous along shore, usually at those spots where the Littoral road runs close to the sea. Reason, of course—high-powered cars to whisk the stuff away to their distribution centres."

"Sounds well organized, sir."

"It is, Sergeant. And Blampignon wondered if we'd like to be in on tonight's little jamboree. We may draw a blank, of course. On the other hand it might be interesting. What's your reaction, m'lad?"

"Bang on, sir!" exclaimed Freddy eagerly. "Should help us to get a line on just how these French cops work."

"Just what I thought. I've already told Blampignon to fit us into the scheme. He's meeting us here at the local police-station round about six. Oh and that's not all. I've had a cable from the Yard about that Colonel chap at Beaulieu."

"Malloy, sir?"

Meredith nodded.

"They've combed through his record at the War Office. A first-rate soldier and dead reliable—that's their considered opinion. So I think we can safely say that Bourmin's the only one at the Villa Valdeblore tied up with this currency-cum-counterfeit job. At any rate I'm going to take a gamble on it."

"Gamble, sir—how do you mean?"

"We're going to drive over to Beaulieu this morning and see Colonel Malloy. I'm going to lay my cards on the table and enlist his help. It's a risk, I admit, but a calculated risk, and it might well bring a very handsome rabbit out of the hat, Sergeant. So get outside that *brioche* as quickly as you can, then nip round and get the car out of the garage."

IV

Providence was certainly at their elbow that Sunday morning. From the outset their little expedition to the Villa Valdeblore ran on oiled wheels. To begin with, when they arrived at the villa, the Rolls was drawn up before the portico, and Bourmin in a bottle-green uniform was ushering a small, wispy woman into its barn-like interior. Meredith felt sure that this was Mrs. Malloy and to judge by her sombre but dressy *ensemble* it looked as if the Colonel's wife were off to church. Anxious that Bourmin should know nothing of this visit, Meredith waited until the Rolls had turned into the main road at the south end of the avenue, then, with Strang at his heels, strode up the short drive to the front entrance.

A few minutes later, their luck still holding, they were shaking hands with Colonel Malloy in his small, book-lined study at the end of the hall. To Meredith it was like stepping out of France into an infinitesimal but unmistakable scrap of the British Empire. It was as one would have expected—regimental groups; a rack of sporting guns; a couple of stuffed salmon; a mantelshelf crowded with silver cups and trophies; and everywhere about the room the indiscriminate *lares et penates* of the Colonel's extensive sojourns in the Orient.

The Colonel, himself, merged into this background like a chameleon. Tall, gaunt, white-haired, with a short bristly moustache on his long upper lip; a profile like a hawk, and steel-blue eyes that looked out on the world with an air of tolerant good humour—Meredith recognized the type at once. Bigoted and conventional, perhaps, but the sort of fellow one could depend on in adversity and honest as the day was long. Having shown his credentials, Meredith explained the reason for his presence in the South of France and outlined the circumstances that had brought about his visit to the Villa Valdeblore. Colonel Malloy listened without comment until Meredith had concluded his explanation. Then he snapped out with a choleric expression:

"So that damned fellow Bourmin's a Bad Hat, eh? Can't say I'm surprised. I've never really trusted him. It was my wife's idea that we should engage him. She liked his manner. But women are more easily taken in by that sort of thing than we are, eh? Now what exactly d'you want me to do, Inspector? Dismiss him? Hand him over to the local police?"

"Good heavens—no! That's the last thing we want. You see, sir, we uphold that Bourmin's only a small cog in a big wheel. We're hoping that now we've taken you into our confidence you'll be able to keep an eye on the chap. For example, if you notice anything suspicious in his actions—"

"I'm to get in touch with you, eh? Well, that makes sense. I'm in a sound strategic position to keep him under observation."

"So we can count you in, sir?"

"Up to the hilt."

"Good enough," said Meredith, delighted with the Colonel's readiness to help. "Now tell me, sir—does Bourmin live on the premises?"

"Yes—he's got a couple of rooms over the garage. He has his meals with the rest of the staff in the kitchen."

"I see. We noticed the car was just leaving as we turned up."

"Quite. My wife attends the English church here. Bourmin always drives her to the service and waits outside the church to drive her back. If it hadn't been for a touch of lumbago, I'd have been there myself."

"What time do you expect them back, sir?"

"Oh, not for another hour and a half at least."

"Do you think we could take a look at these rooms. Quite understand if you object."

"My dear fellow, why not? Bourmin's probably locked the door but I've a duplicate key. I'll take you over at once. Unless, of course, you'd rather—"

"No. I'd like you to come along too, Colonel. But if we *can* investigate the place without being seen by the domestic staff so much the better. Whatever happens we don't want to put Bourmin on his guard."

A few minutes later the three men were climbing the exterior staircase that led up to the chauffeur's snug little flatlet above the garage. Once in the small but comfortably furnished living-room, Meredith explained:

"We're anxious to find out just where and how Bourmin picks up the counterfeit notes as they come off the press. Does he collect the stuff in bulk and store it away until he's unloaded it on his... er... clients? Or does he deal with it in penny packets, so to speak? By the way, Colonel, you allow the fellow to use the car on his half-day off, eh?"

"Yes, confound it! How did you find that out? A concession of my wife's. Can't say I agree with all this spoon-feeding but a good chauffeur's hard to come by these days. It's one of my wife's little whims to keep the fellow 'sweet'. You want me to put a stop to these jaunts—is that it, Inspector?"

"Far from it, sir. I wanted to make sure you *wouldn't* stop them. The Sergeant here has been detailed to tail the chap on these Thursday trips. We're hoping he'll eventually lead us to the nerve-centre of the racket. Now what about a quick comb through of the fellow's effects."

"To see if he's got any of these notes tucked away under the mattress, eh?"

"That's roughly the idea, sir. If he hasn't then he must be making regular contacts somewhere with another member of the gang. O.K., Sergeant, let's get cracking. The usual routine search. You know the procedure."

Together the two officials made a deft and comprehensive search of the chauffeur's two rooms. Luckily Bourmin's personal possessions were meagre to a degree and many of the built-in drawers and cupboards were empty. At the end of twenty minutes Meredith was pretty well satisfied that every possible hiding-place had been thoroughly frisked. He turned to the Colonel.

"Umph—much as I anticipated. No sign of any notes, no documentary evidence, nothing in fact to connect him in any way with the racket. Of course there's always the chance that—"

"Here, hang on a second, sir!" broke in Strang excitedly. "I believe I've hit on something. Take a dekko at this." The Sergeant held out a crumpled, half-torn envelope. "I found it jammed in the window-frame here. It was folded up into a kind of wedge. I suppose the window rattled or something."

Meredith took the tattered envelope and peered inside it.

"But the darn thing's empty, Sergeant!"

"I know, sir. But have a squint at what's on the back of it. Looks like a map of some sort."

Quickly Meredith reversed the envelope and examined the sketch.

"Ump—a street plan by the look of it. Unfortunately the corner's been torn off and half the sketch seems to be missing." Meredith smoothed out the crumpled scrap of paper and placed it on the table. "Let's take a more detailed look at it. You too, Colonel, if you will. You know more about the local topography than we do. Maybe you'll recognize the spot."

For a few moments the three men pored in silence over the crude and mutilated drawing. It encompassed what appeared to be three roads enclosing a small triangle. Opposite the apex of the triangle was inscribed a cross, against which was written C.C. 6a. Pencilled lightly between the lines that represented the widest of the three roads—the one, in fact, that formed the base of the triangle—were the letters ARTE, then a space, followed by the letters QL.

"Well, sir, what do you make of it?" asked Meredith, who'd already whipped out his notebook and made a copy of the plan. "Puzzling, eh?"

The Colonel nodded.

"Pity we can't lay our hands on the missing piece. This semi-circular tear cuts right across the middle of the lettering. And the letters at the base obviously indicate the names of the—" Malloy broke off and added excitedly: "Here, wait a minute! I believe I've hit on a clue."

"Really, sir?"

"Yes—this QL. Notice the space after the Q? Well, I've a shrewd idea that this Q stands for Quai. You follow? Quai something-or-other. And if I'm right... well, you see the implication?"

"We'll locate the spot somewhere near a harbour."

"That's how it strikes me. May be wrong, of course. But it's worth following up. Mind you, there are a good many harbours along this stretch of coastline, but I've no doubt the local police—"

"Exactly. I'll get in touch with them at once."

"And this cross—what do you make of that, sir?" asked Strang.

Meredith winked.

"I've my own ideas about that, but at the moment, Sergeant, I'm just not talking." The Inspector glanced at his watch. "We've still got a bit of time in hand, but I reckon there's nothing more to be gained by hanging about here." He turned to Strang. "Refold that envelope, m'lad, and jam it back in the window-frame just as you found it. Ready, Colonel? Can't say how much I appreciate your co-operation.

But mum's the word, of course. Better if you don't even mention our visit to Mrs. Malloy. You agree, sir?"

"Emphatically!" The colonel's steel-blue eyes twinkled merrily. "Maybe you're familiar with the old French saying, Inspector."

"What saying, sir?"

"A woman's chief weapon is her tongue and she never lets it rust! Apt, eh? Devilish apt!"

CHAPTER IX

THE MAISON TURINI

I

AT SIX O'CLOCK, punctual to the minute, Inspector Blampignon's car drew up outside the *Commissariat de Police* in Menton. Meredith and Strang had already been there some minutes chatting with the Duty Sergeant. Blampignon greeted them boisterously.

"Ah, this is a great pleasure, *mes amis!* It is good that we should all work arm in arm, as you say. Much may happen tonight. Much may not happen. But in our profession it is necessary always to be an optimist." He pivoted on the Duty Sergeant. "A room where we can be alone, perhaps?"

The Sergeant pushed open a door that led out of the main office.

"*Voila, M'sieur L'Inspecteur!*"

Once the door was closed, Blampignon swung round on Meredith and announced with a melodramatic flourish:

"*M'sieur*—we have it!"

Meredith looked blank.

"Have what?"

"The information you wished for... about the little sketch on the envelope. The moment you had rung me off, I collected all the necessary maps. I say to my staff 'Find this place or I cut your throats!' *Mon vieux*—ten minutes before I leave Nice, they find what we look for. Those young men have good sense, eh?"

"You're telling me!" exclaimed Meredith elatedly. "Well, my dear fellow, what's the answer?"

With a flamboyant gesture Blampignon whipped a large-scale map from his pocket and slapped it down on the little table in the centre of the room.

"See here—a street map of Menton." He snatched a pencil from another pocket and stabbed it down on the map. "Here, see... the harbour. And here, a road running beside the harbour. You note its name, Inspector?"

"Quai Bonaparte," read Meredith.

"*Exactement!* To the left of the little triangle, you remember... the letters ARTE. Now we have it! To the right QL. Please to read again."

"Quai Laurenti."

Blampignon shrugged.

"It is simple, eh? All we need to do now is to walk down to the harbour and find out, *précisément,* what this cross, marked C.C. 6a, is meant to indicate. You have an idea already, perhaps?"

"Just a hunch," nodded Meredith.

"A hunch—what is that?" asked Blampignon, puzzled; then with sudden inspiration: "Ah! I have it. A box in which you keep rabbits. But why should this cross represent a—"

Meredith broke in with a laugh.

"Hold hard, my dear chap, or we're going to get in a tangle. A hunch is a... is a..." Meredith glanced despairingly at Strang. "Good lord, Sergeant, how the devil *would* you describe a hunch?"

"An intuitive guess, sir," said Freddy promptly.

"An intuitive—?" began Blampignon, more puzzled than ever.

"O.K. We'll let it pass," cut in Meredith hastily. "But if my theory's correct then I've a pretty shrewd idea that X marks the spot."

"The spot?" demanded Blampignon, still hopelessly at sea.

Meredith nodded.

"The spot where 'Chalky' Cobbett has his hide-out. The spot where he and his little playmates print off their dud notes."

Blampignon whistled.

"*Eh bien,* I admit it is possible."

"Well, if C.C. doesn't stand for 'Chalky' Cobbett," contested Meredith, "then I'm losing my grip. The 6a is probably the number of the house or flat."

"Quite, M'sieur. And this evening before we turn our minds to this other little business, it would be as well for us to take a walk down to the quayside. Always it is like this. For days no progress, then... zut!... everything happen at once." Blampignon refolded the map and thrust it back in his pocket. "*Maintenant, à nos moutons, mes amis...* to tell you what I propose about the little expedition we make tonight. It occur to me that..."

II

It was nearing dusk when the three officials, having parked the car just beyond the market, found themselves sauntering along the Quai de Bonaparte. To Meredith, who'd greatly enjoyed this unique and colourful episode in his long professional career, it was a sobering and nostalgic moment. Within the next half-hour, it was more than possible that his investigations would be at an end. With "Chalky" Cobbett under arrest and the illicit press out of action, the whole counterfeit-cum-currency racket would, *ipso facto,* die a natural death. And it wouldn't be easy, he realized, to take leave of this sunlit, sparkling coast with its terraced vineyards and olive groves, its palms and oleanders, its fantastic cacti, its mimosa-scented streets and impossibly blue seas. He thought of the Old Kent Road on a wet February night and shuddered.

But there it was. Duty was duty. He'd come south to pick up "Chalky" Cobbett and, once he was pulled in, he'd be forced to write Finis to the case, pack up his traps and clear off back to England, Home and Beauty.

It was, therefore, with mixed feelings that Meredith heard Blampignon's announcement:

"That triangular grove of palm trees a little way ahead—that is the place we look for. We turn off here at the left. This is not a good district. It is very poor and very..." Blampignon delicately held his nose. "You have noticed it, *mon ami?*"

Meredith most certainly had! A potpourri of garlic, sewerage and dank rottenness that rose like a miasma from the airless alleyways that zig-zagged in mounting terraces from the waterfront. An atmosphere of poverty and depression hung over the district. Even the little group of palms, beneath which were a few uncomfortable, iron-slatted seats, had the moulting bedraggled look of worn-out feather-dusters.

They had no difficulty in pin-pointing the building that Bourmin had marked with a cross in his little map. It was evidently a kind of tenement-house, and possibly due to wartime neglect the property was sadly in need of repair. Scabs of plaster were peeling away from its sickly green walls and its lop-sided shutters and skimpy iron balconies were rotting and rusting for want of paint. The whole façade was festooned with lines of gaily-coloured undergarments, slung between the balconies like tattered flags. It looked as if a puff of wind would bring the whole place crashing to the ground.

"*Maison Turini,*" read Strang from the chipped stone plaque let into the wall. "Heavens above, sir! what a rabbit warren. I reckon we'll need a ferret to flush 'Chalky' out of this lot."

Blampignon pointed out:

"Remember we have what is no doubt the number of the apartment in which you hope to find your friend. Number 6a was it not? *Alors!* we make an enquiry."

In response to the Inspector's jerk on the rusty bell-push, an aged crone, with a black shawl over her head, her feet encased in carpet slippers, flip-flapped out of a glass-fronted cubby-hole just inside the entrance. She hadn't been alone in the little room. Seated at a table over a bottle of cheap red wine was a wizened, white-bearded little fellow with a face the colour of a walnut. He was chuckling and mumbling to himself with all the unselfconscious naivety of a child in the throes of some imaginary adventure.

"*Pardon, Madame*—you are the *concierge* here?" asked Blampignon.

"Yes, M'sieur." Then catching the Inspector's sidelong glance she added in explanation: "*Hélas,* M'sieur, my husband is no longer able to carry out his duties. He is just a little..." She tapped her forehead significantly. "You understand? *Eh bien,* what is it you wish, M'sieur?"

With the natural politeness of his race, Blampignon explained the reason for his visit and, with the greatest discretion, began to cross-question the old woman. At first she seemed reluctant to talk, but soon—obviously flattered by the charm of the Inspector's approach—her answers grew more and more voluble. As she spoke a kind of *patois* Meredith was unable to grasp even the gist of her remarks. But to judge by the ever-broadening smile that spread over Blampignon's honest, sun-kissed countenance, he was getting the information he was after, plus a full measure of irrelevant gossip! As the old woman's evidence continued, Blampignon's smile gave way to a grin; the grin to a chuckle; and the chuckle to a slowly-mounting roar of laughter that shook his portly frame from head to foot.

"Good heavens, man!" exclaimed Meredith, bewildered by his *confrère's* reaction. "What the devil's the matter? What's the joke?"

"We are the joke, *mon ami,*" gasped Blampignon, the tears trickling down his cheeks. "Perhaps I should be in a bad humour because we have come on—how do you say?—the chase of the wild goose? But sometimes it is better to laugh than to curse."

"You mean we're too late?" shot out Meredith. "Chalky's given us the slip, eh?"

"He was never here, *mon ami.*"

"Never here!"

Blampignon dabbed his eyes and, still chuckling, shook his head.

"C.C. eh? We think, *naturellement,* that it stand for 'Chalky' Cobbett. But this is where we go wrong. I have enquired of Madame who live in apartment number 6a."

"Well?"

"A young woman, M'sieur, by the name of Celeste Chounet. I ask Madame when and how this young lady came to be here. She tell me some two months ago a middle-aged foreigner engage the rooms for her. I ask her to describe this man." Blampignon shrugged.

"*Eh bien,* it is Bourmin without a doubt. She says he come here once or twice a week to visit his little friend upstairs." The inspector winked. "I think perhaps I should have a few words with this Mam'selle Chounet myself, eh? Madame here has been most explicit but always it is wise to check up on such a statement. You will wait here, perhaps?"

"O.K.," chuckled Meredith. "But business before pleasure, remember!"

After Blampignon had ascertained the whereabouts of the girl's apartment and plodded away up the narrow spiral stairway, the *concierge* returned to her cubby-hole. Meredith and Strang began to pace idly up and down the dingy corridor, discussing in low tones the unexpected outcome of this little expedition. Whatever his superior's reactions may have been to this setback, Freddy was elated. Despite the snub that he'd received early that morning outside the Villa Paloma, he still felt that given time and opportunity he could win Miss Westmacott over to a more co-operative frame-of-mind. And with "Chalky" still at large there could as yet be no question of their return to London.

Ten minutes later Blampignon rejoined them. He announced with an expressive roll of his dark and luminous eyes:

"*Tiens!* our friend Bourmin has unquestionably the eye of a connoisseur. A very charming and sensible young woman."

"And her story tallies with that of the old woman?" asked Meredith.

"Absolutely, *mon ami.* Bourmin set her up in this apartment some eight weeks ago. They met one evening in a café at Monte Carlo."

"Did you question her about Bourmin?"

"Yes—but I think it is certain she knows nothing of his criminal activities. Nor does she even seem to know who are his friends. It is clear that he does not come here as often as Mam'selle Chounet would wish." Blampignon shook his head and heaved an elephantine sigh. "I think perhaps she is lonely sometimes. It is very sad, *mon ami.* The beauty of a woman is like that of a flower. It must be looked on often before it withers. *Tout passe, tout change,* as we say. Yes, yes... it is very sad."

III

It was shortly after midnight when they spotted the ghostly outlines of the launch against the dark line of the land. For three solid hours the little police-boat had been patrolling about two hundred yards off-shore between the harbour at Menton and the outermost point of Cap Martin. For the first hour Meredith and Strang had enjoyed the novelty of this maritime beat, but as time dragged on and nothing happened their initial enthusiasm began to wane. Now it looked as if things, with any luck, were about to grow more lively.

It was evident that the launch had slipped into its mooring-place when the police-boat had been at the far end of its patrol, for they were convinced that it hadn't been there when they'd last investigated this particular stretch of coastline.

Hastily throttling back the engine, Blampignon brought the boat round in a wide sweep and headed for a point about a hundred yards away from where the launch was lying at its moorings. He explained in swift undertones:

"We will get ashore, *mes amis,* and see what we can see, eh? But very silently, you understand. I think it is possible that so far we have not been noticed."

Cutting out the engine entirely, Blampignon, with perfect judgment, brought the little craft gently to the shore. There, with surprising agility, the Inspector clambered cautiously on to the rocks and in a few seconds had securely tied off the painter. One by one he helped the others to disembark and silently, in single file, they began to creep towards the launch.

The foreshore at this point was tricky to negotiate in the dark. Beyond the fringe of rocks, a rough grassy bank mounted to the road that, for about half-a-mile or so, ran parallel with the sea along the eastern side of the cape. To make matters worse a canopy of umbrella pines shut out what little light there was, and their roots, thwarted by the stony soil, in many places projected above the ground. And it was in one of these, when they were less than a dozen yards from their objective, that Blampignon unfortunately caught his foot. Even as he measured his length on the ground a low whistle sounded ahead, followed by the scrape of boots sliding over the rocks and the sudden lifting drone of the launch's engine.

"*Vite! Vite!*" yelled Blampignon. "Before they cast off."

"Come on, Strang," snapped Meredith, hastily clicking on his torch. "At the double—but watch out for these confounded roots!"

"O.K., sir."

Aided by the rays of the pocket-lamp they plunged forward, slipping and scrambling over the rocks until they reached the spot where the boat had been moored. But even as Meredith made ready to spring aboard, the launch swung clear of the rocks and, gathering speed, slipped swiftly away into the darkness. Meredith swore fluently.

"So that's that, eh, Sergeant? A couple of seconds sooner and we'd have nabbed 'em." Adding as Blampignon lumbered up out of the gloom gingerly rubbing his barked shins: "What now, my dear fellow? No good giving chase, eh? Too big a start."

Blampignon shook his head despondently:

"It is hopeless, hopeless! But the launch... do you think you could identify it if you saw it again?"

"Sure of it. White-painted hull with two thin scarlet stripes just above the water-line. There was a name on her bows, but unfortunately she was too far out for me to read it."

"A name!" exclaimed Blampignon. "That is very curious. It is usual for these racketeers to avoid such a simple means of identification. There is much about this business, in fact, that I fail to understand. If she was moored here to unload the contraband, why is there no car waiting to collect it?"

"Umph, you've got something there," commented Meredith, slowly swinging the rays of his torch over the surrounding ground. "Nothing's been dumped here either. Another odd factor, eh? After all, they'd have had plenty of time to start landing the stuff before we broke in on the party. As you say—" Meredith broke off and added with a chuckle: "Hullo! Here's a bit of evidence they've left behind anyway. An empty wine bottle by the look of it." He picked up the bottle and examined the label. "Nuits St. Georges, eh? Must have been making a night of it. I suppose we *are* right about this?"

"How do you mean?" asked Blampignon.

"You don't think it was just a picnic party or a courting couple or something of the kind?"

"But if so why did they rush off in such a hurry?" demanded Blampignon. "Oh no, no. Of this I am sure. They were engaged in—now what is the expression?—some shady business, *mon ami.*"

"Quite—but *what* shady business?"

Blampignon shrugged.

"It is incomprehensible, M'sieur. But perhaps, in due course, we find the answer."

"And now?" asked Meredith. "Where do we go from here?"

"Back to Menton. It is useless to continue our patrol. I think it is good time that we tie up the boat and get a little sleep. Tomorrow I will ring you and let you know if any of our patrols have better luck. I am still hoping it is so, M'sieur."

CHAPTER X

PICTURE PUZZLE

I

DIRECTLY AFTER BREAKFAST the following morning Meredith received a 'phone-call from Inspector Blampignon. The news that he had to impart was sensational but puzzling. A coastguard cutter, patrolling some two miles off Cap Ferrat, had actually succeeded in intercepting the cruiser-launch before it had made contact with the smaller craft that had put out from various points to meet it. The crew had been arrested, the contraband impounded by the custom's authorities, and the launch, itself, confiscated. According to Blampignon this ill-fated trip had resulted in a dead loss of some ten million francs to the gang who'd sponsored it. He was convinced that the racket, at any rate for the time being, had been broken wide open.

"But you see what we have to ask ourselves now, *mon ami?* If the launch we see at Cap Martin has no connection with this smuggling, then what precisely was it up to?"

Although they discussed this enigma for some minutes, Meredith had to admit that he was as nonplussed as Blampignon himself. They did advance one possible theory. Had the launch been "borrowed" without the owner's permission? But, as Blampignon pointed out with devastating commonsense, along that crook-infested coast nobody but a fool would leave the engine-casing of his boat unlocked. And apart from this elementary precaution there were a dozen other equally effective methods of immobilizing such craft when lying at their moorings. Meredith concluded:

"So take it all round, we've got to admit we're flummoxed. Well, thanks for ringing, my dear chap. If anything further turns up in this counterfeiting business I'll let you know on the nod. But don't expect miracles, because at the moment we seem to be bogged down. Depressing but true. However, we'll do our best. Can't say more. *Au revoir*, old man."

II

Later that day Meredith was to reflect on this particular statement and chuckle. But that was just how it always ran. Long periods of frustration and inactivity, suddenly alternating with short, sharp bursts of progress.

It was only a few minutes after Blampignon had rung off, in fact, when a totally unexpected development put just such a jerk into his investigation. It was a 'phone-call from the local police-station that first whipped Meredith and Strang out of the doldrums in which for so many days they'd been becalmed. Some information had just come in—significant information. Inspector Gibaud was anxious that his English colleagues should have the details without delay. Could they call round at once?

"Can a duck swim?" exclaimed Meredith, delighted. "Expect us in three minutes. No—cancel that, and make it two!"

Inspector Gibaud, whom Meredith had already met, was waiting impatiently for them in his office. He was the perfect counterpart of Blampignon—a tough, wiry little man, with quick brown eyes and a pair of magnificent handlebar moustaches that he chewed fiercely during moments of reflection. From Meredith's point-of-view Gibaud had one outstanding virtue—he could speak English like a native. The outcome, no doubt, of a long-ago holiday at Folkestone where he'd fallen in love with the receptionist at his hotel and eventually whisked her back over the Channel as his wife.

Waving them to be seated, Gibaud announced brusquely:

"I've some good news for you, Inspector. Some of those counterfeit notes have turned up here in Menton. They were brought along early this morning by a tobacconist called Guillevin. And that's not all!

Guillevin was able to identify the particular customer who passed these notes over the counter."

"The devil he was!" exclaimed Meredith. "And where exactly does this M'sieur Guillevin hang out?"

"At the far end of the Rue de la Republique—near the Old Town."

"I see. And the customer who passed the notes?"

"An odd little fellow by the name of Jacques Dufil. Apparently he always buys his tobacco at Guillevin's. At least," amended Gibaud with a smile, "when he can afford it. Guillevin's known the fellow for years. He lives somewhere up in the Old Town in a single room and ekes out a precarious sort of existence as a painter."

"Jacques Dufil, the artist?" broke in Strang excitedly.

Meredith broke in with a sardonic glance.

"Don't tell me you know the fellow!"

"Well, not exactly, sir. But there was a picture of his in the exhibition I visited the other morning. Pretty duff in my opinion. But, of course, all this ultra-modern, surrealistic stuff leaves me cold."

"Good lord! just listen to it!" snorted Meredith. "These high-brow boys from Hendon!" Adding as he caught Gibaud's expression, "Anything worrying you, Inspector?"

"No, no. I'm surprised to hear that Dufil's showing one of his canvases at the gallery—that's all. No idea he had any standing as an artist. It certainly doesn't fit in with the facts."

"How do you mean?"

"Well, at one time, according to Guillevin, he made a pretty sketchy sort of living touting his masterpieces round the tourist cafés during the holiday months."

Meredith's interest quickened.

"Tourists, eh? You know, Gibaud, I wouldn't be surprised if we hadn't got something here. Has it occurred to you that this picture hawking would provide the perfect alibi for a little shady dealing... er... on the side, as it were?"

"Black Market francs, eh? The point *had* occurred to me. But I'm afraid *that* cat won't jump."

"Won't jump—why?"

"Because for the last six months our friend Dufil hasn't been working the cafés. Apparently he's found a patron who's willing to buy his canvases. Not just an odd one here and there, but his whole output! I don't say the poor devil's made a fortune, but he's certainly had a bit more to spend on tobacco."

"I see," mused Meredith; then, springing up, he added impatiently: "Well, what are we waiting for? We've got to have a word with Dufil. We've got to find out just how these dud notes came into his possession. Point is, until we've cross-questioned him, we can't be sure he isn't tied up with the racket himself. Where does he hang out?"

Gibaud chuckled.

"Although he's a professional man, I'm afraid he doesn't wallow in the luxury of a proper postal address. But Guillevin's explained exactly how we get there. It's off some alleyway in the Old Town. You'd like me to come along as interpreter, perhaps?"

"There's no 'perhaps' about it," admitted Meredith with a rueful smile. "I'd be sunk without you."

"Good enough then," concluded Gibaud briskly. "Let's go."

III

To walk from the broad avenues and sunlit shopping streets of the new town into the sunless chasms between the high shuttered houses of the old was to pass in a few moments from the twentieth century into the Middle Ages. Meredith, who so far hadn't had time to explore this quarter of Menton, found it fascinating. The guide-books, tendering their customary bunch of shop-soiled adjectives, might refer to the Old Town as "quaint", "picturesque", "historic"; but, as they plunged into this labyrinth of narrow streets, it was the word "ageless" that came instinctively into the Inspector's mind. This, one felt, was as it had always been. In these secret, tortuous alleyways nothing had changed. The bare-footed, brown-skinned old harridans gossiping on their doorsteps might well have squatted there when Napoleon's Grand Army tramped along this twelve-foot highway on their victorious march into Italy. Here, felt Meredith, amid this amorphous red-tiled cluster of houses clamped so securely to the naked rock, time and progress had been kept at bay.

But Gibaud allowed his English colleagues little time to stand and stare. With an unerring sense of direction he hustled them briskly through this honeycomb of dark, squalid streets, turned into a vine-shaded courtyard and rapped imperatively on the rickety door of the hunchback's one-roomed lodging. After a moment's silence, they heard the painful shuffling of his footsteps on the creaking stairs and, an instant later, the door was cautiously opened and his head appeared round the corner of it like an apprehensive tortoise. Seeing Gibaud, who was in uniform, Dufil uttered a snarling cry and shrank back, a sullen, suspicious expression on his crooked features.

"What do you want? Why have you come here?" he demanded hoarsely.

"You are Jacques Dufil?" enquired Gibaud politely.

"Yes, M'sieur."

"Very well—we want to have a talk with you."

"A talk with me. What about, M'sieur?"

Gibaud gestured to the staircase.

"Shall we discuss that upstairs, my friend?"

The hunchback lifted his misshapen shoulders.

"But certainly—if it is necessary."

Once up in the gloomy, stone-walled little room, Gibaud, wasting no time in small talk, got down to his cross-examination. At first, still apprehensive and ill-at-ease, Dufil refused to be drawn. But gradually, realizing the impersonal nature of the Inspector's enquiries, his grunted monosyllables gave way to an ever-quickening stream of information. And bit by bit it all came out.

At the end of some fifteen minutes, Gibaud, who'd been hastily jotting down a summary of the hunchback's evidence, turned with a satisfied chuckle to Meredith and demanded:

"Well, how much did you understand of that lot?"

"Not a damned word!" retorted Meredith. "But since you look like a cat that's swallowed the canary, I guess you've learnt plenty. So you'd better give me the low-down, my dear chap. Then if I want to put any questions to our friend here you can tackle him before we leave. O.K.?"

"O.K.," nodded Gibaud. "Well, this briefly is how it runs, About six months ago a fellow named Latour got in touch with Dufil after he'd seen him touting his pictures round the cafés. He asked Dufil if he was prepared, from then on, to sell him every picture that he painted. There was one stipulation. If Dufil accepted the offer he was to keep his mouth shut about this arrangement. At first Dufil thought the fellow must he a dealer and that he was buying in his canvases as a speculation. You know how I mean?—on the offchance that there might be a future vogue for the fellow's work. But he soon realized that Latour had absolutely no knowledge of art. Mind you, our friend here wasn't making a fortune out of this offer. Far from it! Latour made it clear from the start that he was only prepared to pay a cut-throat price. But the point was that the money came in regularly and on the nod. Dufil naturally asked himself why was Latour so anxious to buy up all his output? And why didn't he want anybody to know about it? Well, our friend here may have a queer-shaped head but it's screwed on the right way." Gibaud paused and threw a sidelong glance at the hunchback, who, though not understanding a word of English, had been beaming and nodding as if in complete agreement with the Inspector's narrative. "You're a cunning little fellow, eh, Dufil? Far more intelligent than you look, I reckon." The hunchback's nods grew more emphatic and he chuckled hoarsely. Gibaud turned again to Meredith. "It didn't take him long to dig out the answer to the mystery. Latour was buying in his pictures and fobbing them off as his own. In short, for some private and obviously nefarious reason Latour was posing as an artist. Realizing this Dufil made a few discreet enquiries in the town and soon discovered that Latour was living in the house of an eccentric Englishwoman—a wealthy widow by the name of Hedderwick. It seems that she owns a largish villa here in the Avenue St. Michel."

"Hedderwick! The Avenue St. Michel!" cried Strang excitedly. "Good heavens! it's all beginning to add up."

"Have you gone crazy?" asked Meredith with a withering glance. "What's beginning to add up? I suppose you couldn't possibly let us know what you're blethering about?"

"Well, you see, sir—Miss Westmacott mentioned that there was an artist living in the house. She didn't actually tell me his surname. She just referred to him as Paul. But it *must* be this fellow Latour. It's a staggering coincidence, but there's no getting round it."

"There are times, m'lad," observed Meredith with a glare, "when I could take you by the ears and shake you silly. What the devil are you driving at? Who's Miss Westmacott? Where did you meet her? And what the deuce do *you* know about the Avenue St. Michel?"

Realizing that he could no longer sidestep an explanation, Freddy flushed to the roots of his hair and, taking a deep breath, delivered a garbled and almost incoherent account of his meeting with Miss Westmacott at the exhibition and, later, his encounter with her outside the gates of the Villa Paloma.

"I see," said Meredith at the conclusion of his subordinate's romantic little saga. "The secret love-life of Acting-Sergeant Strang, eh? I thought you said that, on your present pay, wine and women were two of the luxuries you couldn't afford."

"Oh, but this is different, sir," stammered Freddy. "Absolutely it is. Miss Westmacott's a really decent type, if you know what I mean. There's absolutely no—"

"O.K., Sergeant," broke in Meredith with a twinkle. "No need to get hot under the collar. We'll take your word for it. The point is you appear to know something about this set-up at the Villa Paloma and the knowledge might prove useful." He turned to Gibaud. "You agree, Inspector?"

"Well, the Sergeant's information certainly corroborates Dufil's evidence concerning Latour. And from what M'sieur Strang has just told us, it's evident *why* Latour was buying in these pictures."

"You mean he'd persuaded this Hedderwick woman he was an artist down on his luck and needed these pictures to prove it?"

"Exactly. This Englishwoman was acting as his patron. Latour was... now how shall I put it?"

"Sitting pretty," suggested Meredith. "And he was damn well going to make sure he went on sitting pretty. Yes, I see that—but how about these dud notes? Where do they come in? Are you suggesting that Latour's been paying Dufil for these canvases in counterfeit money?"

"No, no—there was a further little twist in the relationship between Latour and our friend here before the counterfeit notes turned up on the scene. It all hinges on the exhibition that the Sergeant mentioned just now—L'Exposition de Peinture Méditerranée at the Menton galleries."

"I don't follow."

"This way, my dear fellow. Dufil here has a great pride in his work. No doubt about that. He has, I think, the faith and integrity of the genuine artist. He puts into his pictures all that is best in himself, even though he's never received the recognition that, in his opinion, is due to him. But Latour, you see, treated the poor devil as if he were a hack, a mere machine to turn out the goods for which he was prepared to pay. Naturally our friend here rebelled against this attitude, and when he heard that this local exhibition was being planned, he cocked a snook at Latour and submitted one of his pictures for the committee's consideration."

"And they accepted it?"

Gibaud nodded.

"With the result that a few days ago Dufil was approached by an art dealer from Cannes. The fellow had evidently taken a fancy to his work and was anxious to act as his agent."

"I see!" whistled Meredith. "And Latour got to know about this, eh? He saw the picture in the exhibition, perhaps, realized that Dufil was now in a position to sell his work elsewhere and—"

"Precisely," cut in Gibaud. "He paid Dufil a flat hundred thousand francs to turn the offer down. Of course Latour was furious with Dufil for submitting the picture, but he wasn't in a position to do anything about it. At first he tried threats, but, as I said before, Dufil's no fool. He knew he held the whip hand and Latour had to climb down. The one thing Dufil didn't anticipate was that Latour would buy him off with a wad of utterly worthless notes. So it rather looks as if Latour gets the last laugh, eh?"

"But does he?" demanded Meredith with a meaning look. "Does he, my dear fellow? You see the implication? If Latour was able to lay his hands on a hundred thousand francs' worth of forged notes, surely he must be tied up with the racket? And since we know just where to find him, I've a feeling that M'sieur Latour's all lined up for a spot of third degree. I don't want to appear unduly optimistic but, in my opinion, this looks like the beginning of the end." He swung round on Strang. "Another couple of days, Sergeant, and I shouldn't be surprised if we're hitting the trail for home. Sorry to nip your little romance in the bud, but there it is. I daresay you'll recover from the shock!"

CHAPTER XI

EVIDENCE IN THE ATTIC

I

PARTING FROM Inspector Gibaud at the steps of the Commissariat, Meredith and Strang set off briskly through the town *en route* for the Avenue St. Michel. It was still a little short of noon and the Inspector was determined to cross-question Latour without a moment's delay.

"There's just one thing, sir," ventured Freddy as they swung into the Avenue de Verdun. "About this girl I met... this... er... Miss Westmacott."

"Oh good lord, yes! I was forgetting, Sergeant. She's Mrs. Hedderwick's niece, isn't she?"

"Yes, sir," gulped Freddy. "But Mrs. Hedderwick doesn't know that I've met her. She might be a bit scratchy about it, if you follow. So... er... if you could sort of—"

Meredith broke in with a laugh.

"I see what you're hinting at, but you can rely on my discretion. My ignorance, when necessary, can be positively abysmal, m'lad. It's all a part of our training, eh?"

A saucy-eyed maid, whom Freddy recognized as the girl he'd seen feeding the kitten in the garage-yard, answered their ring. On learning that Meredith wished to have a word with Mrs. Hedderwick she ushered them into a small but exceedingly elegant little lounge on the right of the hall. It was furnished in the Chinese style, with exquisitely lacquered stools and tables, a couple of glass cabinets filled with porcelain figures, embroidered Chinese hangings in the narrow windows and, underfoot, a silky, lime-green Chinese carpet. The clean faint scent of sandalwood hung on the air. Meredith eyed the room appreciatively. There was nothing he would have enjoyed more than an uninterrupted potter around these collector's pieces, but barely had he set off on a tour of inspection when the door opened and Nesta Hedderwick waddled in like some amiable, bright-plumaged duck. Meredith gave her a little bow.

"Mrs. Hedderwick?"

"That's right," nodded Nesta. "And who exactly...?"

"I'm Inspector Meredith of Scotland Yard and this is my assistant, Sergeant Strang."

Mrs. Hedderwick's reaction to this simple if dramatic announcement took Meredith by surprise. He was accustomed to people, unexpectedly confronted by a member of the Force, displaying a certain understandable anxiety. After all the police were often the unwilling harbingers of bad news. But this was different. Mrs. Hedderwick's smile went out like a snuffed candle and an expression of wild alarm took possession of her monumental features. She gasped out:

"Inspector Meredith! Scotland Yard! But why...? What brings you here? I didn't send for you." Her big flabby face twitched nervously. "There must be some mistake. Who exactly do you wish to see?"

"We'll come to that in a moment, Madam," said Meredith with a reassuring smile. "But before we discuss the reason for my visit perhaps you'd care to see my credentials. You're probably asking yourself what a member of the C.I.D. is doing down in Menton. But let me assure you, Mrs. Hedderwick, I'm acting in collaboration with the French police. I'm here, in fact, on their behalf."

After a casual glance at the official document, Nesta burst out impatiently:

"Yes, yes—I don't question your *bona fides*. But why should the police want to see *me*? There's nothing wrong, is there?"

"Not exactly wrong," said Meredith, more than ever puzzled by the woman's strange uneasiness and suspicion. "But acting on information that we've recently—"

With a spasmodic gesture Nesta stumbled forward, gripped the Inspector by the arm and broke in hoarsely:

"It's Tony, isn't it? Why can't you put me out of this damned suspense? It's Tony Shenton! It is, isn't it?"

"Tony Shenton?" Meredith shook his head. "I've never heard of the gentleman. What made you think we'd come to see Mr. Shenton?"

The transfiguration was little short of miraculous. A flood of relief swept over those raddled but good-natured features. Her grip on the Inspector's arm relaxed.

"You mean it's nothing to do with Tony?" gulped Nesta gratefully. "Oh, thank God for that! I thought perhaps it... it might have been an accident. He's such a reckless fool in a car. I'm always twitting the wretch about it." Nesta, now rapidly regaining control of her feelings, flashed the Inspector a shamefaced smile. "You must excuse my stupidity, officer. So ridiculous of me to fuss over the boy, but I can't help it. Now do please sit down and tell me how I can help you."

"I understand, Mrs. Hedderwick," said Meredith as he dropped into a nearby armchair, "that you've a gentleman living here by the name of Latour."

"That's quite right," nodded Nesta. "Paul Latour. I've allowed him to use one of the upper rooms as a studio. He's an artist."

"So I believe," said Meredith drily. "How long has he been staying here?"

"Oh, about six months. I can't say for certain."

"And you met him—how?"

"Through Colonel Malloy, an old friend of mine. He brought Paul over to dinner one evening."

Meredith glanced up from the notebook which he'd already flipped open on his knee and demanded in surprised tones:

"You mean Colonel Malloy at Beaulieu?"

"Yes—such a darling old bore. He and his wife drive over here for bridge every Friday. Don't tell me you know him!"

Meredith said glibly:

"Oh, just a nodding acquaintance—nothing more. If I remember rightly he owns a Rolls Royce, with a Russian chauffeur to drive it, eh, Mrs. Hedderwick?"

"Yes—an odd creature by the name of Nikolai Bourmin."

"Now you may consider this question irrelevant, but I want you to think carefully before you answer it. Has it ever struck you that this Mr. Latour was... well, how shall I put it?... on intimate terms with Bourmin?"

"Well, if he was," retorted Nesta, "I've certainly never noticed it. Bourmin always sits with the servants on our bridge evenings. Naturally, if Paul made contact with him then I shouldn't know anything about it. You must see that. But why *should* he want to? What on earth could they have in common?"

Nodding his appreciation of this point, Meredith shut his notebook with a snap, stowed it away in his pocket and got to his feet. Looking Nesta squarely in the face he rapped out:

"Mrs. Hedderwick, would it surprise you to know that for the last six months this *protégé* of yours has been living here under false pretences?"

"False pretences!" cried Nesta bewildered. "What exactly do you mean?"

In a few terse sentences Meredith set out the information they'd gleaned that morning from Jacques Dufil, omitting only that part of the hunchback's evidence that dealt with the counterfeit notes. During his explanation his eyes never left the woman's face, but what he read there reassured him of the sincerity of her reactions—an expression of blank incredulity that slowly gave way to a mounting tide of anger. Whatever the reason for Latour's long-standing deception, it was certain that Mrs. Hedderwick had no inkling of the underhand trick he'd played on her. With a congested look, she heaved herself up from her chair and stood there, gasping and quivering, like a trout out of water, speechless with indignation. The instant Meredith concluded his explanation, however, she burst out:

"Oh, the vile ungrateful hypocrite! How dare he! To trade on my generosity, my good-nature. It's unforgivable! But why did he do it? Can you tell me that, Inspector? What was the point of it?"

"We suspect there may be some criminal reason for his actions. I don't say it is so. But that's what I've come here to find out."

"You want to question the wretch—is that it?" Meredith nodded. "Very well," went on Nesta with a vindictive gleam in her eye. "I'll get somebody to show you up to his studio at once. I'd come myself, but all those stairs on top of this upset... I just couldn't face it." With a series of elephantine thuds she stumped to the door. "Excuse me, Inspector. My niece is out on the terrace. I'll ask *her* to escort you."

II

To Acting-Sergeant Freddy Strang that brief hiatus in the unfolding drama of their visit was little short of purgatory. From the instant he'd set foot inside the Villa Paloma he'd been half-dreading and half-hoping that, during the course of their investigation, he'd come face to face with Dilys Westmacott.

And now, thanks to Mrs. Hedderwick's reluctance to negotiate the stairs up to the attic, such an encounter was about to take place. In the light of what had transpired at their last meeting, Freddy had already decided on the attitude he'd adopt towards Miss Westmacott—a certain professional reticence subtly combined with a suggestion of injured innocence.

He could imagine her surprise and confusion when she learnt the true nature of his calling. Sergeant Strang of the C.I.D., eh? That was the sort of title to go over big with a charming girl like Miss Westmacott. She was going to feel pretty foolish when she thought of her previous unworthy suspicions; her high-handed rejection of his perfectly innocent advances. But now he'd got the poor kid at a disadvantage he was quite prepared to be magnanimous. Oh yes, he'd let her see at once that *he* wasn't the sort of chap to harbour vindictiveness. If she cared to apologize... well, that was O.K. by him. Bad show to rake up the past and throw it, so to speak, in her teeth.

But the moment Dilys Westmacott, sponsored by an agitated Aunt Nesta, appeared in the Chinese room, the whole fabric of Freddy's strategy went up in smoke. A proper professional reticence be damned! How could a fellow gaze into Dilys' wide blue eyes and retain that air of detachment and solid common-sense appropriate to a member of the Force? And this was the girl he thought to have at a disadvantage—this lovely creature whose very presence turned him into something akin to a goggling, tongue-tied moron! With a valiant effort Freddy tried to get a grip on his emotions; to arrest the slow, unspeakable blush that so shamefully suffused his features.

He registered her start of surprise, her momentary recoil, as Mrs. Hedderwick boomed forth a hasty introduction.

"This is my niece—Miss Westmacott. Inspector Meredith and Sergeant Strang, darling, of the C.I.D. Now don't keep them waiting, dear. Off you go! And don't fail to let me know, officer, just what that despicable wretch has to say for himself. Provided," added Nesta with an indignant snort, "he has *anything* to say! You'll find me on the terrace."

Ignoring Freddy entirely, Dilys led the way up the wide curving staircase, along a spacious landing, and up a narrower, gloomier set of stairs that mounted to an equally narrow and gloomy passageway. About half-way down the passage was a bright yellow door before which Dilys came to a halt.

"This is the studio, Inspector, but I expect Mr. Latour's still asleep."

"Asleep!" exclaimed Meredith. "At this hour of the morning?"

"Oh, he hardly ever gets up before lunch. But then he never goes to bed until the small hours." Dilys laughed. "Heaven alone knows where he sneaks off to at night. I mean you don't usually paint pictures in the dark, do you? It's always puzzled me."

Meredith thought to himself:

"Out all night, eh? A pretty suggestive factor in the circumstances."
Aloud he said: "O.K., Miss Westmacott. We'll give him a knock-up.
He won't relish being yanked out of his beauty sleep, but time's a
commodity I'm not prepared to waste."

Dilys asked tactfully:

"Would you rather I faded out? I mean, perhaps, you'd—?"

"No. I'd like you to hang on a minute, if you don't mind, young
lady."

Lifting his hand Meredith rapped sharply on the door, paused
for a moment, listened, then rapped again. No answer. He called
impatiently: "M'sieur Latour, open up, will you? It's the police."
All remained dead quiet inside the room—not even the rustle of
bedclothes or a creaking of springs. Meredith glanced meaningly at
Strang, then, turning the handle and finding the door unlocked, he
entered the studio.

The place was in chaos. Drawers and cupboards gaped open, papers
lay scattered about the floor, the bed was unmade. On the dressing-
table stood an empty brandy bottle, a broken glass, a half-filled packet
of Gauloises cigarettes. A single comprehensive glance told Meredith
all he wanted to know. There was no dodging the evidence. For some
reason, Paul Latour had snatched up his personal impedimenta,
rammed it in a suitcase and cleared out of the Villa Paloma!

With a sour expression the Inspector turned to the bewildered
couple peering over his shoulder.

"Too late, confound it! The bird's flown. And, if I'm not very much
mistaken, Miss Westmacott, neither you nor your aunt are likely to
set eyes on the fellow again."

"But... but why?" stammered Dilys. "Why should he leave in
such a hurry?"

"I've my own ideas about that, young lady, but at the moment I'd
rather not discuss 'em. Tell me, when did you last see Latour?"

"Last night at dinner," said Dilys, adding after a moment's swift
reflection: "No, wait! He didn't come in to dinner. I remember my

aunt was rather riled about it. When I come to think of it I don't believe I've seen him since Saturday evening."

"The night *before* last, eh?" Meredith whistled and turned to his assistant. "I want you to interrogate everybody in the house about this particular point, Sergeant. Understand? I'm going to make a thorough search of this room. I've no doubt Miss Westmacott will show you around the place and put you in touch with the various members of the household—also be kind enough to act as interpreter where the domestics are concerned."

"Yes, of course, Inspector."

"Oh, and Sergeant," added Meredith as the couple made to move off along the passage, "find out from the staff if Latour was in the habit of making contact with our friend Bourmin on Friday nights. That's the night when the Colonel and his wife come over here for bridge."

"Very good," gulped Freddy. "Is that all, sir?"

Meredith shot him a swift, sly glance and winked.

"As far as I'm concerned—yes, Sergeant. But if anything else occurs to you... well, use your own initiative. Private enterprise, eh?" Meredith winked again. "See how I mean?"

"Yes, sir," said Freddy, for the second time that morning flushing to the roots of his hair. "I think I get the... er... general idea."

III

"Well," murmured Dilys, coming to an ominous stop on the first-floor landing, "I must say this is a bit of a shock. You might have warned me that you were coming."

"But I didn't know myself until about an hour ago," protested Freddy. "Honestly, Miss Westmacott, I didn't mean to kid you about all this. Just couldn't help myself. I mean to say, I'd had strict orders to preserve my incognito. So of course..."

"But Mr. John Smith!" exclaimed Dilys with a censorious shake of her head. "You might have thought up a better one than that."

"Yes, it was a trifle unenterprising," admitted Freddy ruefully. "But now you know who I really am and why I couldn't come clean about it when we first met...?"

"Well, it naturally makes a difference."

"Good!" said Freddy. "I hoped perhaps it would."

"I suppose I ought to apologize for being so absurdly suspicious?"

"Apologize!" cried Freddy in shocked tones. "What on earth for? It wasn't your fault. Good heavens—no! *I'm* the one who ought to apologize."

"But why? I quite see now that you couldn't help acting as you did."

"Yes—but to lead a girl up the garden path, just when we seemed to be... be..."

"When we seemed to be... what?" asked Dilys with a mocking, utterly demoralizing glance.

"Well, you know," floundered Freddy. "Sort of getting together and... well, making a pass at each—No, dammit! I don't mean that exactly. I mean..." He gazed at her appealingly. "Oh lord! can't you give me a bit of a leg up, Miss Westmacott?"

"I might," she smiled. "If you could possibly bring yourself to call me Dilys."

With an impetuous whoop, utterly forgetful of his surroundings and that professional reticence proper to a policeman in the execution of his duty, Freddy fumbled for her hand and squeezed it warmly.

"Heck! that would come easy, if you really meant it, Miss Westmacott. It's 'Dilys' from now on. And in case you didn't know, I'm Freddy. Ridiculous sort of moniker, I admit, but—"

"One better than John Smith," said Dilys with a teasing look; adding on a more practical note as she gently freed her hand: "Now we really must be sensible. The Inspector will be absolutely furious if you—"

"Back on the beat, eh?" growled Freddy. "O.K. But before we break up the party there's just one suggestion that occurs to me."

"And that?"

"Why shouldn't we have another stab at getting together on the Casino terrace—say, twelve o'clock tomorrow, eh?"

"Twelve o'clock tomorrow!" echoed Dilys.

Freddy nodded emphatically.

"Is it a bet?"

"I don't see why not."

"The lord be praised!" said Freddy, ostentatiously mopping his brow with an invisible handkerchief. "And now, having cleared up this little misunderstanding, what about showing me round the domestic quarters? Quite an experience to see a pukka C.I.D. wallah in action!" Freddy cleared his throat and with a passable imitation of his superior's finest official manner, rapped out: "Now tell me, young lady, when did you last see that blighter, Dillon? I want you to think carefully, because if he's been getting fresh with you—!"

But Dilys, fearful that her aunt might suddenly appear from the terrace, was already half-way down the stairs.

CHAPTER XII

L'HIRONDELLE

I

FOR TWO SOLID HOURS that afternoon Meredith sat at the table in his hotel bedroom poring over the notes and depositions that he and the Sergeant had brought back from the Villa Paloma. The heat, which seemed to slither into the half-darkened room through the slats of the closed shutters, was shattering. Although Meredith had yanked off his coat, rolled up his shirt sleeves and loosened his collar, he was still perspiring profusely. Even the glass of iced lager at his elbow brought little relief.

But for all his bodily discomfort, his mental processes were ticking over with their customary smoothness and precision. Little by little he was sorting out the relevant data from the disjointed scraps of information that he and the Sergeant, like a couple of scavenging hens, had picked up from the various members of the Hedderwick household.

One point stood out sharply from this welter of facts. Latour had "moonlighted" from the villa—presumably some time during the course of the previous twenty-four hours—i.e. Sunday. Admittedly neither Mrs. Hedderwick nor her niece had seen him since Saturday evening, but both the cook and the parlour-maid had heard him coming down the back-stairs just before lunch on Sunday. Lisette, the maid, had actually seen him crossing the yard to the back-gate. According to the Sergeant's excellent notes, the girl was convinced that Latour wasn't portering any form of luggage. So much for that.

But late last night, or rather during the small hours of the morning, Miss Pilligrew had wakened from an uneasy slumber with a touch of indigestion. Unable to get off to sleep again she'd switched on her bedside lamp and started to read. A few minutes later she'd heard sounds coming from Latour's studio, which was directly above her own room. She thought little of it because Latour often sneaked into the house during the small hours and went up to bed via the back-stairs. According to Miss Pilligrew the time when she'd heard these noises was just after one a.m. Although there was no other witness to corroborate this statement, Meredith felt certain that Miss Pilligrew's evidence could be accepted as reliable. So Latour had left the villa shortly before lunch on Sunday and re-entered it some time after midnight. And there was little doubt that on his return to the villa he'd immediately packed his belongings and cleared out of the place as quickly as he could.

But why? That was the real teaser.

Even if he were a member of the counterfeit gang—as Meredith now firmly believed—what had driven him to make this sudden flit? Presumably something that he'd learnt between noon and midnight the previous day. Some move on the part of the police, perhaps, acting as a straw in the wind. But if so who had warned the fellow of the investigations that were afoot? Had he made this discovery for himself or had the information been handed on by A. N. Other? Bourmin, perhaps? Not that Meredith had any proof that Bourmin and Latour were acquainted. Strang's enquiries among the domestic staff, in fact, had clearly revealed that Latour had never made contact with the chauffeur when he was over at the villa on Fridays. Moreover, as far as Meredith knew, Bourmin had no inkling that he'd been tailed in Monte Carlo. Nor did he know anything of their visit to his rooms above the Colonel's garage. Unless, of course, Malloy was double-crossing him—a theory that Meredith flatly refused to consider. Besides, would Bourmin have had the opportunity to get in touch with Latour after their interview with Malloy on Sunday morning? Well, a 'phone-call to the Villa Valdeblore would soon settle this little point. At the same time it would be just as well to find out how Malloy had made first contact with Latour. After all, it was the Colonel who'd introduced him to Mrs. Hedderwick—presumably in all good faith. He decided to ring Malloy there and then.

Ten minutes later he was back in his room with the answers, so to speak, in his pocket. Malloy's explanation of his chance meeting with Latour in a Nice café seemed perfectly feasible and above-board. There was absolutely no suggestion that, when he'd introduced the fellow to his old friend Mrs. Hedderwick, he'd any inkling of Latour's real character. So much for that. His statement concerning the chauffeur's movements was equally clear and convincing. Bourmin hadn't left the Villa Valdeblore, except when on duty at the wheel, during the course of Sunday afternoon or evening. Malloy was emphatic. Bourmin had spent the afternoon chatting with the maids in the kitchen. In the evening he'd driven the Colonel and his wife over to Antibes where they were dining with friends. They hadn't arrived back at Beaulieu until well past eleven. So what? That was one cat, at any rate, that wouldn't jump.

What else had they done the previous day? Met Blampignon, of course, at the local Commissariat to discuss plans for that night's coastal patrol in connection with the smuggling racket. And, by Jove, yes! that visit to the tenement-house near the Quai de Bonaparte—the "chase of the wild goose", as Blampignon had voiced it—that had led them, not to "Chalky" Cobbett, but to Nikolai Bourmin's mistress! Was this where Latour had picked up his information? Was it Mam'selle Chounet who'd tipped him the wink? True, Blampignon had given her no hint of the business that had brought them to the Maison Turini, but she was probably quite intelligent enough to put two and—

Meredith swore under his breath. What the devil was he blethering about? Hadn't Blampignon satisfied himself that the girl knew nothing of Bourmin's criminal activities? Which included, *ipso facto,* the counterfeit racket. And what Blampignon held to be true Meredith was unprepared to refute. Was this just another obstinate cat that wouldn't jump?

He thought: "But hang on a minute! What about the old woman in the carpet slippers, the *concierge*? She must have guessed from our interrogation that the police were interested in Bourmin. Was *she* responsible for the leakage? More than possible, eh? It all boils down to this. Did Latour visit the tenement yesterday some time between noon and midnight? Better check up on this. Get Gibaud to come down with me this afternoon and make the necessary enquiries."

II

With the cunning and sagacity nurtured by long experience of criminal investigation, Meredith suggested that Gibaud should refrain from questioning the old woman until he'd interrogated other, presumably disinterested, witnesses living in the building. Before leaving the Villa Paloma that morning he'd obtained an excellent photograph of Latour from Mrs. Hedderwick. As they neared the Maison Turini Meredith handed this photograph over to Gibaud.

"I'm going to sit down under these palm-trees, my dear chap, and smoke a pipe. Point is if I show up the old girl's bound to recognize me, and at the moment we don't want to put her on her guard. All you've got to do is to walk slap by her cubby-hole and start making enquiries round the ground-floor rooms. Find out if anybody's seen Latour hanging about the place. If they have then rejoin me here and we'll tackle the *concierge* together. Agreed?"

Gibaud, who was in plain clothes, wasted no time. Making straight tracks for the building, he mounted the steps and disappeared swiftly through the open door. Five, ten, fifteen minutes passed. Meredith shifted uncomfortably on the iron-slatted seat, trying to curb his impatience. A great deal, he felt, depended on his colleague's enquiries. If only it could be proved that Latour was in the habit of—

He glanced up quickly. Gibaud was almost trotting up the road towards the oasis of palms. Long before he reached the spot Meredith could see that he had a grin on his ferret-like features worthy of the Cheshire Cat. He jumped up and hurried forward eagerly to meet him.

"Well?"

"We're on to something here!" shot out Gibaud. "I found no less than four witnesses who're prepared to swear that they'd seen Latour about the place."

"The devil you did!" exclaimed Meredith, unable to conceal his elation at the news. "And yesterday?"

"He turned up about ten p.m., stayed chatting for about twenty minutes with the old woman in her cubicle and then left in a hurry."

"It's always the old woman he comes to see?"

"Yes—invariably. None of the witnesses I questioned has ever actually spoken to the fellow—just noticed him in conversation with the *concierge* as they were entering or leaving the building."

"What about the girl—Celeste Chounet?"

"I asked about her. They were certain Latour had never gone up to her room. They've never seen them together at any time."

"I see. Well, it's obvious what we've got to do now. Stick that photograph under the old woman's nose and ask her point-blank if she can identify the fellow. If she hedges or denies that she knows Latour, then, by heaven, we've got her in a cleft stick!"

And five minutes later that was just where they'd got the old biddy. Quietly but relentlessly, in the little glass-fronted cubby-hole, Gibaud grilled her to a turn; breaking off every now and then to put Meredith *au fait* with the progress of his interrogation. Throughout the interview her husband sat at the table, chuckling and nodding and talking to himself in some strange, incomprehensible lingo.

Once she realized that her denials were cutting no ice, Madame Grignot trotted out her explanation readily enough. The facts, as she related them, were simple. Thirty years ago, in an obscure little village on the outskirts of Dijon, she'd taken a position as nurse to the Latours' three children. Paul, her eldest charge, was then three. She'd stayed with the family until Paul's father had died; and then, since his mother could no longer afford to pay her wages, she'd taken another situation near Aix-en-Provence. Paul, who'd been devoted to her, was then fourteen and, although he'd seen little of her in the intervening years, he'd never failed to keep in touch with her. Just after he'd come to live at Menton, she wrote asking if Paul could find her a job and it was through his good offices that she'd eventually obtained the post of *concierge* at the Maison Turini. He often called round to have a chat with her about old times and to bring her poor demented husband a bottle of wine. Then why, demanded Gibaud, had she gone to the trouble of denying that she knew M'sieur Latour? *Eh bien!* that too was simple. Only the day before the Englishman had called round with an Inspector of police and they'd asked her many searching questions about a M'sieur Bourmin. And now, today, he was here again, and they were asking many questions about M'sieur Latour. Was it not natural that she should refuse to give to the police information which might cause trouble for poor M'sieur Latour? Was it not natural that she should pretend not to know him?

III

"Well," demanded Gibaud, as they turned into the Quai de Bonaparte and began to stroll at a leisurely pace along the waterfront, "what do you make of our dear Madame Grignot? Do you think her explanation holds water?"

Meredith said cautiously:

"Well, yes and no. A subtle mixture of fact and fiction—at least, that's how it struck me."

"I don't quite follow," said Gibaud, unable to see how Meredith had arrived at this conclusion. "Her story seemed perfectly feasible. She certainly rattled it off without any hesitation."

"Exactly!" exclaimed Meredith. "That's just what makes it suspect. When Blampignon questioned her about Bourmin... well, you should have heard the old biddy! The facts were so thickly encrusted with embellishment that it was darn difficult to isolate the evidence we were after. She just couldn't keep to the point. If you ask me, my dear chap, today's story was a trifle *too* pat. Rather as if she'd learnt it off by heart, eh?"

"You mean Latour had more or less primed her with what to say in case we should ever question her?"

"Just that," nodded Meredith. "I don't say the general facts aren't true. It's quite possible that she *was* the family nurse. But I'm darned if I'll accept her explanation for Latour's recent visits. The old lady knows plenty and I'll wager a week's wages that it was she who tipped him the wink to get clear while the going was good. You see, our enquiries about Bourmin would naturally—" Meredith broke off and stood there in the middle of the pavement, his mouth agape, a look of wild incredulity on his aquiline features. "Well, I'll be—!"

"What the devil's the matter with you?" asked Gibaud, bewildered.

"That launch, moored over there against the harbour arm," pointed out Meredith. "The one with the two thin scarlet stripes painted on its hull..."

"Well, what about it?"

In a few curt sentences Meredith described their Saturday night encounter over at Cap Martin. Gibaud whistled.

"And you think this is the same boat, eh?"

"Certain of it. Here, quick! Let's take a walk out on to the breakwater. Somebody's sure to know who owns the confounded thing."

In this assumption Meredith was right. A group of swarthy, barefooted fishermen were just swarming ashore off one of the many gondola-prowed fishing-boats tied off along the quayside. In answer to Gibaud's enquiries they broke into voluble and concerted explanations. When at length the babble had died down, Gibaud turned to his colleague who'd been teetering with impatience at his elbow. Meredith rapped out:

"Well?"

"She's a privately owned pleasure launch by the name of *L'Hirondelle*. A pretty roomy and luxurious affair according to these fellows."

"But who owns her?" snapped Meredith. "That's what interests me."
Gibaud smiled.

"You'd better take a grip on yourself. You're going to get a high-voltage shock."

"Oh for crying aloud, man! don't keep me dangling."

"Well, believe it or not, it's that wealthy countrywoman of yours."

"By heaven!" gasped Meredith. "Mrs. Hedderwick! Now what in the name of thunder...?"

IV

Thanking Gibaud for his help, Meredith parted from him at the steps of the Commissariat, and for the second time that day headed for the Villa Paloma. A dozen questions were queueing up in his mind demanding attention. If it was *L'Hirondelle* that they'd seen moored under the rocks at Cap Martin (and Meredith felt sure it was), had it made the trip with Mrs. Hedderwick's permission? And who exactly had been aboard her? In the flurry of their attempt to detain the launch, Meredith had only caught a fleeting glimpse of the figure so frantically casting off. In the rays of his torch the man's features had been indistinguishable. One thing was certain. There must have been at least two men aboard the craft, for even as the fellow in the stern was loosing the painter the engine had been started up amidships. O.K. Accept a maximum of two. The question remained—who? Latour? Bourmin? But could the latter have got over from Beaulieu? Latour then?

Meredith clicked his fingers. Heavens, yes! Hadn't Miss Westmacott mentioned his mysterious, nocturnal sallies from the villa? And did Latour on these occasions make for the *Hirondelle*? Reason—he was tied up, not only with the counterfeiting gang, but with the cigarette racket. Perhaps Blampignon was wrong. Perhaps the same gang *was* responsible for both forms of criminal activity. Well, he knew what his next move must be. He'd get Mrs. Hedderwick's permission to examine the launch in the hope of picking up a clue that would transmute his assumption into a proven fact.

Ten minutes later he was sitting opposite the widow in the Chinese room. Although somewhat surprised to see him back again so soon at the villa, Nesta answered his questions both promptly and frankly. The facts that emerged were these:—

1. Apart from herself, two other members of the household had the keys to *L'Hirondelle*'s engine-casing and cabins—Shenton and Latour.

2. Both had permission to use the launch when they wished, though if *L'Hirondelle* had been used at night Mrs. Hedderwick knew nothing about it. She certainly had no idea it was out on Saturday night.

3. Mrs. Hedderwick had a few guests in on Saturday night and the party hadn't broken up until after 1 a.m. Shenton was present throughout. But Latour left the villa shortly after dinner.

So much for that, thought Meredith, as he strolled down the Avenue St. Michel on his way back to the harbour. Three people had keys of the launch—two had an alibi for Saturday night. So, *ipso facto,* everything pointed to Latour. And the man with him was either Bourmin or A. N. Other, who so far hadn't come under suspicion.

But the question remained—what the deuce was Latour doing out at Cap Martin? Landing contraband? But no contraband had been dumped near the mooring-place, and the full cargo of illicit cigarettes had been found on the smugglers' launch *before* they'd had time to split up the consignment among the smaller craft. Was there a woman in the case? Was the other member of the crew a female?

Still pondering over these tantalizing problems Meredith arrived back at the steps of the Commissariat de Police. Luckily Gibaud was still in the building and more than ready to accompany Meredith back to the harbour. On their way down through the cavernous alleys of the Old Town, Meredith brought his French colleague up-to-date with the progress of his enquiry.

"And what exactly do you want me for?" asked Gibaud, when Meredith had concluded his report.

"Well, it struck me that somebody may have seen the *Hirondelle* being boarded on Saturday night. Always a few loafers hanging around the quayside. We might be able to pick up a description of the crew who took her out of harbour. I reckon she left somewhere between ten and midnight. In the meantime I'm going to take a snoop round the launch herself. The old girl's loaned me the keys and given me full permission to do as I please. I reckon her readiness to help places Mrs. Hedderwick beyond suspicion."

Turning into the Quai Monleon, Meredith swung right to continue on his way along the harbour-arm, leaving Gibaud to start his enquiries among the many bars and cafés along the waterfront. A couple of minutes later Meredith was aboard *L'Hirondelle* and his investigations were under way. The Inspector was no nautical man. He'd only a layman's knowledge of things maritime, but even he was able to appreciate the trim and graceful lines, the excellent finish and surprising roominess of the launch. Unlocking the door to the main cabin amidships, Meredith quickly began to examine the various bunks and lockers on the look-out for anything that might suggest some secret or concealed compartment. Gradually, with his customary efficiency and caution, he combed through every nook and cranny of the boat, until he was satisfied that every cubic foot of space had been accounted for. In the cockpit aft he sounded and took a dip of the twin petrol-tanks. In a gloomy recess off the for'ard cabin, discovering a fair-sized tank, he lifted the galvanized lid and flashed his torch inside it. But again there was nothing to rouse his suspicions. The tank, as one might have expected, was filled, not with packets of Chesterfields or Lucky Strike, but drinking water! He even thrust an arm down the bell-mouthed ventilators that projected through the cabin roof. But all to no avail. At the end of an hour's meticulous, high-pressure search, he was forced to admit that there was absolutely nothing suspicious about the launch's design or lay-out.

He stumbled, in fact, on only one small clue. Under a bunk in the for'ard cabin he unearthed a half-filled crate of empty wine bottles labelled Nuits St. George. And thinking back to Saturday night Meredith recalled that the empty bottle they'd noticed on the rocks at Cap Martin had borne the same label. Nothing startling, of course, but at least it helped to corroborate his belief that the launch lying up under the umbrella pines *was* the *Hirondelle*.

Relocking the cabin and engine-casing, he was just clambering up on to the quayside when he saw Gibaud coming at a brisk pace along the harbour-arm. Guessing from the Inspector's hasty approach that he'd got something to tell him, Meredith hurried forward to meet his colleague.

"Well," he demanded eagerly, "any luck?"

Gibaud nodded.

"The devil's own if you ask me! Latour was seen by two witnesses boarding the *Hirondelle* about ten-thirty on Saturday night. I picked up the information from a couple of longshoremen in one of the waterfront *bistros*. No doubt about it. They've often seen and spoken to the fellow. As a matter of fact, they seemed to know quite a bit about him."

"You mean this isn't the first time they've spotted Latour boarding the launch?"

"Far from it. Apparently these nocturnal trips in the *Hirondelle* have been going on for about two months—at least once or twice a week."

"The deuce they have!" exclaimed Meredith as they set off in step back along the wide stone pier towards the town. "Have your witnesses any idea *why* Latour chooses to put out of harbour after dark?"

Gibaud chuckled with cynical amusement.

"Well, I can tell you what he told them and leave you to judge whether he was telling the truth or not. Wasn't it Hitler who said 'the bigger the lie the greater the chance of it being believed'? Latour obviously works on the same principle."

"How do you mean?"

"Guess what he told these fellows! That he was painting a series of pictures depicting the various coast towns at night—street illuminations and all that as seen from off-shore."

"And knowing as we do now that he couldn't paint a damn picture..." Meredith whistled. "No question that he was up to some sort of skullduggery. Tell me—last Saturday night—was Latour the only person seen boarding the launch?"

"No. He had a companion. According to my witnesses the same companion who always accompanied him on these shifty expeditions. An elderly, white-bearded man, in a long black cloak and wide-brimmed black sombrero."

"Good heavens," grunted Meredith. "Sounds like the villain in an old-fashioned cloak-and-dagger drama!"

"To you—yes," agreed Gibaud with a smile. "But down here on the Midi we're accustomed to this kind of sartorial eccentricity. Personally I don't consider there's anything really odd about the old fellow's get-up."

"And his identity?" asked Meredith eagerly.

"There, I'm afraid, we've run up against a blank wall. The longshoremen haven't the faintest idea who he is. They've never been able to see his features under the shadow of his outsized hat. On the few occasions when Latour's stopped to exchange a word with them, his companion's always hurried on without speaking."

"Puzzling," commented Meredith.

"Not to a Frenchman!" retorted Gibaud with a twinkling glance. "You can guess what the locals have to say about it."

"*Cherchez la femme,* eh?"

"Precisely. The white beard, the long cloak, the sombrero—in their opinion the perfect disguise beneath which to conceal the... er... shall we say? tell-tale idiosyncrasies of the female form. And personally," added Gibaud as they crossed once more into the Quai Monleon, "I think they've hit on a very possible explanation!"

CHAPTER XIII

CLUE ON CAP MARTIN

I

DURING THE NEXT twenty-four hours, after the week-end spurt, Meredith's investigations dropped, so to speak, into bottom gear. No further developments. No further information. No word of the missing Latour, for whose apprehension a general call had gone out to all police-stations in the district. Yet Meredith was far from idle. A further exhaustible interview with Mrs. Hedderwick had enabled him to draw up a series of fairly comprehensive case-histories of the various members of her household. All the womenfolk and this fellow they were always bumping into, Bill Dillon, seemed, on the face of it, to be utterly beyond suspicion.

But in the case of Tony Shenton Meredith hesitated to make up his mind. He had no real reason for this hesitation, just a hunch that the fellow, whom he'd cross-questioned on his first visit to the villa, was a bad egg. There was something shifty and slick about him; a decided whiff of the playboy that immediately put the Inspector on his guard. He had the curious impression that the young man's face was familiar. But if so—why? Meredith smiled to himself. Well, whenever a C.I.D. bloke claimed to recognize a face it was usually because the chap in question had a criminal record. A cynical admission, perhaps, but that was how it ticked.

Was it worth, he wondered, following up this hunch and air-mailing a photo of Shenton to the Records Department at the Yard? Time and again he'd known these long shots in the dark to find their billet. What was it his old mentor "Tubby" Hart used to say? "The conscientious detective leaves no stone unturned and no avenue unexplored in the interests of his investigation."

Meredith argued thus:—Latour had been living at the villa under false pretences. Now he was suspected of having a tie-up with a for-gery gang and, having been tipped the wink concerning the recent activities of the police, he'd scapa-ed in a hurry. A young man living in the same villa has a face that seems familiar to a member of the C.I.D. And if that didn't add up to something pretty significant then pigs had wings!

By midday that Tuesday morning, a photo of Shenton, together with the Inspector's covering remarks, was on its way to the Yard. The matter was marked—*Urgent*.

II

For Acting-Sergeant Strang that particular Tuesday marked a blissful and memorable hiatus between two slices of high-pressure activity. Meredith, engrossed in a routine check-up of the evidence now to hand, was more than tolerably disposed to let his subordinate off the official leash. Much as he appreciated the lad's keenness and efficiency there were times when his high-spirited chatter and unbounded zeal were a trifle distracting. Perhaps, too, a certain deep-bedded sentimental streak in the Inspector's make-up was partly responsible for his decision to let Freddy have a day off-duty. A day that Freddy was determined to devote entirely to Dilys Westmacott. Provided, of course, that she was prepared to co-operate.

After their prearranged meeting on the terrace of the Menton Casino their resuscitated friendship got away to a flying start. And with Dilys' co-operation assured, they agreed to meet directly after lunch and take a walk out to Cap Martin.

The cloudless weather was still holding. The air had a sparkle in it like a dry and tingling wine. The blue waters of the Mediterranean, shading to exquisite purples and greens close inshore, lapped at that sun-drenched coastline as gently as a kitten at a saucer of milk. Beneath the umbrella pines the shadows lay cool and heavy, with here and there a band of brilliant light scored across the undulating road along the edge of the cape. Clear of the pines the couple deserted the road and began to clamber out over the rocks to where the tip of the headland plunged like a dagger into the sea. A few fishermen were perched like large black gulls here and there along the water's edge. Chancing to notice them, Dilys enquired anxiously:

"Are you keen on fishing, Freddy?"

"Me? Good lord, no!" retorted Freddy scornfully. "I'm all for an active life. Can't see the point of sitting on a large damp rock, baiting a hook with a large damp worm in the forlorn hope of catching a small damp fish. Besides, I haven't got the right temperament—far too impatient. Daresay you've noticed it."

"Wouldn't 'impetuous' be a better word?" smiled Dilys. "But I'm glad you're no angler. Tony's mad about it."

"Tony?"

"Tony Shenton—you met him yesterday when you were asking all those questions up at the villa."

"Oh, I get you—the big blond chap who runs that crimson Vedette. Honestly, Dilys, I can't say I liked the cut of his jib." Then suddenly recollecting the scene he'd witnessed in the garage-yard, he added unthinkingly: "Of course he's a fisherman. I remember now. He had a rod and creel with him at the time."

Dilys dumped herself down on the nearest rock and stared at him in bewilderment.

"What on earth are you talking about? I'd no idea you'd met Tony before yesterday. Am I allowed to ask *where* you met him, or is that another of your wretched professional secrets?"

"Oh good lord, no!" protested Freddy breezily. "It's all quite simple and above-board. You see, I happened to be—" He gaped like a gaffed pike, swallowed hard and looked at Dilys with an expression of anguished dismay. "Oh heck! I've properly put my foot in it this time. Don't quite know what to say. It's damned awkward. You see, I shouldn't actually have been there... I mean, eavesdropping like that... quite definitely a bad show. But the point is..."

And courageously taking the bull by the horns, Freddy blurted out a full confession of his early morning patrol in the Avenue St. Michel. And realizing that he'd been there, not by chance, but in the hope of seeing something of her, Dilys was naturally flattered and delighted. Profoundly relieved to find that she wasn't going to tear a strip off him, Freddy regaled her with the full story of what had transpired outside the garage.

"You mean that all Tony had got in that basket was an ordinary lump of rock?" asked Dilys incredulously.

"Just that. Curious, eh? The poor mutt must be ga-ga or something. Does he often nip out during the early hours for a spot of fishing?"

"Oh, about once or twice a week. It's always puzzled me. Fishing and Tony don't seem to go together."

"How long has he been interested in this odious form of sport?" asked Freddy, idly picking up a small pebble to throw at an empty wine bottle that was stuck up precariously on a nearby rock.

"Oh, it's quite a recent fad of his."

Freddy groped round for a second suitably-sized missile.

"How do you mean by recent?"

"Well, it must have been about a couple of months ago when he started—" Dilys broke off and glanced at Freddy suspiciously. "Look here, you wretch, are these questions the outcome of natural curiosity or are they part of a very subtle cross-examination?" She sighed. "You're a bit of a trial, Freddy. Can't you ever forget that you're a policeman?"

"Sorry," grinned Freddy. "Force of habit, I'm afraid." He picked up a third pebble and this time, more by luck than judgement, hit the wine bottle square amidships. He uttered a whoop of triumph. "Got it! Third go. Not so duff, eh?"

"But terribly thoughtless," pointed out Dilys practically. "Now there'll be hundreds of nasty jagged bits of—" She broke off and stared at him in alarm: "Freddy! What is it? What's the matter?"

He was standing there transfixed, his eyes glued to a spot a few yards ahead of him across the intervening jumble of grey, water-smooth boulders. With an effort he withdrew his gaze from the object that had so unexpectedly riveted his attention and said with a reassuring smile:

"Oh... er... nothing really. Just an odd little idea that came into my head. Nothing to do with you, I assure you. Just something that started up a pretty startling train of thought."

"The great detective at work!" exclaimed Dilys teasingly. "I shall have to get used to these moments of inspired revelation, Freddy. At present I find them rather shattering." She raised her hands to be helped up from the rock. "Now what about concentrating on me for a change."

With an amiable chuckle, Freddy grasped her hands and hauled her to her feet.

"I'm a whale of a chap for doing anything that comes easily! As a matter of fact..." he glanced around cautiously, "if it wasn't for these wide open spaces..."

He made a hurried attempt to snatch a kiss but, losing his balance, slipped sideways and sprawled in undignified embarrassment at his enamorata's feet. A bungled performance, to say the least of it, but one that Freddy more than redeemed by a masterly and highly successful repeat performance under the screening branches of the umbrella pines. Thereafter he saved shoe leather. For as they returned, tired but happy, along the sun-baked promenade, Freddy walked on air.

III

Taking reluctant leave of Dilys outside the Villa Paloma, Freddy hurried back through the town to the Hotel Louis. Racked with impatience he went up to Meredith's room and rapped on the door.

"*Qui est là?*" sang out Meredith in his stubbornly insular accent.

"Strang, sir. Can I have a word with you?"

"O.K. The door's not locked."

Meredith, coatless, with his shirt-sleeves rolled up, was sitting in an aura of tobacco smoke, poring over the various documents that littered the table before him. On seeing Strang he grinned broadly.

"Well, my little Casanova, how's life been treating you? To judge by the hectic flush and dishevelled hair I should say you'd had a very interesting afternoon. Nice walk, eh?"

Freddy smiled sheepishly.

"Bang on, sir—thanks. But I didn't actually barge in here to worry you with my private affairs."

"No worry, Sergeant, I assure you. As your superior officer I've naturally been following the progress of your little romance with the keenest interest. But if you didn't come here to talk about that young woman, then what the—?"

Freddy broke in eagerly:

"Look here, sir, do you mind if I borrow the car?"

"What on earth for?"

"Well, sir, I've got a hunch and I want to follow it up. I may be right off the rails, but I've a sneaking idea that I've hit on the *modus operandi* of this forgery business."

"The devil you have!" whistled Meredith. "Just like that, eh? O.K. Sergeant. Pull up a chair and give me the gen. Any sort of hunch at this stage of our investigation is just about synonymous with manna in the wilderness. Right—fire ahead!"

For some fifteen minutes Freddy talked and Meredith, save for an occasional pertinent question, listened intently. At the end of that time he sprang to his feet, rolled down his sleeves and reached for his jacket. Then, unhooking his hat from the door, he clapped it on his head and rapped out:

"Nip down to the garage, m'lad, and get the car out at once. I'm coming along with you. I've just got to tidy up these papers and get 'em under lock and key. Meet me outside the front entrance in thirty seconds. O.K.—jump to it!"

As Meredith was hurrying by the reception-desk in the hotel lobby, however, he was intercepted by the *maître d'hôtel.*

"An urgent 'phone-call for you, M'sieur. I've had it put through as usual to my private office. It's Inspector Gibaud ringing from the Commissariat."

"Thanks," nodded Meredith. "I'll take it at once. By the way, I want you to do me a favour."

"Certainly, M'sieur—anything you wish."

"I want you to dig out a bottle of Nuits St. George—an empty bottle. Can do?"

The *maître d'hôtel* goggled.

"An *empty* bottle, M'sieur?"

"That's the idea," nodded Meredith.

"Very well, M'sieur. It is certainly a strange request, but I will fetch it for you at once."

When, five minutes later, Meredith, with the wine bottle under his arm, went through the swing-doors to where Strang was waiting in the car, the latter realized at once that something was wrong. The Inspector looked as if he'd just been forced to swallow the juice of an unripe lemon.

As Meredith clambered sullenly into the driving-seat, Strang asked politely:

"Anything the matter, sir?"

"The matter!" snorted Meredith. "I'll say there is." He slammed in a gear with a vicious jerk and let out the clutch. "I ought to have thought of it, Sergeant. I'm losing my grip. *Anno domini,* I suppose. Not that *that's* any excuse."

"I don't get it, sir."

"Don't you? Then I'll put you wise. Gibaud has rung through to say that he's just received information from some blokes down at the harbour that the *Hirondelle* put out to sea last night about eleven p.m. His witnesses swear that one of the men to board her was Latour."

"Latour!" exclaimed Strang. "But I thought—"

"So did we all!" retorted Meredith. "That's just where we tripped up. We naturally thought Latour would have cleared out of Menton. Instead, like the sly devil he is, he's evidently been lying low right under our confounded noses."

"He was alone, sir?"

"He was not!" snapped Meredith. "He was accompanied by that curious chap in the long black cloak that I was telling you about last night. Heaven knows, I could kick myself. I ought to have got Gibaud to post a chap on the quayside to keep the launch under observation. That's the second time we've let Latour slip through our fingers. At any rate I've fixed for a watch to be posted down there tonight."

"But look here, sir!" cried Strang, as Meredith swung the car into the Avenue de Verdun and headed for the Promenade du Midi. "This unexpected bit of news ties up perfectly with this new theory of mine. I mean if Latour took the boat out last night, it would account for—"

Meredith cut in with a sudden lifting of his previous ill-temper.

"By Jove—yes! That particular point hadn't occurred to me." Adding with seeming irrelevance: "By the way, did you notice what had happened to the bottle we spotted on Saturday night? You must have passed the spot where the launch was moored on your walk this afternoon."

Freddy nodded solemnly.

"I did, sir. *It was gone!*"

Meredith gave a long low whistle; then, with a sudden burst of optimism, declared:

"By heaven, Strang! I think we've got 'em. We've got 'em by the short hairs, m'lad."

IV

Cap Martin; the Villa Valdeblore at Beaulieu; then over to Menton and the Villa Paloma—it was long past dinner time when Meredith and Strang arrived back at the Hotel Louis. But a word to the *maître d'hôtel* and the couple were soon sitting down in the deserted dining-room to an excellent if belated meal. They were in a jubilant mood; a mood that gained lustre from the bottle of Beaujolais that Meredith had ordered to celebrate the occasion. Their evening's investigations had brought in results that, in the light of Meredith's previous depression, seemed little short of miraculous. It was Freddy's hunch that had set the ball rolling, and their subsequent enquiries at the Villas Valdeblore and Paloma had increased its impetus. Suddenly, as if by magic, a series of uncorrelated clues had clicked together to form a clear and revealing pattern. Events which had previously baffled them could now be explained away with startling simplicity. It was always the case, thought Meredith—once one had discovered the solution to a problem it was hard to believe that a problem had ever existed.

But the Inspector was in no mood to waste time on an analysis of their good fortune. Although it was then past ten o'clock he was far too keyed-up to call a halt to the day's investigations. Hastily finishing his coffee, Meredith nodded to Strang and together they hurried out to the car.

A three-minute dash through the emptying streets brought them down to the harbour. The constable whom Gibaud had detailed to keep watch on the *Hirondelle* was standing back in the deep shadows formed by the high stone breakwater of the harbour-arm, only a few yards from where the launch was riding at her moorings.

"*Eh bien?*" demanded Meredith.

"*Pas de personne, M'sieur.*"

"*Bon!*" said Meredith curtly.

It wasn't exactly a loquacious exchange but one, thought Meredith, that was well within the scope of his linguistic abilities. At any rate it told him all he wanted to know. He turned to Strang.

"O.K. Sergeant—let's get aboard."

To Meredith, of course, this exhaustive search was a repetition of his previous day's exploration aboard the *Hirondelle*. But now, convinced that he'd overlooked some vital clue, his investigations were even more prolonged and meticulous. Flicking on his torch and ordering the Sergeant to do the same, he unlocked the cabins and, together, they got down to work.

At the end of half-an-hour, puzzled and dejected, they'd arrived nowhere. Meredith glared at Strang and shook his head.

"Can't make it out, Sergeant. I could have sworn our theory was a winner. I'm damned if I can see where we've slipped up. After all, when I searched the launch yesterday I didn't know what I was looking for. Just any sort of clue, eh? But now we're looking for a specific object that, *ipso facto,* must occupy a specific amount of space. And that definitely limits the area of our search. It's got me hipped. Don't mind admitting it."

"Going to call it a day, sir?"

"No, m'lad, I'm not," retorted Meredith with a stubborn look. "We're going to start all over again. Come on, let's get for'ard and work our way back to the cockpit. We've all night before us."

This wasn't the first time that Meredith's obstinacy and thoroughness had brought home the bacon. Some twenty minutes after they'd started their second examination they hit on the solution to the problem that had been puzzling them.

"Well, well, well!" chuckled Meredith, delightedly. "What do you know about that, Sergeant? Ingenious, eh? Must give the devil his due. You realize what this discovery means, of course?"

"That we've broken the racket wide open, sir."

"Just that, I reckon. Blampignon's now in a position to draw up the necessary warrants of arrest. A useful and highly satisfactory day's work, m'lad. Except for one outstanding exception we've now got the gang more or less in the bag."

"The exception being 'Chalky' Cobbett, sir?"

"Exactly, Strang. The man we were sent over here to trace and apprehend. Disappointing, eh? I hate having a loose end lying around in a case." Meredith turned aside to lock the door of the for'ard cabin. "Still, sufficient unto the day is the progress thereof. We mustn't expect miracles. Ready, Sergeant? Time we got back and caught up on our sleep. We're all lined up for a pretty exhaustive pow-wow tomorrow with our good friend Blampignon. I guess he's going to be tickled to death!"

CHAPTER XIV

NOTES IN CIRCULATION

I

AN EARLY 'PHONE-CALL to Nice brought Inspector Blampignon hell-for-leather over to Menton. Gibaud had placed his office at their disposal and shortly after ten o'clock that Wednesday morning Meredith, Strang, Blampignon and Gibaud himself were seated in the small, business-like, first-floor room at the local Commissariat de Police.

Very naturally the atmosphere of the conference was one of suppressed excitement. For after weeks of indifferent progress the case had suddenly reached that conclusive phase where proven facts could be substituted for unproven, if plausible, speculation. Blampignon, his round, good-natured face wreathed in smiles, was like a cat on hot bricks. Racked with impatience, it was all he could do to tether himself to his chair. Barely had Gibaud closed the door and dropped into his seat behind the desk, when Blampignon burst out explosively:

"*Mon Dieu!* is it necessary that we waste time like this? Do you wish me to die of suspense, *mes amis?* Tell me now, what exactly is it you have managed to find out?"

"Darn nearly everything!" grinned Meredith, who with an irritating lack of haste was setting a match to the bowl of his pipe. "But don't look to me to start the ball rolling. That's the Sergeant's pidgin. He's the fellow who first set the match to the fuse and with your permission, gentlemen, I'm going to ask him to open the proceedings. Agreed?" The two French Inspectors nodded. "O.K. Sergeant. Fire ahead—it's all yours."

"But... but where exactly do you want me to begin?" stammered Freddy, somewhat overwhelmed by the responsibility that had suddenly been thrust upon him.

"Begin at the beginning, m'lad," suggested Meredith drily. "It's always a sound idea."

"You mean with what I happened to see that morning in the garage-yard at the Villa Paloma?" Meredith nodded. "O.K. sir. Well, early last Sunday morning I..."

And without more ado Freddy described in detail all that he'd witnessed through his peep-hole in the lattice gate—Shenton's arrival in the Vedette; the strange "catch" that he appeared to have brought back from his early-morning fishing expedition; his hasty conceal-ment of the tar-spotted boulder when the maid had come out into the yard. Every now and then, at Blampignon's request, he had to break off so that Gibaud could translate some phrase that his colleague was unable to grasp. Freddy then turned to the walk he'd taken with Dilys Westmacott the previous afternoon. After describing the route they'd followed out to Cap Martin, he went on:

"We clambered out over the rocks to a point only a few yards from the sea. Miss Westmacott sat for a moment and we started chatting. Well, to cut a long story short, I happened to notice an empty wine-bottle stuck up on a rock a few yards ahead of us." Freddy grinned. "Naturally I couldn't resist the invitation, and I began chucking peb-bles at the thing. At the third shot I hit it fair and square. And then, just close to it, I spotted the boulder."

"The boulder?" enquired Blampignon. "What is?" Gibaud explained. "Ah! the piece of rock. And what is the significance of your discovery, *mon ami?*"

"Well, sir, I noticed that it had tar-stains on it like the one Shenton had taken from his creel. *And the arrangement of the stains—five dots like a lopsided domino-five—was identical!*"

"*Mon Dieu!*" breathed Blampignon gustily. "Go on! Go on!"

"I realized at once that these five dots couldn't have got there by chance—I mean exactly the same number and arrangement in both cases. It seemed pretty obvious that they'd been *painted* on. And then it struck me that the up-ended bottle might have some connection with the boulder—that it might have been set up there as a kind of marker. Without Miss Westmacott realizing I managed to decipher the label on one of the broken pieces. Nuits St. George, sir."

"Nuits St. George!" echoed Blampignon excitedly as he turned to Meredith. "But that was the label on the empty bottle you saw on the rocks after we surprise the launch on Saturday night!"

"Exactly," nodded Meredith. "And it was there for the same reason—to pin-point the spot where one of these specially marked and specially designed boulders had been set ashore off the launch. Yesterday, when Strang passed the spot, he noticed that the bottle had gone. Presumably the boulder had been collected in the interim and the bottle thrown into the sea or hidden in the undergrowth."

"But why... what...?" floundered Blampignon with a blank, almost imbecile, expression on his swarthy features.

Meredith laughed.

"Let me tidy it up for you, my dear fellow. Mind if I take over now, Sergeant? Right! Then let's get down to the fundamental facts of the mystery. The launch we surprised on Saturday night *was* the *Hirondelle*—no mistake about that. Latour was aboard her with A. N. Other—this enigmatic figure in cloak and wide-brimmed hat whom my good friend Gibaud here claims to be a woman. Latour was there for one reason and one reason only—to land one of these curiously marked boulders and to mark its position with an empty bottle of Nuits St. George. Aboard the launch, by the way, I found a crate half-full of these empty bottles."

"*Mon Dieu!*" cried Blampignon, clapping his hands despairingly to his head. "Do not let us worry about these bottles. It is the pieces of rock I do not understand."

"Neither did we at first," admitted Meredith. "Until we laid our hands on one and succeeded in opening it."

"Opening it?" demanded Gibaud, bewildered. "What the devil do you mean?"

"Fixed under the centre dot of the domino-five was a perfectly concealed spring-catch. By luck I pressed the right spot and the top of the contraption hinged back. Inside, of course, it was hollow. A thick lead plate was let into the base of the rock to counteract the loss of weight due to this hollow. Neat, eh? To all appearances the lump of rock both looked and felt genuine."

"And the hollow," asked Blampignon, "for what was it made?"

"To conceal a nice thick wad of counterfeit notes all fresh and crackling from the press, my dear fellow."

Blampignon jumped to his feet.

"So that is how they work it! The press was on board *L'Hirondelle*—is that how you mean?"

"Ingenious, eh?" chuckled Meredith. "What better place to set it up? All Latour had to do was to cruise around off-shore at night, print off a prearranged consignment of dud notes, slap 'em into one of these boulder affairs and dump the stuff at some lonely spot along the nearby coastline."

"But why these elaborate precautions?" asked Gibaud. "Why not walk off the launch with the notes in his pocket?"

"Because there was always a chance that the police might grow suspicious of his nocturnal trips in the *Hirondelle*. If the launch was searched or Latour frisked as he came ashore... well, he'd have as much chance of getting away with it as an icicle in hell! That money was hot, and Latour wasn't going to risk handling it. Sensible, you'll admit. With their particular *modus operandi* there was absolutely nothing to connect the Hedderwick launch with any sort of racket."

"Nothing? Nothing?" cried Blampignon, who was now striding about the room in a perfect dither of excitement. "How do you mean... nothing? What about the printing-press? Are we so stupid, we police, that if we see a printing-press on a boat we ask no questions? *Merdre!* I do not believe that one, *mon vieux*."

"Hang on! Not so fast," chuckled Meredith. "You Frenchmen

always pride yourselves on your logicality. Well, let's look at this from a logical point of view."

"*Eh bien,* that is just what I do!" protested Blampignon.

"Not entirely," corrected Meredith. "Now be honest, old man. You wouldn't start searching the launch for an illicit printing-press unless you had definite proof that Latour was a member of a gang. And if neither he nor any member of his crew were caught with the notes on their person—I mean as they came ashore—would you honestly suspect that the counterfeiting was being worked from the *Hirondelle*? Owned, remember, by the highly respectable Mrs. Hedderwick."

"No," admitted Blampignon with a hangdog look. "That is true. Without we catch him coming off the boat with the notes on him, how should we suspect?"

"Precisely. Don't forget that when we *did* catch up with Latour it was via Guillevin, the tobacconist, and Jacques Dufil, the hunchback. It was sheer crazy carelessness on Latour's part to bribe Dufil with forged notes. And even then we shouldn't have associated the racket with the *Hirondelle* if we hadn't had that chance encounter with the launch off Cap Martin on Saturday night. Agreed?"

"*Mais oui,*" said Blampignon sheepishly. "That is good sense."

"Well, that's my first point. Now for the second. Even when my investigations *did* lead me to the *Hirondelle,* I found absolutely nothing suspicious about her. Admittedly, when I searched the boat on Monday I wasn't specifically looking for a printing-press, because I'd no idea then how the trick was being worked. You follow?"

"*Oui, oui—parfaitement,*" nodded Blampignon.

"But last night, when Strang and I searched the launch again, we boarded her *expecting* to unearth the press. But even then, if it hadn't been for a fortunate mishap I guess we'd have chucked our theory overboard and kidded ourselves that the press *wasn't* aboard the *Hirondelle.*"

"And when you did find it?" asked Gibaud eagerly. "Where exactly—?"

Meredith cut in with a malicious twinkle:

"Oh, no—I'm not going to spoon-feed you fellows. When we're through with this pow-wow we're driving down to the harbour and I'm going to give you and Blampignon a chance to discover the darn thing for yourselves! But before we do that let's return to the receiving-end of the set-up—the collecting and disposal of the notes once they'd come off the press. As far as the Sergeant and I have been able to ascertain there are only three men working the racket—four, if we include the elusive 'Chalky'."

"And those?" enquired Gibaud.

"Latour, Shenton and Bourmin. Latour, printing; Shenton, collecting; Bourmin, disposing. And of these three, I've a very strong suspicion that the Englishman's the one behind the organization. Now for the details. You recall the Sergeant's evidence concerning Shenton's early-morning fishing expeditions?" The two Inspectors nodded. "Well, that was the alibi he employed when picking up the notes. Simple, eh? A bit of fishing, say, off Cap Martin or wherever they'd agreed to put ashore the notes. A quick look around for the empty wine-bottle. Another casual glance around in the vicinity of the marker for a medium-sized boulder bearing five tar stains. Even if there were other anglers out on the rocks it would be perfectly easy for Shenton to slip the boulder unnoticed into his creel."

Gibaud protested:

"I still think it sounds damnably over-complicated."

"Not a bit of it. The notes had to be set ashore in some sort of container. And that container had to merge into the surrounding landscape like a chameleon. What better than one more lump of rock amid a million others? Actually there's more to it than that, but I'll deal with this in due course. Anyway, we've now got irrefutable evidence that this was the way Shenton worked it. Yesterday evening when we drove over to Cap Martin we took with us an empty bottle of Nuits St. George. This we set up on the rock where the Sergeant had spotted the original marker—the one he smashed with that pebble! To allay all suspicion we picked up every piece of broken glass. Later, at the Villa Paloma, I had a private word with Miss Westmacott. I asked her to keep watch from her window to see if Shenton set out early this morning on one of his little angling jaunts. If so, she was to ring me at my hotel."

"And she did?" asked Blampignon.

"Yes—he left about six-thirty. And if that isn't conclusive proof, then I'll grow a beard and like it!" chuckled Meredith. "So much for that. Once the Sergeant had stumbled on the boulder clue the remaining links in our chain of evidence snapped very neatly into place. We drove over to Malloy's villa at Beaulieu and found just what we were looking for—a five-spot, perfectly natural-looking lump of rock that was used to prop open one of the garage doors."

"But how did it get there?" demanded Blampignon instantly. "This Bourmin disposes of the notes. He does not collect them. At least that is what you tell us just now."

"Quite, my dear chap. We asked ourselves the same question. How did Bourmin pick up the notes from Shenton over at Menton? Did Shenton deliver them in person? If so, when and where? It struck us that it wouldn't be easy for Shenton and Bourmin to arrange a rendez-vous. Bourmin never knew when exactly he'd be on duty. The Colonel made that point clear. The chauffeur was often called out at a moment's notice. Besides it wouldn't be easy for Shenton, with a pretty full private life, to nip away from the villa just when he pleased." Meredith turned to Strang. "And then we hit on the explanation, eh, Sergeant?"

"A winner all the way, sir!" exclaimed Strang.

"You see," went on Meredith, "we found out that every Friday night Bourmin drove the Malloys over to the Villa Paloma for an evening's bridge. And it struck us at once that this was the link we were looking for. Here was a chance for Bourmin to collect the specie without rousing the slightest suspicion. Nobody, in fact, even suggested that Bourmin knew either Latour or Shenton."

"And you find out that your theory was right... how?" asked Blampignon.

"From Beaulieu we drove direct to Mrs. Hedderwick's. In the garage-yard there we found an identical boulder employed in exactly the same way. You see the beautiful simplicity of it all? Bourmin slips the empty boulder into the Rolls—probably under the driving-seat or some other suitable spot. After dropping the Malloys at the front-door, he parks the Rolls in the garage-yard at the rear of the villa. There he substitutes the empty boulder for the one that Shenton has placed ready for him. Doubtless Latour was responsible for conveying the empty containers from the villa to the boat—presumably in the rucksack that, according to Miss Westmacott, he used for carrying his painting gear. As I see it, there was a chain of boulders kept in continuous motion. Villa to boat, boat to shore, shore back to Villa Paloma, Paloma to Valdeblore, Valdeblore back to Paloma and so on and so on." Meredith paused, pulled out a handkerchief, mopped his brow and turned with a triumphant expression to his French *confrères*. "Well, gentlemen, that's our story and we hope you like it. Now before we drive down to the *Hirondelle* are there any—?"

There was a rap on the door.

"*Entrez!*" sang out Gibaud.

A constable entered.

"*Pour M'sieur Meredith.*"

He held out the cablegram which had been sent round post-haste to the Commissariat by the manager of the Hotel Louis.

"Ah, thanks," nodded Meredith. "I was expecting this." Adding the moment the constable had closed the door: "A little enquiry I made at the Yard concerning our friend Shenton." Hastily slitting open the envelope, he scanned the enclosed message and emitted a low whistle. "Well, well—what do you know? Just listen to this, gentlemen—*Reference your enquiry stop person in question served six months Wormwood Scrubs 1939 stop theft West-end night-club stop charged under name referred your cable but at time trial suspected to be alias stop this never proved stop.*" Meredith glanced round with a self-satisfied smile, slipped the cablegram back into the envelope and thrust it in his pocket. "So my feelings about that young fellow weren't misplaced. As I suspected, a Bad Hat. I felt sure I'd seen his face before and I probably had... in the Rogues' Gallery at the Yard!" Meredith paused to relight his pipe, then added: "Now before we drive down to the *Hirondelle,* are there any questions, gentlemen?"

"*Mais oui,*" nodded Blampignon. "Just one little question. This figure in the cloak—you say Gibaud here suspect that it is a woman. And by the way you say it, *mon ami,* I think you do not agree, eh?"

"I do not!" said Meredith emphatically. "And for one very good reason. Now that we know for certain that the notes were being run off the press aboard the launch, I'm convinced that Latour's companion was a man."

"A man?" asked Blampignon impatiently. "But what man?"

"A man who was indispensable to the working of that press. A man upon whose expert knowledge and technical skill Latour would be forced to rely. The king-pin, in fact, of the whole shady set-up."

"*Sacré nom!*" exclaimed Blampignon, with an upward roll of his dark expressive eyes. "'Chalky' Cobbett himself!"

"Exactly," smiled Meredith. "The gentleman I was sent down here to collect."

II

"Well," called down Meredith from the quayside, "any luck, m'lads?"

Blampignon stuck a flushed and sheepish face out of the cabin-door and, glancing up at his tormentor, shook his fist.

"One half of an hour and we find nothing—nothing, *mon vieux! C'est incroyable.* But I have no more patience to continue the search. You have had your little laugh, perhaps?"

"And how!" chuckled Meredith maliciously. He nodded to Strang, who was squatting on a nearby bollard. "O.K. Let's get aboard and put 'em out of their misery."

Dropping lightly on to the deck of the launch, Meredith and Strang, followed by the two French Inspectors, passed through into the for'ard cabin. There Meredith flicked on his pocket-torch and opened up a dark, deeply-recessed locker let into the starboard side of the boat beyond the double-tiered berths. Motioning his colleagues forward, Meredith announced with a dramatic flourish of his hand:

"*Voilà, messieurs!* The answer to the mystery!"

"The fresh-water tank!" exclaimed Gibaud. "But confound it, we lifted the lid and looked inside it. The darn thing's brimful of water."

"That's what *we* thought," admitted Meredith. "I even shone my torch inside to make sure. If I hadn't done so, we'd still be groping, eh, Strang?"

"You mean you see something strange about the tank that awake your suspicion?" asked Blampignon.

Meredith shook his head.

"No—even then I spotted nothing odd about it."

"Then how the devil…?" began Gibaud, bewildered.

"My torch slipped out of my hand and fell into the water—that's all." Meredith groped in his pocket and pulled out a chip of stone that he'd picked up on the quayside. He handed it to Blampignon. "Just drop this in and watch carefully, my dear fellow."

As Meredith directed the rays of his torch down into the tank, Blampignon dropped the stone into it with a gentle plop. It descended for about eighteen inches and then, as if affected by some incalculable freak of gravity, appeared to remain suspended in the water.

"But, *mon Dieu!*" exclaimed Blampignon, "it is not natural! What is the explanation?"

"This," said Meredith curtly.

Reaching forward, whilst Strang kept the lid hinged back as far as it would go, Meredith cautiously gripped the rim of the tank and lifted out the false tank that was cunningly fitted into the top of the receptacle. Beneath it was a deep recess, insulated from the outer sides of the tank by a kind of four-inch water-jacket. Inside this recess was the printing-press!

"Good heavens!" cried Gibaud. "No wonder we didn't tumble to it. We sounded the tank, of course, to make sure that it wasn't hollow."

"Quite," nodded Meredith. "And you suspected nothing because of this ingenious idea of fitting a second smaller tank inside the first and filling the space between 'em with water. We got caught the same way. We've certainly got to hand it to 'Chalky', because I'll wager a week's wages that he was the blighter who hit on the idea. All he and Latour had to do was to lift the press out of the recess, print off the notes, lift the press back in again and refit this tray of water into the top of the tank. I imagine the base of the tray escaped our attention because the light of the torch was reflected from the surface of the water and acted as a blinder. At any rate, that's how the trick was worked. And the only outstanding problem we've got on our hands is this—where the deuce is 'Chalky' Cobbett? Find the answer to that one and we're all set, I imagine, to pull in the wanted men."

CHAPTER XV

THE SHUFFLING COCKNEY

I

BACK ONCE MORE in Gibaud's office the little group of officials went into another extended huddle. They still had to decide on the best scheme for the arrest of the wanted men. In Meredith's opinion it would be fatal to pull in Shenton and Bourmin before they'd discovered the whereabouts of Latour and the elusive "Chalky". It was certain the couple would get to hear of the arrests, and, the moment they had, they'd melt away like a couple of snowflakes on a griddle. True, Latour had already cleared out of the villa because he suspected the police had learnt something of the gang's activities—but even Latour had no precise idea of just how much the police had succeeded in finding out. After all, hadn't he taken the launch out *after* his flit from the villa? And hadn't Shenton collected the latest batch of forged notes only that morning? Latour and Cobbett might be on their guard. They might even lie low for a period. But it was obvious that, at present, they'd no intention of abandoning their very profitable enterprise. As for Bourmin and Shenton, they were still blissfully ignorant of the fact that they'd come under suspicion. They had absolutely no reason to suspect that they'd been linked up either with the racket or with each other.

"So what is it you have to suggest, *mon ami?*" asked Blampignon, after an exhaustive discussion of this somewhat ticklish problem.

"Well, it's not for me to say, my dear chap. The actual arrests are *your* pidgin. But weighing up the pros and cons I'm against any immediate action. Risky, I admit. If we postpone the arrests of Bourmin and Shenton, say, for forty-eight hours, then we stand a chance, in the interim, of laying our hands on Latour and Cobbett. On the other hand if Bourmin and Shenton *do* happen to find out that we've got a line on 'em, then this very delay would enable them to get cracking while the going's still good. There's always a chance that they might pick up information about our recent investigations in the district—our interest in the *Hirondelle,* for example. It boils down to this. If we delay a couple of days we stand a chance of pulling in all four of 'em—or, if our luck's out, of allowing the whole boiling to slip through our fingers. That's our problem in a nutshell. But I must leave the final decision to you and Gibaud."

"*Eh bien,*" nodded Blampignon, still obviously vacillating. "What is your idea about this, Gibaud?"

Gibaud shrugged.

"Two birds in the hand are worth four in the bush," he declared with an oracular air. "On the other hand... I'm pretty sure Meredith's got the right idea. Yes—take it all round, I'm for delaying the arrests."

"*Bon!*" exclaimed Blampignon, his good-natured face suddenly wreathed in smiles. "Then I will agree to it. We will allow ourselves forty-eight hours in which to find Latour and Cobbett. It is what you call a long shot, eh? But, *tiens!* that is how we will decide."

Unrealized by the little group in Gibaud's office, it was a decision that was to bear in its train many unexpected and unhappy consequences.

II

Before separating for lunch the Inspectors decided on the line of their future investigation. Gibaud made himself responsible for the day and night watch that was to be kept on *L'Hirondelle.* He'd already drawn up a duty roster and detailed a couple of plain-clothes men from the local force to carry out the job. The extended search for Latour and Cobbett was to be undertaken by Gibaud himself, in concert with Meredith and Strang. They arranged to meet at the Commissariat at two o'clock.

After a hasty lunch, therefore, the Englishmen found themselves once again in Gibaud's office deep in discussion.

"I don't know how you feel about it," said Meredith, "but in my opinion, we ought to make a house-to-house comb-out along the waterfront. At least, for a start. After all, if 'Chalky's' been making frequent trips aboard the launch, it's pretty well certain that he must have his hide-out in the vicinity of the harbour. Far easier and far less risky if he was more or less on the spot. Agreed?"

Gibaud nodded.

"And our Number One Priority, I imagine, is the Maison Turini. We know Latour's been making contact there with old Madame Grignot, the *concierge*. And since birds of a feather—"

"Exactly," cut in Meredith. "There's a fair chance that 'Chalky's' been very successfully tucked away in one of the apartments—either by himself or with some unsuspecting family in the tenement. Well, there's our starting-point, my dear chap. If we draw a blank there, we'll damn well search every likely house and café along the quayside."

A swift run in the car brought them to the Quai de Bonaparte, and a few minutes later, after a further exhaustive cross-examination of Madame Grignot, their search of the building was under way. It was a long and arduous task demanding infinite tact and patience. The onus of the work naturally fell on Gibaud since all the various interrogations had to be carried on in French—but Meredith and Strang were by no means idle. Not only was it necessary to cross-question the inmates of the various apartments, but a thorough search of every likely hiding-place was equally essential. After all, Latour might have bribed some occupant to keep his or her mouth shut about the presence of the wanted man, and their knock on the door might have sent the fellow scuttling into some prearranged place of concealment.

From the first floor they moved up to the second; from the second to the third and fourth; from the fourth to the extensive cellars that formed a kind of semi-basement to the building. *En route* Mam'selle Chounet was, for the second time, put through the hoop. But she, like Madame Grignot and every other occupant of the place, swore that she'd never seen anybody answering to "Chalky's" description either in or near the Maison Turini. At the end of three hours' solid and unremitting labour they were forced to admit that they'd got precisely nowhere!

Dropping into a nearby café for a hasty snack and a well-deserved *apéritif* they set out to extend their enquiries along the Quai de Bonaparte. Two hours later, depressed and wilting, they moved along to the Quai Laurenti. But always to be met with the same blank stares and emphatic headshakes; the same negative answers and infuriating irrelevances. For a chap who must have been passing constantly up and down the quayside on his way to and from *L'Hirondelle,* probably for weeks on end, "Chalky" Cobbett appeared to have taken on the miraculous attributes of the Invisible Man! In brief—nobody had seen him in the district, far less spoken to him or made his acquaintance. What was more, nobody had ever heard any gossip about the fellow.

It was this last factor that really puzzled Meredith. "Chalky" may have been a topline forger, but he was certainly no linguist. It would be utterly impossible for him to conceal the fact that he was English, or at any rate a foreigner. Moreover, "Chalky" was a pint-sized sort of chap—a little over five feet in his socks—with that dead white complexion which had originally earned him his nickname. And if an undersized, white-faced little rat of a foreigner could have been wandering about this district for weeks on end without causing comment then something was very definitely screwy. There seemed to be only one logical answer to the enigma. "Chalky" hadn't been noticed along the waterfront for the very simple reason that he'd *not* been living near the harbour. In short, their investigations had been a damnable waste of time!

It was long after dusk before the three officials retraced their steps along the Quai Laurenti and headed for the parked car. Jaded, leg-weary, and disheartened, they spoke little as they jogged by the garishly-lit little shops and cafés that shouldered each other along the gently curving waterfront. Even for a Mediterranean night the air was exceptionally clear and balmy. Quite a number of people were strolling up and down the broad pavements or sitting over their drinks at the little marble-topped tables outside the cafés. Pausing a moment to light his pipe, Meredith temporarily dropped behind his companions, who, busy with their own reflections, plodded on towards the car.

The Inspector was just flicking out the spent match, when a small boy, chased by an irate, gesticulating woman, shot out of a nearby *pâtisserie* like a greyhound from a trap. In view of the lad's violently masticating jaws, it was pretty obvious that the owner had caught him pilfering her stock-in-trade. His precipitate appearance on the pavement resulted in a head-on collision with a bent, wizened little man who was shuffling by the shop with his eyes seemingly fixed on the ground. The outcome of the impact, from Meredith's point-of-view, was startling. In a flash of ill-temper the little fellow made a wild attempt to fetch the urchin a clout on the head.

"'Ere! watch aht!—blast yer!"

In the circumstances this censure was admittedly justifiable but why the devil, wondered Meredith, had the old man lashed out in English? English, moreover, that had about it the unmistakable clipped and nasal twang of the Cockney? He swung round sharply and took a closer look at the elderly white-bearded figure. Then he suffered a shock. There was no mistaking the man's features as, muttering under his breath, he started off again on his interrupted shuffle along the brightly-lit sidewalk. It was M'sieur Grignot—the half-witted husband of the *concierge* at the Maison Turini!

So Grignot could speak English, could he? *Cockney* English! And when the need arose his mind could work as quickly and clearly as the next man's. What the deuce did it mean? That Grignot's insanity was assumed? That the fellow, for all his mumbling and chuckling and head-nodding, was merely laying on an act?

And then, like a bolt from the blue, Meredith hit on the explanation for the old fellow's behaviour; a startling theory that whipped him into a mood of ever-mounting excitement. Good God, yes! it all added up. The simulated craziness; the inarticulate babblings; the uncomprehending glances—what better alibi for a man who wished to conceal his identity? Frenchman by name but Englishman by birth, eh? Simple to hide the fact that he couldn't speak or understand a word of French behind this façade of idiocy. And hadn't Latour been in the habit of paying regular visits to M'sieur and Madame Grignot in their little glass-fronted cubby-hole? And wasn't the Maison Turini within a stone's throw of the harbour? Above all, wasn't this M'sieur Grignot a pocket-sized little chip of a chap, who displayed, in moments of forgetfulness, an easy command of Cockney vituperation?

By heaven, yes! there was absolutely no doubt about it. The search for the elusive "Chalky" was at an end. He could be picked up now whenever they wished at the Maison Turini!

III

By ten-thirty that evening, after a dash over to Nice, concerted plans had been worked out for the arrest of the wanted men. The dead-line was fixed for ten-thirty the following morning. Blampignon was to pick up Bourmin at Beaulieu, and a 'phone-call had been put through to Colonel Malloy at the Villa Valdeblore asking him to make sure that the chauffeur would be on the premises at the appointed time. Meredith, Strang and Gibaud were to deal with Cobbett at the Maison Turini; and, immediately after his arrest, they were to go direct to the Villa Paloma to pull in Shenton.

Over the providential and unexpected discovery of "Chalky's" whereabouts Blampignon was jubilant.

"You have no doubt about this, *mon ami*? There is no chance that we arrest an innocent man?"

Meredith shook his head emphatically.

"None whatever! The devil only knows why I didn't rumble the trick before. Of course the beard and the olive-skinned complexion helped to pull the wool over my eyes. His assumed craziness did the rest. Clever, you'll admit. Latour knew he could trust the old woman, and I imagine when he fixed for her to take up that *concierge* job at the Maison Turini, he kidded the owners of the place that she was actually married to this halfwit. All 'Chalky' had to do as a preliminary was to let his beard grow and darken that dead-white pan of his with some suitable stain. The idea of acting ga-ga, of course, was to overcome the lingo difficulty and prevent people from asking awkward questions. Ourselves included! Neat, eh? Naturally when we made enquiries this afternoon to find out if anybody had seen or heard anything of a five-foot, white-faced Englishman in the district we drew a blank. But I'll wager every darn witness we questioned had seen Madame Grignot's crazy 'husband' shuffling and muttering around the streets. If you ask me, 'Chalky' had hit on the all but perfect alibi. If it hadn't been for that youngster... well, the chances are we'd still be groping. Bourmin, Shenton and now Cobbett. Three in the bag, eh? A pity we can't lay our hands on Latour. Can't bear to have loose ends lying around and Latour's one of 'em. However..." Meredith lifted his shoulders, "this looks like the wind-up of my assignment down here. And I don't mind telling you, my dear Blampignon, that I've enjoyed every minute of it. The *entente cordiale,* eh? I shall miss your sunny, Provençal smile back at the Yard!"

CHAPTER XVI

THE MISSING PLAYBOY

I

"CHALKY'S" arrest the following morning was effected without a hitch. The job was done so quietly and efficiently that nobody in or near the Maison Turini realized what was happening. "Chalky", himself, caught on the wrong foot, made no serious attempt to deny his identity. A moment's bluster, a few querulous protests and, recognizing the hopelessness of his position, he threw in the towel. Seated between Meredith and Strang in the back of the local police-car, he was whisked off through the sunlit streets to the Commissariat, where he was to be placed under lock and key until Blampignon arrived to take him over to Nice. On the steps of the Maison Turini, Madame Grignot, with much wringing of hands, watched her erstwhile "husband" pass out of her life—presumably for ever. She'd been warned to hold herself in readiness for further cross-examination. Gibaud had made it clear that she might be charged for withholding information from the police and as an accessory both before and after the fact.

Once "Chalky" had been safely deposited in the lock-up, the three officials returned post-haste to the car and drove all out for the Villa Paloma. After all, they weren't going to have that redoubtable old harridan, Madame Grignot, tipping the wink to Shenton. They'd been caught that way in the case of Latour.

Parking the car just short of the villa gates in the Avenue St. Michel, Meredith detailed Strang to take up his position in the garage-yard and ordered him to keep a close watch on the rear of the building. As the Inspector pointed out there was always the chance that Shenton might smell a rat and endeavour to make a bolt for it. The moment Strang had slipped in through the wicket-gate, Meredith turned to Gibaud.

"All set?" Gibaud nodded. "O.K. Let's go."

As on his previous visit, it was Lisette who answered the Inspector's ring at the front door. But on enquiring if Mr. Shenton were in the girl threw him an evasive glance and said haltingly:

"I am sorry, M'sieur—but... but I think M'sieur Shenton is not here."

Meredith rapped out anxiously:

"You mean he's away—on a visit somewhere?"

"No—not exactly, M'sieur."

"Just out and about somewhere, is that it?"

The girl's embarrassment increased.

"Well, no, M'sieur. I think that he..." She broke off and concluded with a little rush: "Perhaps you would care to see Madame Hedderwick? It is better, perhaps, that she should explain."

"Very well," agreed Meredith, puzzled by the girl's strangely hesitant manner. "Kindly tell her it's Inspector Meredith, will you?"

Once the girl had ushered them into the Chinese room and retired, Gibaud observed:

"There's something odd about this. Either the fellow's here or he isn't."

"Quite. Can't make out why the girl was hedging. Anyway, we'll see what Mrs. Hedderwick has to say."

Nesta Hedderwick, as it transpired, had plenty to say! She was in a state of considerable agitation. With her customary directness she came to the cause of her perturbation without delay. The outstanding points of her non-stop narrative were these—Shenton hadn't come down to breakfast. Half an hour ago she'd gone up to his room and discovered that his bed hadn't been slept in. His car was gone from the garage. She'd questioned the other members of her household but apparently nobody had set eyes on Shenton since dinner the previous evening. Madame Bonnet, the cook, however, was convinced that she'd heard him starting up the Vedette shortly after 9 p.m. So it *was* possible that he'd gone out for a drive and the car had broken down.

But if so why hadn't he telephoned to say that he'd be spending the night away from the villa? It was unlike him, declared Nesta, to leave her in suspense, knowing how anxious she'd be. It was strange that the police should have turned up, as she was just about to put through a call to the Commissariat.

"And now that you *have* turned up," asked Nesta shortly, "what do you want with Mr. Shenton?"

"A private matter," said Meredith vaguely. "We just want to ask him a few questions—that's all."

"Well, you can't if he's not here!" retorted Nesta acidly. Then with a sudden change of mood, she went on: "I can't help wondering if he's had an accident. It's something I've always dreaded. But I suppose if there *had* been an accident—" Nesta, aware that the door had opened behind her, glanced over her shoulder and demanded tartly: "Well, Lisette, what is it?"

"Please, Madame, M'sieur Gibaud is wanted on the telephone. It is the Commissariat, M'sieur."

Mrs. Hedderwick uttered a thin wail of alarm.

"There, what did I tell you? I knew I was right! I had a premonition. Something dreadful's happened. I'm sure of it."

During his colleague's absence, Meredith did his utmost to reassure the distracted woman, but when, in a few moments, Gibaud returned, Meredith realized at once that something was definitely wrong.

"I'm afraid I've some rather disturbing news for you, Madame."

Nesta shrank back in her chair with an inarticulate cry and gasped out:

"It's Tony, isn't it? There *has* been an accident. I knew it! I knew it! He's... he's not...?"

Gibaud shook his head.

"No, not exactly an accident, Madame. But a report has just come in that his Vedette was found abandoned this morning out on Cap Martin. The Desk Sergeant knew I was here so he rang me direct."

"But Tony...?" enquired Nesta faintly. "Have they no news?"

Gibaud lifted his shoulders, hesitated a moment, and then announced quietly:

"A man's béret was found on the rocks close to the sea, about a hundred yards from the point where the car had been parked. A black béret, Madame, decorated with a red pompom and silver badge of the English Air Force."

With a shivery moan, Nesta buried her distorted face in her hands.

"Yes... yes... it's Tony's. There... there can't be any mistake. Oh, what does it mean? What does it mean, Inspector?"

"That," said Gibaud with a sympathetic headshake, "is something that we still have to find out. We have a car outside, so with your permission, Madame, I suggest we drive out to Cap Martin without delay."

II

The manager of one of the hotels perched on the rocky escarpment overlooking the cape had sent in the information concerning the abandoned car. It had first been noticed by a member of the staff cycling out from Menton about six-thirty that morning. The manager hadn't telephoned immediately, thinking that the owner of the car might have been taking an early-morning walk in the vicinity. But when, later, he himself had strolled down and found the car still there, he'd come to the conclusion that the matter should be reported without delay. A further factor lent urgency to his decision. *The running-board opposite the driving-seat was spattered with blood!*

There and then he got in touch with the local *gendarme,* who, after inspecting the Vedette for himself, rang the Commissariat at Menton. It was this *gendarme* who'd picked up the black béret on the edge of the rocks, opposite the spot where the car had been abandoned.

When Meredith, Gibaud and Strang arrived on the scene, they found the fellow on duty by the Vedette. After Gibaud had heard his report, the two Inspectors got down to a thorough examination of the car. There was no questioning the veracity of the manager's evidence. Several small bloodstains were visible on the off-side running-board, and a closer inspection revealed further spots of blood on the actual bodywork just above the running-board. At a casual glance, due to the crimson paintwork, these stains had been practically invisible.

"Well," demanded Gibaud, as they straightened up from their preliminary investigation, "what do you make of it?"

"Curious, to say the least of it. No bloodstains anywhere inside the car. Merely these scattered spots along the side opposite the driving-seat. If there's been foul play of any sort... well, you see the implication?"

"You mean that if Shenton *were* attacked the assault must have taken place after he'd got out of the car?"

Meredith nodded.

"And the moment we assume that, we're up against another peculiar factor."

"And that?"

"The bloodstains are on the side *opposite* the driving-seat—that is to say on the right of the car. And since Shenton would obviously get out on the left, it suggests he must have walked completely round the car before he was attacked. Peculiar, eh? You'd have thought his assailant would have nobbled him as he was actually clambering out—that's to say, when he had him at a disadvantage. A small point, I admit, but one worth remembering."

"Quite," agreed Gibaud. "And assuming Shenton's been scuppered it's reasonable to suppose that his assailant then carried his body across the rocks and dumped it in the sea. *En route* his béret fell off and—"

"Whoa! Whoa!" cut in Meredith sharply. "Not so fast, my dear fellow. Presuming this is the spot where the attack was carried out why aren't there any bloodstains on the road? I know damn well there aren't because I've been looking for 'em."

"There is that," admitted Gibaud with a crestfallen look. "Then what's your explanation?"

"That *if* Shenton's been murdered—and, for heaven's sake, let's keep that 'if' bang in front of our noses—then the job was done elsewhere. The murderer merely used the Vedette to convey the body to this particular spot. Probably, as you suggest, to dump the remains in the sea."

"Well, it might explain away the hood," agreed Gibaud.

"The hood?"

"Yes. It struck me at once. An open car with its hood raised and its side-windows fixed in place is a rarity in these parts. As far as I can recall, we haven't had a drop of rain for a fortnight. There was certainly no rain last night. As a matter of fact, it was exceptionally warm and windless."

Meredith nodded.

"I get your point. The hood was up and the screens in place because the murderer wanted to conceal the fact that there was a corpse in the back-seat. There may be something to it. Though I can't help feeling that if he'd shoved the body in the well and covered it with a coat, all this palaver wouldn't have been necessary. After all, his one thought must have been to get away from the scene of the crime as quickly as possible."

Strang, who throughout this exchange had been listening with both ears wide open, put in deferentially:

"And there's another point, sir."

"Well, Sergeant?"

"Well, sir, it's that idea of the body being dumped in the sea."

"You don't like it, eh?"

"No, I'm darned if I do, sir. You see, when Miss Westmacott and I walked out over the rocks yesterday we found it pretty hard going. Devilish difficult to keep your feet in daylight. But for a chap to negotiate them at night carrying a dead weight, say, of twelve stone... well, he'd be lucky if he didn't break his leg, let alone his neck!"

Meredith nodded his approval of this point.

"Quite an intelligent appreciation of the facts, m'lad." He turned to Gibaud. "You agree?"

"As a matter of fact," said Gibaud, "since I put forward the theory I've had some second thoughts about it myself."

"How do you mean?"

"A question of the tides. Along this stretch of the coast they're practically non-existent. Not a bit like your English tides. Even if the body were carried out from the rocks, I'm pretty certain it would be washed ashore again in a few hours."

"More sound sense, eh? And there's yet another fact that helps to put the kibosh on this 'dumping' theory."

Strang asked:

"What's that, sir?"

"Good heavens! don't you get it? The Vedette! If the murderer hoped to dispose of the evidence in this way why abandon the car about a hundred yards from the spot where the body was dropped into the water? Crazy, eh? It's simply drawing attention to the very thing he was anxious to conceal."

"*Exactement!*" exclaimed Gibaud. "But the béret? Mrs. Hedderwick was convinced that it belonged to Shenton."

"I think it did," said Meredith. "But isn't it possible that the béret was planted out on the rocks *deliberately?*"

"You mean as a red-herring, sir?"

"Precisely, Sergeant. The set-up as I see it is this. A murder is committed at Point A. The murderer's car is abandoned at Point B. And the body is concealed at Point C. Always assuming," added Meredith with his usual caution, "that a murder *has* been committed. And always bearing in mind that if it *has* the victim may *not* be Tony Shenton."

III

But for all Meredith's conviction that the body *hadn't* been dumped in the sea, they very sensibly made a long and exhaustive search along the rocky shores of the outermost point of the cape. They found nothing.

Not even a bloodstain to suggest that the body had been man-handled from the road to the water's edge. It was just as they'd anticipated.

With Gibaud at the wheel of the Vedette and Meredith and Strang in the police-car, they drove back along the coast-road to the Villa Paloma. While Gibaud was telephoning Blampignon about these latest developments, Meredith seized on the chance to have a further talk with Nesta Hedderwick.

Certain now that her forebodings hadn't led her astray, the poor woman was on the verge of a collapse. Although the Inspector was careful to avoid the suggestion, she quickly grasped the fact that the police, after their visit to Cap Martin, now suspected foul play. With an effort, however, she managed to pull herself together and answer Meredith's questions with reasonable composure.

From the Inspector's point-of-view this interview was highly successful. Quite a lot of significant information was forthcoming. When Mrs. Hedderwick claimed that nobody had seen Shenton since dinner the previous evening, it now seemed that the statement was not strictly accurate. Admittedly, when she'd discovered that Shenton's bed hadn't been slept in, she'd trailed round the house asking everybody if they'd seen anything of him. But there were two members of the household whom she hadn't been able to question for the simple reason that they weren't there. Directly after breakfast that morning, Kitty Linden and this fellow, Dillon, had driven off in the latter's car to spend a day up in the mountains. According to Mrs. Hedderwick they'd taken a picnic lunch—so the chances were that they wouldn't be available for cross-examination until some time that evening. So much for that.

Questioning the unhappy woman about the relationship between these young people, Meredith found himself face to face with a really significant clue. During the last few days there'd been a marked cool-ness between Kitty Linden and Shenton, though previously they'd been more or less living in each other's pockets. There was no doubt in Mrs. Hedderwick's mind that Kitty was hopelessly infatuated with

Shenton, a feeling that to a certain extent the young man had reciprocated. Now they'd evidently had a drastic quarrel and Kitty, that
morning, had gone off for the day with Dillon. Was there anything
in it? wondered Meredith. Here, at any rate, was the familiar and
everlasting triangle that time and again had supplied a motive for
murder. And in this case? Was it outside the bounds of reason that
Dillon, consumed by jealousy, had quarrelled with his rival and in a
blind and impassioned moment stabbed him? Well, such things had
happened before and they'd happen again. It would be interesting to
know if Dillon could have made contact with Shenton the previous
evening, possibly, somewhere outside the villa.

But here Mrs. Hedderwick proved a broken reed. Immediately
after dinner she'd gone up to her bedroom with a headache. She'd no
idea whether Dillon had left the house or not during the remainder
of the evening. But why not ask her niece? She would probably know.

He found the girl out on the terrace, more or less entwined with
Acting-Sergeant Strang. Apart from this visual clue, their embarrassment at his unheralded appearance clearly showed that they hadn't
been wasting their time. And Meredith was equally determined not
to waste his! A few deft questions and his interest in Dillon as a possible suspect was injected with a new liveliness. The girl's evidence
was clear and to the point. Summarized in the Inspector's notebook
it read thus:—

*9 o'clock (circa) Madame Bonnet, the cook, heard Shenton drive
off in the Vedette.*

*9.30 (circa) Dillon seen leaving house by Dilys W. When ques-
tioned by girl stated he was going to take stroll down to sea to get
some fresh air.*

*10.40—Dillon returned and joined girl and Kitty Linden in
lounge. After a brief chat and drink went up to bed.*

11.10—Dilys and Kitty went up to bed. Dilys heard sound of running water in wash-basin of Dillon's room. Called out "Good-night". Dillon answered.

Thanking the young woman for her co-operation, Meredith, followed somewhat reluctantly by his chastened subordinate, strolled out to the car where Gibaud was already seated at the wheel.

"Well," demanded Meredith, "how did our good friend Blampignon react to the news?"

"He's coming over without delay. One good bit of news anyway. Bourmin's been pulled in without any trouble. But this latest twist had got poor Blampignon thoroughly rattled. He suggests we have a scrambled lunch and meet him in my office at one-thirty. Can you make it?"

Meredith glanced at his watch.

"Five past one." He grinned. "Five minutes to reach the hotel, leaving us twenty minutes to get outside a four course lunch! Well, I suppose it *can* be done. Don't worry, my dear fellow, we'll be there."

CHAPTER XVII

FATAL PLUNGE

I

PUNCTUAL TO THE MINUTE, having forgone that four course lunch for a deliciously fluffy *omelette aux fines herbes,* Meredith and Strang joined their French colleagues in Gibaud's office. For once the smile on Blampignon's moon-like countenance was conspicuously absent. He slumped in his chair, contemplating his upturned feet with the disgruntled expression of a small boy, who, at the last minute, had been deprived of some long anticipated treat. He grunted without preliminary:

"This is bad news, *mes amis.* It is a complication we did not anticipate. You have no doubt that Shenton has been murdered, eh?"

"Well, if the bloodstains on the car are anything to go by *somebody's* been murdered—or at any rate pretty badly wounded. But I'm not saying, *ipso facto,* this 'somebody's' Shenton."

"What have you learnt since Gibaud rang me from the villa?"

Meredith gave details of the information he'd picked up during his interviews with Mrs. Hedderwick and her niece. He went on:

"If we assume that Shenton's kaput, then we can't shut our eyes to the significance of Miss Westmacott's evidence concerning Dillon's movements after dinner last night. After all, if the fellow's in love with the Linden girl... well, there's a possible motive for the crime."

"*Mais oui*—the motive," agreed Blampignon. "But what of the *modus operandi?* Consider the facts. The car is found out on Cap Martin and it is quite a long distance from the Avenue St. Michel to Cap Martin. And what is the time available? You say Dillon leave the villa at nine-thirty and return a little after ten-thirty. One hour, eh? Is it possible that Dillon could have been there and back in the time?"

Meredith pulled a wry grimace.

"On the face of it—no. But taking into consideration all the known facts, I still think we can put forward a plausible reconstruction of the crime. This way. Suppose Dillon had arranged to meet Shenton outside the villa—perhaps to discuss their relationship in regard to the Linden girl. And suppose Shenton was standing beside his parked car when Dillon showed up. The roads in the vicinity of the Villa Paloma, I imagine, would be fairly dark and deserted at night. O.K. then. Dillon draws a knife, stabs Shenton before he can defend himself, and conceals his body at some suitable spot nearby—retaining, of course, that tell-tale black béret. He then drives the Vedette hell-for-leather out to Cap Martin, abandons it by the roadside, and plants the béret on the rocks to suggest the body's been dumped in the sea." Meredith turned to Gibaud. "How far do you reckon it is from the Avenue St. Michel to the point where the car was discovered?"

Gibaud made a quick mental calculation and announced:

"At a rough estimate about two and a half kilometres. That's to say a little over a mile and a half."

"So by ten o'clock, I reckon Dillon could have been all set for his homeward journey, leaving him about thirty-five minutes in hand."

"And no car," put in Blampignon instantly.

"Quite," nodded Meredith. "But even if he failed to cadge a lift or pick up a providential 'bus, I still think he could have covered the distance quite easily on foot... I mean, of course, in the time available. He's an athletic type and from what I've seen of him in pretty good trim." Meredith glanced round enquiringly. "Well, gentlemen, what do you think of it? Any objections?"

"Well, I don't exactly want to butt in, sir," put in Freddy deferentially.

"Well, Sergeant?"

"If Shenton was stabbed beside his car wouldn't there be blood-stains on the road or pavement at the spot where the poor devil must have collapsed?"

"Perhaps there are," contested Meredith succinctly. "So far we haven't looked. It might be a sound scheme if we did."

"Quite apart from searching the environs of the villa for the missing body," suggested Gibaud. "Not that I'm criticizing your excellent reconstruction, my dear fellow. It certainly forms a working basis for our immediate investigation." He turned to Blampignon. "You agree, sir?"

Blampignon hesitated a moment, then said with a lugubrious air of caution:

"I am not so sure of it, Gibaud. There are many little points to consider. The blood on the clothes of M'sieur Dillon, *par exemple.* Mam'selle Westmacott make no mention of this, but *sacré nom!* they would have been there! Nor does Mam'selle Westmacott tell us that he was in a state of agitation when he returns to the villa. She say nothing about this. But a man who has just committed a murder and walked, perhaps, some two and a half kilometres in—" There was a rap on the door. "*Entrez!*" sang out Blampignon. "*Eh bien?*"

"M'sieur Meredith is wanted on the telephone. It is Mam'selle Westmacott, M'sieur."

"Your inamorata, eh, Sergeant?" said Meredith with a malicious glance. "I wonder what the devil *she* wants? Excuse me, gentlemen. Shan't be a minute."

In this Meredith underestimated the duration of his absence. It was a full five minutes before he returned to Gibaud's office. As he glanced slowly round the circle of enquiring faces, there was a grim expression on his aquiline features.

"*Eh bien?*" shot out Blampignon impatiently. "What is it? You look as if you have heard bad news, *mon ami.*"

"I have," said Meredith curtly.

"Well?" demanded Gibaud.

"*About an hour ago our friend Dillon committed suicide!*"

"Suicide!" exclaimed Blampignon, springing up in amazement. Meredith nodded.

"He threw himself over a precipice!"

Blampignon was the first to recover from the shock of Meredith's unexpected announcement.

"How did Mam'selle Westmacott learn of this?"

"Kitty Linden's just been brought back to the villa in a state of collapse. She was picked up in a fainting condition somewhere near a spot called the Col de Braus by an American tourist. The girl was evidently able to gasp out what had happened and give her address before she passed out completely."

"*Tiens!*" exclaimed Blampignon. "And this American?"

"He's driving round here straight away. He's promised Miss Westmacott to pilot us to the place where the tragedy occurred. So far the body hasn't been recovered. I reckon that unfortunate lady's got a tidy lot on her plate this morning—what with her aunt on the verge of hysterics and this Linden wench flat out on the sofa. Just didn't know where to turn for help. That's why she rang me."

"Suicide, eh?" put in Gibaud with a sagacious nod. "Accepting your theory that Dillon's responsible for Shenton's disappearance, this might be the logical outcome of his actions."

Meredith observed:

"Death due to a guilty conscience, eh? The same thought occurred to me. But until we—"

All further speculation was cut short by the entry of the Desk Sergeant with the news that an American gentleman by the name of M'sieur Bucknell had called to see Inspector Meredith.

"*Très bien,*" said Blampignon. "The Inspector will join him in a moment." He turned to Meredith. "It is necessary that I return to Nice for a conference, *mon ami.* You will let me know the details of what happen this morning up on the Col de Braus. Also what progress you make in the case of the missing Shenton. I understand, *naturelle-ment,* that now you have made the arrest of Cobbett, your assignment is officially at an end. But I am ringing the Yard at once to ask the

Commissioner if he will not allow you and Sergeant Strang to stay on here until we solve the puzzle of Shenton. You are agreeable to this?"

"Nothing I'd like better, my dear fellow, if the A.C.'s prepared to play."

"*Bon!* Then that is settled." Blampignon swung round on Gibaud. "I wish for Cobbett to be taken out to my car—hooded and hand-cuffed. You understand? Perhaps when we have—how do you say?—grilled him a little he will tell us where we may find M'sieur Latour! We must not forget that he is still at large. Nor must we forget the possibility that *he* might have knifed our friend Shenton. For reasons that, at the moment," concluded Blampignon, "are not apparent to us."

III

Bucknell's car, a long sleek glittering saloon, took the gradients up from Menton like a thoroughbred. The American handled the car with the casual ease of a man who has spent a lifetime crossing continents and mountains behind a steering-wheel. He was an uninhibited, talkative sort of chap and, in the first ten minutes, Meredith had learnt quite a bit about him. He was on his way to Rome for an international get-together of *hoteliers,* having nosed his way over the Alpes Maritimes via Grenoble. The fact that his journey south had been interrupted by this unexpected contretemps left him utterly unruffled.

Some little way beyond Castillon, Bucknell slowed down and pointed out the spot where he'd found the girl slumped by the roadside.

"I noticed the parked auto about a mile up the road. I guess that marks the actual spot where this guy, Dillon, went over the edge."

"Wonder why the girl didn't make use of the car?" observed Meredith.

"I asked her that myself. Seems that she can't drive. If you ask me it's darned lucky I happened along when I did. Not exactly a traffic jam up here, huh?"

Bucknell was right about that. It was strange, after the colourful activity of the coast towns, to find oneself after a comparatively short run amid the grandeur and desolation of the mountains. When a few minutes later Bucknell pulled in beside the parked car and Meredith stepped out, the panorama stretched out before him took his breath away. The road at this point, curving round a spur of the mountainside with a precipice dropping away sheer on its outer edge, formed a kind of natural look-out. Dillon's Stanmobile had been parked in a providential recess on the inner side of the road, and since a large tartan rug had been spread out on the rocky verge beside the car it was obvious that the couple had selected this spot for their picnic lunch. Meredith noticed that a low wooden fence had been erected, presumably by the local authorities, along the outer curve of the road. As Strang, who'd been sitting in the back of the car, came forward to join him, Meredith observed:

"Well, this precludes the possibility of accident. The fence isn't particularly high, I admit, but nobody could go over the edge without first climbing it. I couldn't see why the girl was so certain that Dillon threw himself over deliberately. Now it's obvious."

Cautiously climbing the fence, Meredith inched his way to the brink of the precipice and gazed down. Admittedly the Inspector had a good head for heights, but even he was affected by a momentary vertigo as his eyes raked the rock-strewn valley below for any sign of the body. Then suddenly, as his head cleared, he saw a gleam of white against the dun-coloured background of rock and scrub.

He announced grimly:

"The poor devil's there all right. But how the deuce we're going to—" He broke off and added excitedly: "No—wait! There seems to be a rough track running up the valley. Looks like a mule-track or something of the kind." Climbing back over the fence, Meredith whipped out the large scale map that Gibaud had sensibly thrust into his pocket before leaving the Commissariat. For a moment he studied it intently; then he rapped out: "Yes—it's a mule-track right enough. See here—it's clearly marked."

"And by the look of it, sir," put in Strang, who was now at Meredith's elbow craning over the map, "it links up with this road here, running down to L'Escarene."

Meredith turned to the American.

"Look here, Mr. Bucknell, it seems unnecessary to take up any more of your time. We may be up here for at least a couple of hours. And if we do manage to reach the poor devil... well, it won't be a particularly pleasant sight. And now that Dillon's car's available..."

"I guess you're right," nodded Bucknell. "No real point in me hanging on." He pushed out a large and friendly hand. "Well, it's been a pleasure to meet you, Inspector. I guess the folks back home'll be tickled to death when I tell 'em I've met a real live guy from Scotland Yard."

After thanking him for his co-operation and helping the American to back his car to a place where it was possible to turn it, Meredith and Strang hastened back to the Stanmobile. Folding up the rug and throwing it on to the back seat, Strang took his place beside Meredith, who was already at the wheel. A few hundred yards ahead they came to a weather-beaten signpost and, forking left, began the slow and tortuous descent towards the distant village of L'Escarene. For a time the road seemed to swing away from the great buttress of rock that formed the precipice. Then, to Meredith's satisfaction, it doubled back and headed directly for the base of the crag. A moment or so later Meredith braked up hard and brought the Stanmobile to a slithering standstill.

"There's our mule-track, Sergeant. Damn nearly wide enough to get the car along, I reckon, but we'd better not risk it. If the track narrows we shan't be able to turn."

Jumping from the Stanmobile they set off briskly along the loose and stony surface of the glorified bridle-path; Strang, at Meredith's suggestion, carrying the folded rug over his arm. Then only a short distance from the road, rounding a bulky outcrop of rock, they came on the body of the unfortunate Dillon.

He was sprawling face-downward; one arm flung out, the other doubled under his chest. He was dressed in a bleached khaki bush-shirt, white shorts and rubber-soled shoes. On his back, still securely strapped in place, was a large and serviceable rucksack.

Gingerly Meredith rolled the body over and together he and Strang gazed down into what had once been the dead man's face. Hardened as he was to such physical horrors, Meredith was unable to repress a shudder of revulsion.

"Umph," he commented, swallowing hard, "not particularly pleasant, eh Sergeant?"

"Ghastly, sir. Anyway, he couldn't have known much about it. That's one consolation. The poor devil certainly picked the right place to scupper himself."

"So appropriate," agreed Meredith, "that I think we can safely rule out the assumption that he acted on impulse. If you ask me, Dillon was familiar with the lie of the land around the Col de Braus and this morning, when he set off with the girl, he *deliberately* headed for this particular—" Meredith broke off abruptly and, dropping on one knee, placed his ear to the dead man's left wrist. "Well, can you beat that, Sergeant! His watch is still going—glass isn't even broken." Unbuckling the pigskin strap Meredith examined the watch more closely. Then, straightening up, he said sharply: "Good heavens! take a look at the inscription on the back of it."

"*To Bill from his loving wife, Kitty,*" read Strang. "But... but what the blazes does it mean, sir?"

"Precisely what it says, Sergeant. No mistake about it. Unless they've been divorced in the interim, it means that Miss Kitty Linden's *actually Bill Dillon's wife.* At least," amended Meredith with a nod towards the mutilated figure slumped at his feet, "she *was* his wife until her husband decided to chuck himself off that crag!"

CHAPTER XVIII

THE PARKED VEDETTE

I

WITH THE MORTAL REMAINS of Bill Dillon swathed in the tartan rug and accommodated in the back of the car, Meredith set off on the homeward run. Strang, sensitive to his superior's unpredictable change of mood, tactfully refrained from discussing the latest developments in the day's fast-flowing stream of events. It was evident that behind his sweetly-drawing pipe the Inspector was engaged in a spot of high-pressure thinking.

Meredith's thoughts, in fact, were in a state of flux. The totally unexpected discovery that Kitty and Bill Dillon were man and wife forced him to reorient his earlier views concerning the motive for the young man's suicide. What if he were wrong? What if Dillon's fatal act had nothing to do with Shenton's ominous disappearance? In short, what if it were connected, not with Shenton, but with Kitty?

Here was an explosive set-up that might well drive an honest chap like Dillon to take his own life. Look at it this way. Kitty was infatuated with Shenton (that much *was* certain since Mrs. Hedderwick had gone out of her way to stress the fact). Dillon, learning that his wife was staying at the Villa Paloma, rushes down to Menton, doubtless hoping to break up this illicit and, to him, odious relationship. He tries to persuade Kitty to return to him. She refuses. O.K.—what then? Dillon persuades the girl to drive with him up into the mountains—on the pretext, no doubt, of a last desperate attempt to repair the breach between them—and there, up on the Col de Braus, with a final perverse and melodramatic gesture, he forces the girl to witness the ultimate outcome of her infidelity. In brief—Dillon hadn't committed suicide to escape from the hauntings of a guilty conscience, but to free himself from a situation that had become intolerable.

Well, argued Meredith, there might be something in it. Kitty's refusal to return to him might well be the *prima facie* motive for the suicide. But here was another point to consider. What if Dillon, knowing that he was about to take his own life, decided to erase Shenton before executing his own obliteration? Motive, of course, jealousy—a desire to revenge himself on the man who'd broken up his marriage and more or less run off with his wife.

Assuming that Dillon *had* killed Shenton, they'd already discussed, of course, the possible *modus operandi* of the murder. Gibaud, in fact, following up Meredith's theory that the actual stabbing had taken place in the vicinity of the Villa Paloma, had promised to instigate an immediate investigation of the nearby roads and gardens. Doubtless, this investigation was already under way. They had three definite objects in view. (A) To ascertain if there were bloodstains on the road or pavement where the murder had actually been committed. (B) To carry out enquiries among the neighbouring villas to see if anybody had noticed the parked Vedette or anything, in fact, that might corroborate their theory. (C) To comb through all possible places of concealment in the locality in the hope of unearthing the body of the missing Shenton.

It was possible, thought Meredith, that by the time they reached Menton, Gibaud might have already picked up a worth-while clue.

II

When he arrived back at the Commissariat, however, he learnt from the Desk Sergeant that Gibaud and two plainclothes constables were still out on safari. He was anxious that Dillon's body should be removed from the back of the Stanmobile and placed in the mortuary, but discovering that the Sergeant couldn't understand a word of English Meredith found himself in a quandary. He made one or two stilted attempts in his execrable French to explain the situation. The Sergeant, however, remained dismally unresponsive. A hasty flick through his pocket phrase-book convinced Meredith that the editor had failed miserably to provide a phrase suitable to the occasion. To order a taxi; to ask the time; to comment on the weather; to argue with a disobliging porter—yes! But when it came to the conveyance of corpses to the public mortuary the editor was infuriatingly reserved. Meredith was just trying out:—

"*Voulez-vous transporter le cadavre dans l'automobile au le mortuary publique,*" when to his intense relief Gibaud strode briskly into the office.

"Ah, thank God you've turned up!" exclaimed Meredith with a look of relief.

"Why—what's wrong?" enquired Gibaud.

In a few sentences Meredith outlined the results of their run up to the Col de Braus and explained to Gibaud that the body of the unfortunate Dillon was still in the back of the car.

"And you want the remains removed to the mortuary, is that it?" Meredith nodded. "O.K. I'll deal with this. Go through to my office. I'll join you in a minute. I've some sizzling hot news for you."

Meredith barely had time to fill and light his pipe before Gibaud came through from the main-office and flung himself, with a sigh of exhaustion, into his desk-chair.

"Phew! Quite a relief to take the weight off my feet. Been out on the beat ever since you left."

"Well?" demanded Meredith impatiently.

"Well... what?"

"This sizzling hot news of yours."

"Oh that!" chuckled Gibaud, with an exasperating inability to come to the point. "Now don't get me wrong. We've seen no sign of bloodstains anywhere in the vicinity of the villa and we haven't found the missing body. But we *have* picked up some pretty useful information."

"Then, for crying aloud!" exploded Meredith. "Why not let me in on it?"

"Very well—I will. At about eleven p.m. last night a certain M'sieur Picard, who owns a villa not far from the Hedderwick establishment, noticed a car parked by the kerb at the corner of the Avenue St. Michel and the Avenue St. Jeannet. The fellow was returning home on foot after a visit to some friends in the Avenue Thier."

"Well?"

"The car was a crimson Vedette."

"A crimson Vedette!" echoed Meredith excitedly.

"Yes, and that's not all," smiled Gibaud with a certain justifiable smugness. "Picard noticed it particularly for two good reasons. (A) Its hood was raised. (B) Its side screens were fixed in place."

"The devil they were! How did you get hold of this information?"

"A house to house enquiry. Luckily I caught Picard just after he'd got back from his office."

"You think his evidence can be relied on?"

"I'm sure of it."

"Did he notice if there was anybody in the car?"

"Yes, I asked him about that. He's not prepared to swear to it because the street lights were reflected back from the screens and it was difficult to see into the interior. And, in any case, he only took a casual glance as he went by."

"Well?"

"He'd an idea there *was* somebody sitting in one of the front-seats. But, as I said before, Picard's not prepared to commit himself to a definite answer."

For a moment Meredith, who was standing by the window, turned and gazed down reflectively into the busy street below. Then suddenly swinging round he announced in puzzled tones:

"I just don't get it. If this *was* Shenton's car—and on the face of the evidence it *must* have been—what the deuce was it doing on the corner of the Avenue St. Michel at eleven p.m.?"

"I don't follow."

"Good heavens, man, isn't it obvious? If the Vedette was parked a few hundred yards from the Villa Paloma at that particular hour of the evening, then my beautiful assumption that Dillon murdered Shenton and drove the car out to Cap Martin goes up the spout. Damn it all, both Kitty Linden and the Westmacott girl swore that Dillon was back in the house by ten-forty. And according to my reconstruction of the crime the car must have been abandoned out on the cape somewhere around ten o'clock. As I said before, I just don't get it."

"If Picard *did* see a figure in the car do you think it was Shenton?"

Meredith nodded.

"Who else could it be? Confound it all, Gibaud, it was Shenton's car."

"But if the fellow was still alive at eleven p.m. *when* was he murdered?"

"Ask me another. Quite frankly I'm beginning to wonder if we haven't made a thumping big mistake."

"Over what?"

"In convincing ourselves that because Shenton's disappeared he must, *ipso facto,* have been murdered."

Gibaud stared at his colleague in astonishment.

"*Mon Dieu!* you actually think he's still alive?"

"After taking Picard's evidence into consideration... yes. The one clue suggestive of murder is those bloodstains on the bodywork and running-board of the Vedette. Take those away and what have we? An abandoned car and a painfully obvious red-herring in the shape of a black béret with a red pom-pom picked up on the rocks out at Cap Martin."

"Look here," said Gibaud with a disgruntled expression, "I may be inordinately stupid but if Shenton's still alive and kicking, who parked his Vedette out on the headland? And who placed that tell-tale béret on the rocks?"

"I've a very strong suspicion," said Meredith in measured tones, "that Shenton did himself."

"Shenton!" cried Gibaud. "But why?"

"Because he was anxious to kid the world that he *had* been scuppered. I may be wrong about this just as I was wrong over my reconstruction of Dillon's movements last night. A great deal depends on Kitty Linden's behaviour during the next few days."

"What on earth are you driving at?" demanded Gibaud impatiently. "What's the Linden girl got to do with the case?"

"As I see it... everything. She was infatuated with Shenton. According to Mrs. Hedderwick the fellow more or less reciprocated her feelings. That's two sides of the eternal triangle. The third, of course, is supplied by Dillon. You see, during this afternoon's investigations I discovered that Dillon and the Linden wench were married."

"Married!" exclaimed Gibaud. "But how the deuce—?"

Hastily Meredith described the way he'd stumbled on this unexpected scrap of information. He went on:

"Suppose Shenton and the girl wanted to get married—and suppose Dillon refused to divorce his wife. A pretty dynamic set-up, eh? With only one logical way out of the *impasse,* my dear fellow. Now do you get it?"

"*Mon Dieu*—yes! You're suggesting Dillon didn't commit suicide. He was deliberately pushed over the crag up on the Col de Braus."

"Exactly. Shenton had fixed for the girl to lure Dillon to that particular spot, where he was already lying in wait. Hence his attempt to hoodwink us into believing that he himself had been the victim of foul play. After all, my dear Gibaud, dead men don't commit murders. Persuade the world you're dead and you've got just about the finest alibi on the market. See the point? Of course, as an alibi it has one inescapable disadvantage. After committing the crime you've got to *stay* dead. In other words you've got to clear out of the locality where the crime occurred and start up afresh under an assumed name. That's why I suggested that Kitty Linden's behaviour during the next few days should give us a pointer as to whether we're thinking along the right lines. If the girl suddenly packs up, leaves the villa and melts away into the blue, then it's a penny to the Bank of England that she's gone to keep a rendezvous with that exceptionally dead man, Tony Shenton." Meredith paused, yanked out a handkerchief and vigorously mopped his brow. "Well, what's your reaction? Any comebacks?"

"Snag One," grinned Gibaud. "What about the bloodstains on the car?"

"Like the black béret on the rocks, perhaps... deliberately planted there. Probably animal blood. Why not a cat or a dog?"

"Well, that's something we *can* decide one way or the other. Easy for the laboratory wallahs at Lyons to make an analytical test of the stains. Do you want it put in hand?"

"At once, if possible. Any further objections?"

"Yes—a rather crushing one, I'm afraid. Didn't Mrs. Hedderwick stress the fact that Shenton and the girl seemed to have been at loggerheads these last few days? The suggestion of a slap-up quarrel, eh? Well, if the couple were up against each other would they suddenly come together and collaborate in a major crime? Doesn't sound particularly feasible to me."

"Umph," reflected Meredith, somewhat deflated by this perfectly logical argument. "You've got something there, confound you! That bit of evidence had slipped my memory." Then brightening a little, he added: "Of course they might have been putting up an act. Anyway, it's crazy to accept or dismiss my pretty theory at the moment. We've got to interrogate the girl herself, and the sooner the better. Suppose I ring the villa now and see if she's sufficiently recovered to make a statement. Is that O.K. by you?"

"Of course," nodded Gibaud. "And what about the identification of the body? Admittedly both you and Strang have met Dillon more than once, but from the official point of view I reckon we ought to have the corroboration of somebody outside police circles, eh?"

"But heavens above!" protested Meredith. "Surely we needn't drag the poor kid down to the mortuary to view the remains? Facial identification's out of the question anyway. After all if the girl *saw* him go over the edge... well, you see the point?"

"Yes, of course," agreed Gibaud. "It should be enough to get a detailed description of what he was wearing, colour of hair, eyes, any distinguishing marks and so forth. In any case we can check up on her information with his passport. Better see if you can lay your hands on the document. It wasn't on the body."

"Then there's the question of getting in touch with his next-of-kin," pointed out Meredith. "The Yard should be able to help us there. I'll have a word with Blampignon once I've interviewed the girl. You see," added Meredith with a wry smile, "it's well on the cards that the A.C. may decide I'm wanted back home now that 'Chalky's' been pulled in. This Shenton-Dillon affair's merely a postscript to my original assignment. Now suppose I put through that call to the villa."

CHAPTER XIX

WHOSE BODY?

I

ON LEARNING from Dilys Westmacott that Kitty, although still badly shaken by the morning's experience, was now prepared to make a statement, Meredith ordered Strang to collect the dead man's effects and hastened off to the Villa Paloma. He found the girl stretched out listlessly on a settee in the lounge, a haunted expression in her big dark eyes, her features blanched and haggard in the bright evening sunlight that streamed through the french-windows. There was something so forlorn and defenceless about the young woman that Meredith was moved to pity as he crossed the room to greet her.

But the moment Dilys had withdrawn, closing the door behind her, he pulled up a chair and, stifling his feelings, made ready to begin his interrogation. The questioning of a witness still under the stress of recent shock was something he'd always abominated. But duty was duty and if the job had to be done the sooner it was over the better. For all that he refused to stampede the girl. After a few quiet words of sympathy for the ordeal she'd been through, he gently led her on to tell him the story of the morning's tragedy.

Little by little it all came out—the drive up into the mountains; the halt near the Col de Braus for lunch; after the meal, Dillon crossing the road ostensibly to take a look at the view; Kitty smoking a cigarette on the rug spread out beside the car; her sudden realization that Dillon had climbed the fence and was standing on the very brink of the precipice; her warning cry; her attempt to reach him before he fell; his tortured cry as he plunged into space; the horror and panic that overwhelmed her as she stumbled off blindly down the road in search of help; and finally her collapse by the roadside and Bucknell's providential arrival in his car.

It was all very much as he'd anticipated. The details of her story tallied exactly with those he'd already harvested for himself. But why no mention of the relationship that had clearly existed between her and the dead man? Quietly, unemotionally, almost without the girl realizing it, Meredith began his cross-examination.

"You've known Mr. Dillon for some time, Miss Linden?"

Uncertain whether the Inspector meant this as a statement or a question, Kitty glanced up with a startled look. For an instant she hesitated, then she said in a flat voice:

"No—only since he came to stay at the villa."

"Why exactly did Mr. Dillon ask you to accompany him this morning?"

"Because he thought I'd enjoy the drive. It was just a casual, friendly sort of invitation."

"He had no definite reason for asking you?"

"Reason?" Again the gleam of apprehension in the girl's dark eyes. "What do you mean?"

"Just this, young lady. I suspect that Mr. Dillon asked you to join him because he was anxious to discuss something with you. A highly intimate matter that he couldn't very well discuss except when you were alone."

With a pathetic attempt to brazen it out, Kitty flashed the Inspector a hollow smile.

"Really, Inspector, I don't know how you pick up these fanciful ideas."

"By observation and deduction," said Meredith with a meaning glance. "By putting two and two together, Miss Linden. By asking questions. By poking my official nose into what you would call 'other people's business'. Your business, young lady. Your relationship with Mr. Shenton, for example."

Kitty looked up sharply and demanded with a sudden show of spirit:

"What do you know about Tony Shenton? What's he got to do with it? I really don't see why you should drag Tony—"

"Now be sensible, Miss Linden. You were in love with the fellow. I say 'were' advisedly because I happen to know that quite recently you'd quarrelled. And that's less than half of what I know." Groping in his pocket, Meredith pulled out the silver wrist-watch and held it out on the palm of his hand. "Ever seen this before?"

The girl uttered a cry and shrank back against the cushions.

"Yes—it's Bill's—Mr. Dillon's! Where... where did you find it? Was he wearing it when you... when you...?"

Meredith nodded and observed quietly:

"I unstrapped it from his wrist, Mrs. Dillon."

"Mrs. Dillon!" gasped Kitty, dumbfounded. "Then you...?"

"Yes, I read the inscription on the back," Meredith smiled wryly. "Now suppose we stop fencing with each other, young lady, and get down to brass tacks. Why not be frank with me? Far better all round, y'know. Why didn't you tell me at once that you and Bill Dillon were married?"

"Yes, I suppose it was silly of me. It was just that I'd got so used to thinking of myself as Miss Linden... of playing a part that... that..."

"You couldn't bring yourself to tell the truth, eh?" put in Meredith helpfully. "Well, why not take me into your confidence, my dear? It'll clear the air."

"Very well," mumbled Kitty, "now that you've found out I suppose there's little point in holding my tongue."

And once again it all came out—her unhappy marriage; her extra-marital friendship with Tony Shenton; her acceptance of his invitation to join him in Menton; her husband's unexpected arrival on the scene; his efforts to win her back; the dreadful realization that she was going to have a baby and that Shenton was the father; Dillon's willingness to divorce her and her anguished appeal to Shenton that, since she was bearing his child, he should marry her; his blunt and angry refusal; the bitter knowledge that although she was desperately in love with him he'd never really been in love with her.

"And your husband knew just how you felt about Shenton, about this baby, Mrs. Dillon?" Biting her lip to keep back her tears, Kitty inclined her head. "He took it badly, eh?"

Kitty said in a choking voice:

"Yes, naturally. But he was so desperately in love with me that even then he... he was prepared to give me my divorce if Tony would marry me."

"I see. And you still uphold that your husband didn't suggest this morning's expedition in order to discuss these matters?"

"No—I lied to you about that," admitted Kitty. "Tony must have told my husband that he'd refused to marry me. Anyway Bill was terribly unhappy about it all. He asked me again if I'd go back to him." Overwhelmed with misery the tears started to the girl's eyes and she gulped out: "But I couldn't, Inspector! I couldn't! I knew it wouldn't work out. Do you blame me for being honest with him? If I'd gone back to him because of this child it would have meant living a lie, because I knew I didn't love him, that I never had... that I never could! Oh, I've behaved vilely to him. If it hadn't been for me all this would never have happened. Don't you see, Inspector? He took his life because... because he knew that, no matter what happened, I'd never, never go back to him!"

Sobbing bitterly, the girl fell back limply against the cushions burying her distorted face in her hands. For a moment Meredith remained silent, then he said slowly:

"There's just one other little question. Did you at any time this morning see anything of Tony Shenton?"

"Tony!" cried the girl brokenly. "But how *could* I have seen him? I thought he was—"

"Missing, eh? Yes—quite. But you still haven't answered my question, Mrs. Dillon."

"I haven't seen Tony since dinner last night. I swear I haven't, Inspector. I've no idea where he is or what's happened to him. That's the truth. You must, must believe me, Inspector!"

Realizing the girl was at the end of her tether, Meredith sensibly decided to bring the interview to a close. Before he took leave of her, however, he jotted down the details relevant to the identification of the body and made an enquiry about Dillon's next-of-kin. According to the young woman both her husband's parents were dead and the only relation he'd ever mentioned was an uncle living in the Isle of Man. Thanking the girl for her frankness and co-operation Meredith went in search of Mrs. Hedderwick. He was anxious to lay hands on the young man's passport. Encountering Dilys in the hall, he learnt that her aunt, succumbing to the shock of the day's events, had retired to bed. It was Dilys, therefore, who showed him up to Dillon's room and helped him search his belongings for the passport. But to Meredith's surprise the document appeared to be missing.

"Curious," he thought. "The confounded thing must be somewhere. He couldn't have got around without one. For one thing he'd have to produce his passport at the bank when changing his traveller's cheques. And since it wasn't on the body, I wonder...?"

II

Anxious to snatch a few uninterrupted minutes from the whirl of the day's events, the Inspector returned at a leisurely pace to the Commissariat. How much of the girl's story had been true and how much careful and calculated prevarication? That she *was* going to have this baby Meredith didn't doubt; nor did he question her declaration that Shenton was the father of the child. This just wasn't the sort of thing a young woman would attempt to make up. No—with regard to the explosive set-up between her and the two men she'd unquestionably been frank to the point of indiscretion. But had she been equally frank about the series of events that had led up to Dillon's suicide? True, the details of her halting narrative fitted in with what he'd already learnt for himself about the morning's expedition. But the question remained—Had Shenton been on the spot when Dillon went over the crag and was the missing man actually responsible for the fatal fall?

After all, Shenton must be *somewhere*. Already Meredith felt sure that when M'sieur Picard had seen the Vedette parked near the Villa Paloma at eleven p.m. the previous evening Shenton had been sitting in the vehicle. So at that hour of the evening the fellow was evidently still alive and kicking. By that time Dillon was back in the villa; where, after a brief chat with Dilys and Kitty, he'd gone up to bed. So if Shenton had been murdered some time after 11 p.m. Dillon, on the face of it, wasn't the killer. Then who? Was it Latour? He'd disappeared from the villa on Sunday night and nothing had been seen of him since. So Latour *was* a possible suspect. Motive, of course, unknown.

On the other hand, until they actually discovered the whereabouts of Shenton's body it was utterly impossible to say whether the fellow had been murdered or not. That was the stumbling block in the pursuit of any feasible deduction.

"Very well," thought Meredith, "for the moment I'll assume the fellow's alive, and that he killed Dillon by shoving him over that precipice. Motive, of course, to get Dillon out of the way so that he could marry the girl. But does this motive really stand on its own legs? Isn't Kitty's explanation about his *refusal* to marry her more in line with Shenton's character? Certainly it explains away their recent coolness towards each other. And again, she claimed that Dillon, knowing this kid was on the way, actually offered to stand aside, give the girl her divorce, so that Shenton *could* marry her. And what I've seen of Dillon suggests that this is equally 'in character'. So what? If the girl's story's true then Shenton would have no motive for killing Dillon. But if Dillon *knew* Shenton had refused to marry Kitty then, by heaven, Dillon certainly had motive for erasing Shenton!"

Meredith stopped dead in his tracks and stood for a moment in the middle of the pavement oblivious of the curious stares of the passers-by. A staggering idea had just flashed through his mind; an idea so fantastic that it hardly seemed worth a second thought. And yet he gave it not only a second thought, but a third and a fourth. From that moment until he arrived back at the Commissariat de Police and found Gibaud waiting for him in his office, Meredith didn't cease from analysing and enlarging on this sudden electrifying idea.

Gibaud rapped out:

"Hey! come alive, old man. What's up? Seen a ghost? Had a revelation?"

"A revelation!" exclaimed Meredith. "That's just about what I have had. Do you realize, Gibaud, that we may be labouring under an inexcusable delusion?"

"About what?"

Meredith strode over to the rear window of the office and, with a dramatic gesture, pointed down into the courtyard.

"The body that's lying down there on the mortuary slab."

"You mean Dillon's body?"

"Yes—but is it?" cried Meredith, suddenly swinging round on his bewildered colleague. "*Is it Dillon's body?*"

Gibaud said with an ironic lift of his brows:

"Is this over-indulgence or a touch of the sun? Damn it all! you collected the remains yourself from the foot of that crag, didn't you? Are you suggesting that by some miraculous piece of legerdemain I substituted another corpse for Dillon's when I was having the body moved from the car to the mortuary?"

Meredith said grimly:

"No, I'm serious about this, Gibaud. Do you realize that it may *not* have been Dillon who went over the brink of that precipice."

"But his clothes," protested Gibaud. "You got a full description of Dillon's attire from the girl, eh?"

"I did. And it tallies exactly with the clothes found on the body. Khaki bush-shirt, white shorts, gym shoes and so forth. But remember, my dear fellow, clothes don't make the man. This rig-out may have come from Dillon's wardrobe but it doesn't follow that the man inside 'em was actually Dillon. Think of the poor devil's face."

Gibaud shuddered.

"Practically unrecognizable—I admit it."

"No—not 'practically'," corrected Meredith. "Completely unrecognizable. Don't forget I'd met Dillon, and if I had to base my identification of the remains on facial recognition... well, frankly, I couldn't do it. Nor could Mrs. Dillon or anybody else for the matter of that."

Still obviously unconvinced, Gibaud chuckled:

"You've been reading too many detective yarns—that's your trouble."

"What do you mean?"

"Well, it's a well-worn double-cross, isn't it? Whenever a corpse turns up in a crime story with its face battered beyond recognition, you can bet your bottom dollar that it isn't the corpse you think it is. Don't mind confessing it. I've been diddled that way myself. But we happen to be dealing with facts not fiction."

"Quite. But I still think I may be right."

"But, good heavens, if it isn't Dillon out there in the mortuary, who the hell is it?" demanded Gibaud with a sudden crackle of irritation.

"Shenton," said Meredith tersely.

"Shenton!" echoed Gibaud. "How could it be?"

"Easily!" snapped Meredith. "Shenton's missing—suspected murder. No sign of the body. No clue, at present, to suggest the actual locale of the murder. Suppose the girl lied to me when she swore she hadn't set eyes on Shenton since last night. Suppose Shenton did show up on the Col de Braus and, after a violent scene, Dillon threw him over the edge of the crag. Not actually meaning to murder the fellow. Result—panic. A determination to cover up if possible all traces of the tragedy. Helped by his wife Dillon drives down to the spot where the body is lying, realizes that Shenton's features are unrecognizable and suddenly sees the perfect way out of his dilemma." Meredith paused a moment, mopped his perspiring brow and went on: "Don't forget I met Shenton at the villa and it struck me at the time that the two fellows were very much alike in physique and general appearance.

Same blonde hair and blue eyes, eh? Well, the same thought might have occurred to Dillon. So with the girl's help he strips the body and substitutes his clothes for Shenton's. Then he takes off his easily identifiable watch and straps it on Shenton's wrist and fixes the rucksack on his shoulders. He then drives the car back up on to the Col de Braus and, dressed in Shenton's clothes, sets off on foot across the mountains, leaving the girl to broadcast the yarn of his 'suicide'. In short, the young woman's been laying on a very clever and convincing act."

"But would she?" objected Gibaud. "I thought she hated her husband. Damn it all! hadn't she left him for Shenton?"

"Maybe, but when she found Shenton, having got her with child, wasn't prepared to marry her she may have suffered a sudden change of heart."

"Eh? What's all this? A kid on the way?"

"I was forgetting," said Meredith. "I picked up the information this evening from the girl herself." Deftly Meredith outlined the main details of Kitty Dillon's evidence and went on: "And there's another little factor that seems to underline the probability of my theory."

"Oh?"

"Dillon's passport appears to be missing. And if he's trying to get to hell out of the country, it's the one thing he'd hang on to, eh? The one thing he *couldn't* leave on the body. Well, what's your reaction to my little assumption?"

"Lukewarm," said Gibaud succinctly. "It *could* be possible but I don't think it is. To begin with there's the time-factor. Those clothes couldn't have been changed in a few seconds. You try undressing a corpse and see for yourself."

"But hang it all!" argued Meredith, "we don't know what time Dillon and the girl arrived up on the Col de Braus. We do know they left the villa immediately after breakfast and if they'd gone direct to the spot where we found the parked car then they'd have had several hours in hand. Don't forget it was early afternoon before Bucknell landed the girl back at the villa."

"But what about the abandoned Vedette and the black béret—the clues that you claim were deliberately planted to suggest that Shenton had disappeared off Cap Martin? Your theory was that he'd staged a vanishing-act because he was out to murder Dillon. Now you say Dillon has murdered *him*. You can't have it both ways."

"Quite. But Shenton may have met the couple up on the Col de Braus meaning to commit a murder. In the subsequent struggle he got the worst of it—that's all."

Gibaud shook his head and declared obstinately:

"I still don't like it. You'll never persuade me that Dillon thought up such a complicated alibi on the spur of the moment. At any rate it all boils down to the identification of the remains. Same coloured hair and eyes, same build, but what about distinguishing marks? Maybe Dillon's had his appendix out and Shenton hasn't. Or *vice versa.*"

"Well, there's only one witness who could probably put us wise about any kind of physical peculiarities... I mean, in both cases. And *she's* not likely to talk."

"Kitty Dillon?"

Meredith nodded.

"But I'm darned if I'm going to badger the poor kid again tonight. Suppose we sleep on this latest theory of mine. Maybe it'll look different in the morning. Things often do, you know. Anyway I'm going to ring the Yard at once and get them to make contact with the Hawland Aircraft Company. They may be able to tell us something of Dillon's background. He was employed there in the research department." Meredith reached for his hat. "By the way, have you had dinner?" Gibaud shook his head. "Then why not join us at our hotel? Expect Strang's wondering where the devil I've got to."

"Thanks," said Gibaud. "I'd like to—on one condition."

"Well?"

"That we don't ruin a good meal by talking shop!"

CHAPTER XX

THE BAR ST. RAPHAEL

I

AFTER AN EXCELLENT dinner at the Hotel Louis, Meredith suggested that the three of them should forgather in his bedroom for a brief, informal pow-wow before the party broke up. To this Gibaud readily agreed, but as they were crossing the hall *en route* for Meredith's room they were waylaid by the reception-clerk.

"M'sieur Gibaud?"

"That's me," nodded the inspector.

"You're wanted on the telephone, M'sieur."

"Thanks." He turned to Meredith. "It's probably the Desk Sergeant. I told him where he could get in touch with me. I'll be up in a moment."

Once in his room, Meredith asked:

"By the way, Strang, what about the effects collected from the body?"

"I've listed the articles as you said, sir. Practically nothing in the pockets—unmarked white handkerchief, small pocketknife, matches and a packet of French cigarettes. That's about the lot."

"And in the rucksack?"

"I've got it in my room, sir. Empty quart-sized Thermos, two or three screwed up paper-bags and some pieces of orange peel."

"Umph—tidy-minded chap, eh? Wasn't going to litter up the countryside. Funny he should think of a practical thing like that a few moments before he chucked himself over that precipice." He swung round. "Ah, come in, my dear Gibaud! Not been called away, I hope. I've had this bottle of cognac sent up especially in your honour."

"No, it's nothing exactly urgent. The Desk Sergeant, as I anticipated. I'd set one of my worthies on to a routine check-up round the Menton bars and cafés. He's just slammed in a pretty hot report."

"A check-up—on what?"

"Shenton," replied Gibaud tersely. "It struck me that when he left the villa after dinner last night he might have headed for one of the local high-spots."

"And he did?"

"The Bar St. Raphael."

"Where's that?"

"A small chromium-plated dive off the Rue Partouneau. According to the proprietor it's one of Shenton's stamping-grounds. He showed up there about ten past nine, so I reckon he must have driven straight there from the Villa Paloma."

"But how exactly is this going to—?"

"Wait!" cautioned Gibaud with a smile. "I haven't come to it yet. About twenty to ten a fellow came in and joined Shenton at the bar. They had several drinks and left the place together at about ten-thirty."

"But, confound it!" said Meredith testily, "I still don't see—"

"Don't you?" grinned Gibaud with irritating complacency. "Then, let me put you wise. The fellow who joined Shenton at the bar *was unquestionably young Dillon!*"

"Dillon!" exclaimed Meredith and Strang in unison.

"Now do you get the implication? Shenton drove Dillon back to the villa in the Vedette and then parked the car, for some enigmatic reason, at the corner of the Avenue St. Michel. When Picard passed the car about eleven, Shenton was sitting inside it. Why? Was he waiting for somebody? If so, who? Dillon? Dillon's wife? The Westmacott girl? And why in the name of thunder did Dillon meet Shenton, presumably by appointment, in the Bar St. Raphael?"

"I think I can answer that one," said Meredith promptly. "Dillon had arranged to meet Shenton to discuss their relationship in regard to Kitty. He probably went there to find out if Shenton was prepared to marry the girl, once her divorce had gone through."

"Something in that, I admit," put in Gibaud. "The proprietor mentioned a pretty heated discussion. At one time he thought they were going to fly at each other's throats. Shenton was evidently in truculent mood. No doubt that by the time he left the bar he was a trifle lit up."

"Perhaps that's why he didn't go straight into the villa, sir," suggested Strang. "He parked the car so that he could sober up a bit. Maybe when that Picard chap saw him he was sleeping it off."

"It's an idea, Sergeant. But as far as we know he never entered the villa last night. The next thing we heard of the Vedette was of its discovery out on Cap Martin."

"Hey! wait a bit," chuckled Gibaud. "I haven't quite finished putting in my report. The Desk Sergeant was just going to ring me about the Bar St. Raphael incident when a call came in from the local constable at Monti."

"Monti? Where the devil's that?" asked Meredith.

"A small mountain village half-way between Menton and Castillon."

"Well?"

"Shortly before two a.m. in the early hours of this morning a crimson Vedette, with its hood up and side-screens in place, passed through Monti on its way down to Menton."

Meredith whistled.

"You'd put out a general call for information on this point, eh?"

"Yes—together with the number and description of the car."

"But what does it mean?" asked Meredith bewildered. "Did the constable notice if there was anybody in the car apart from the driver?"

"Just," grinned Gibaud. "It evidently came through the village like a hurricane. Just one man at the wheel—that's all."

"No hope of a description?"

"None."

"I see," mused Meredith. "So after hanging about at the corner of the Avenue St. Michel Shenton must have suddenly taken it into his head to drive up into the mountains. Why?"

"Well, sir," put in Strang tentatively, "there may not be anything in it... but if he was on the Castillon road—"

"The Col de Braus!" broke in Meredith excitedly. "Of course, Sergeant. But what would Shenton be doing up there in the small hours of the morning? I just don't get it. Strikes me, the more we learn the less we know! Is Shenton alive or dead? That's the first outstanding question. If dead, then was it Shenton's body we found at the foot of the Col de Braus? Or was it, as we naturally assumed, Dillon's? Did Dillon commit suicide after murdering Shenton? Or did Shenton murder Dillon? Or did Latour murder Shenton?" Meredith chuckled ironically. "Good heavens! I could go on like this all night." He gestured to the glasses set out on the table. "Well, suppose we have a drink and settle down to a further analysis of the known facts. We might in the long run evolve a theory that won't fall down every time we breathe on it!" He raised his glass. "Well, here's to us and the solution to this damned tantalizing problem!"

II

Before Meredith was half-way through breakfast the following morning, he was called away twice to answer the telephone in the manager's private office. The first call was from Blampignon at Nice. He'd been in touch with the Assistant Commissioner at the Yard and the A.C. was quite ready to extend the duration of Meredith's assignment on the Midi. Had Meredith made any further progress in the case of the missing Shenton? If so could he drive over later that morning to Nice and put in an up-to-the-minute report?

The second call was from Gibaud. Could Meredith get round to the Commissariat at the double? Information had come in that very definitely knocked one of Meredith's pet theories slap on the head. Which theory? demanded Meredith. But with an irritating laugh Gibaud hung up and left him crackling with suspense.

Hurrying back to the dining-room, the Inspector swallowed down a final cup of coffee and hustled Strang out to the garage to fetch the car. Ten minutes later they were seated in Gibaud's office, waiting on tenterhooks for the Inspector to hand on the information that had just come in.

"Sorry to drag you round here so bright and early, but it looks as if we've managed to pick up a really sensational bit of evidence. About an hour ago police H.Q. at Monte Carlo rang through to ask us if we'd heard anything of a suicide incident up on the Col de Braus. I explained that we'd already been informed and had the matter fully in hand. I asked them how they'd got to hear about the affair. And this, my dear fellow, is where I began to sit up and take notice."

"Well, go on," urged Meredith impatiently.

"They claimed to have an informant with them at that moment who'd actually witnessed the incident!"

"What!" cried Meredith. "You mean to say—?"

Gibaud nodded.

"A young chap by the name of Edouard Hamel. They're sending him over to us at once. But I thought you'd like to have the main details of his deposition before he showed up. The young man, by the way, is a keen amateur botanist. I reckon that's why he was up near the Col de Braus yesterday morning."

"But why has he only just reported the incident?" asked Meredith, puzzled.

"I'll come to that in a minute. The main point is that at the time Hamel was sitting about a couple of hundred yards above the spot where Dillon went over the edge. He was taking a look at the view through his field-glasses. He could see the outer edge of the road below. The inner side, of course, was blocked by the buttress of rock round which the road has been built."

"So Hamel could see nothing of the parked car—is that what you're getting at?"

"Exactly," nodded Gibaud. "So when Dillon came into view on the far side of the road Hamel thought he was alone. He'd no idea the girl was sitting beside the car on the near side. You follow?"

"I'm ahead of you!"

"Right! Well, to cut the cackle and come to the goose. Hamel wasn't particularly interested in Dillon until he saw him climb the fence. Even then he wasn't exactly perturbed. But with very natural curiosity he levelled his glasses on the spot and brought the figure into focus. He saw the fellow turn, look back for an instant, then throw up his arms and leap out over the cliff. Now this is the point. As he turned, Hamel got a clear view of the fellow's features—*a close up view, in fact, through his binoculars.* Now do you see why I referred to this unexpected bit of evidence as sensational?"

"Good God—yes!" exclaimed Meredith, springing to his feet. "He's in a position to identify the person in question. We've only got to confront him with photos of Dillon and Shenton to know, without any shadow of doubt, whose body we've got out there in the mortuary! But why the devil didn't he come forward at once? It would have saved us a helluva lot of idle speculation."

"Not his fault, poor chap. When he saw what had happened he naturally jumped up and started off down the slope at the double. But he'd only gone a few yards when he tripped over a rock and twisted his ankle. It must have been pretty painful because the poor devil passed out on the spot. He's evidently picked up a nasty gash on the side of his head, so maybe he also suffered a touch of concussion. That explains, of course, why he never made contact with the girl. By the time he'd come to and hobbled down to the car, the girl was already on her way down to Menton. Unfortunately Hamel couldn't drive, so he set off down the Escarene road to try and get help. It's obvious that before you took the same road to search for the body, Hamel must have got beyond the point where you turned off along the mule-track. It also meant that he missed the American on the upper road. Well, to cut a long story short, he eventually fetched up at an isolated cottage and promptly passed out again. He stayed the night there and, this morning, the peasant who owns the place drove him down to Monte Carlo in his mule-cart. And that more or less—" Gibaud broke off, crossed to the window and glanced down into the street. "A police car, eh? This looks like M'sieur Hamel himself. Have you got the necessary photos to hand?"

"Yes—in my wallet. But hang on! I want to make absolutely certain that we can rely on Hamel's identification. Can you rumble up, say, another half-dozen portraits from your local Rogues' Gallery?"

"Yes, of course," said Gibaud as he made for the door. "I'll pick 'em up in the main-office before I have Hamel shown in here. By the way, he doesn't speak English, so I imagine you'll want me to explain what we're after."

When Gibaud returned, Meredith set out the photos in a row on the Inspector's desk and, a few moments later, Hamel, accompanied by the Sergeant who'd driven him over from Monte Carlo, hobbled slowly into the office. He was a frail, studious-looking chap, with bright intelligent eyes beneath a high forehead. It was evident by the way he contracted his pallid features at every step that his ankle was still paining him. With the help of two sticks and the Sergeant's strong right arm, he crossed to the chair Meredith had placed ready for him and collapsed on it with a sigh of relief.

Meredith turned to Gibaud.

"O. K. Inspector. Fire ahead."

In a few rapid sentences Gibaud explained to the young fellow why he'd been asked to come over to Menton. Would he make a careful scrutiny of the photos laid out on the desk and see if he recognized the portrait of the man he'd noticed up on the Col de Braus. With an effort Hamel twisted round in his chair and, one by one, closely studied the photographs. Then suddenly his arm shot out and he placed a finger on the third portrait from the right.

"*Voilà, M'sieur.*"

Meredith craned forward and exchanged a meaning glance with Gibaud.

"So my Shenton theory goes up the spout, eh? It *was* Dillon's body at the foot of the crag, and the girl *wasn't* lying. He's absolutely sure about it?"

Gibaud levelled a few staccato questions at Hamel, who answered them promptly and emphatically.

"There's no shifting him," said Gibaud in English. "He's convinced he's right. And personally I'm prepared to accept his evidence lock, stock and barrel. Agreed?"

Meredith nodded dourly. He was asking himself, with justifiable chagrin, where the deuce do we go from here? This latest information had completely sabotaged the one promising theory left in the bag. It was certain now that Shenton had nothing to do with Dillon's death. But was it still possible that Dillon had committed suicide after murdering Shenton? But if so—when? At 2 a.m. that morning Shenton had evidently been driving down off the Col de Braus in the direction of Menton. Or rather, *en route* for Cap Martin, since his crimson Vedette was found abandoned there at 6.30, some four and a half hours later. So if Dillon *had* killed Shenton the murder must have been committed sometime between two and six-thirty. Could Dillon have crept out of the villa and done the job? But how was he to know where Shenton was to be found? After all, the fellow seemed to have spent the night doing a hell-for-leather and utterly irresponsible Cook's tour in and around the neighbourhood. Even if Dillon had made contact with and murdered Shenton, where was the body? Above all, what had taken Shenton on that enigmatic drive up into the mountains after his long wait in the parked car at the corner of the Avenue St. Michel?

In Meredith's opinion he was faced with one of the toughest problems of his long and arduous career. Lashings of information. A plethora of first-rate clues. Evidence galore. And not a single theory on which to base the next phase of his investigation!

CHAPTER XXI

THE RUCKSACK RIDDLE

I

"By the way," said Gibaud, after Hamel had hobbled down to the waiting car, "I had that blood test put in hand. The result should come through this morning."

"Blood test?" enquired Meredith with a puzzled look.

"In connection with the stains on the side of the Vedette. You suggested they might have been planted there to mislead us—that it might have been animal blood."

"Oh, I get you," nodded Meredith. "My theory that Shenton was anxious for us to *think* he'd been scuppered, so that he should have a watertight alibi for the murder of Dillon. But, hang it all, we know now that he *couldn't* have killed Dillon."

"So the chances are," put in Gibaud, "that it *is* human blood."

"Exactly."

"Then how did the bloodstains get on the car?"

"Eh?"

"You heard me," grinned Gibaud.

Meredith inelegantly scratched his head with the stem of his pipe.

"Umph... puzzling, eh? It brings us back to our old assumption that Dillon *did* murder Shenton and then took his own life. And we know now that the only time he could have committed the murder was between the hours of two and six-thirty ack emma yesterday morning."

"Quite. And during these hours he was fast asleep in bed at the villa. At least, that's what we're bound to assume from the evidence to hand."

"O.K.," said Meredith briskly. "Suppose we *don't* assume it. Suppose we assume that Dillon crept out of the house during the small hours, managed somehow to make contact with Shenton—perhaps after

Shenton had driven down from the mountains—and then stabbed him. Isn't it possible that some member of the Hedderwick household heard the fellow sneak out?" Meredith swung round on Strang. "Look here, Sergeant, I've got to get over to Nice to see Blampignon. No need for you to come along. I want you to get up to the Villa Paloma without delay and make very careful enquiries about this point. Understand?"

"Yes, sir."

"We'll meet for lunch at the *Poisson D'Or* and you can report to me there. *Poisson D'Or...* one o'clock."

"Right, sir. Just one other small matter... Dillon's personal effects. The rucksack, that Thermos-flask and—"

"Oh, hand 'em over to Miss Westmacott. She can keep them with the rest of his belongings until we can trace his next-of-kin and have the whole lot sent on."

"Very good, sir."

II

It was strange that this casual decision was destined to alter the whole aspect of their investigation. It was, in fact, the quart-sized scarlet Thermos-flask found in Dillon's rucksack that was to lead Meredith eventually to a final solution of the problems confronting him. The point was that when Dilys took the flask through to the kitchens, Madame Bonnet, the cook, failed to recognize it. She was emphatic. The flask that she'd filled with coffee before the young couple had set off the previous morning on their ill-fated expedition to the Col de Braus was, admittedly, a quart-sized flask—but it was *blue,* not red! There wasn't, in fact, a scarlet Thermos-flask in the house.

"But she's crackers!" declared Freddy bluntly, when Dilys had rejoined him on the terrace. "It *must* be the flask she filled. She put up their lunch, didn't she?"

"Yes—in Bill Dillon's rucksack. As a matter of fact, Kitty handed me the rucksack and I took it through to the kitchen myself."

"And it was this particular rucksack?" asked Freddy.

"Yes—or one exactly like it."

"Look here," said Freddy with a solemn expression, "d'you mind shooting a few questions at Madame Bonnet for me? We've got to get to the bottom of this. There's something screwy about it."

And when Freddy, with the aid of his charming interpreter, had concluded the brief interrogation, two further facts emerged that considerably deepened the mystery. Certainly Madame Bonnet claimed to recognize the rucksack as the one handed to her by Miss Westmacott, but the crumpled paper-bags and the bits of orange peel... how, she demanded, had they come there? She had packed the sandwiches in greaseproof paper, together with a carton of *gâteau* and *petits fours,* but certainly no oranges. If this *was* the rucksack found on poor M'sieur Dillon's body then what could have happened to change the blue flask to a red and the grease-paper into paper-bags?

Learning that Kitty was spending the morning in bed, Freddy got Dilys to slip up and see her. He was anxious to check up on Madame Bonnet's statement. After all, it was Kitty who must have opened up the rucksack prior to that picnic meal up on the Col de Braus.

It was some ten minutes later when Dilys rejoined him in the lounge.

"Well, what's she got to say about it?"

"The same as Madame Bonnet," said Dilys, dumping the rucksack on a chair. "*Blue* Thermos-flask, sandwiches wrapped in greaseproof and *no* oranges. When they'd finished the meal, Kitty replaced the Thermos in the rucksack, together with all the litter, and handed the rucksack to Bill."

"And he restrapped it on his shoulders there and then, eh?"

"I asked her about that. And as far as Kitty can remember, he didn't. He walked over to the car with it."

"In his hand?"

"Yes. Kitty sat on the rug for a time smoking a cigarette. When Bill rejoined her a few minutes later the rucksack was on his back."

Freddy shook his head.

"You know, darling, the more we probe into this the more crazy it gets. If poor old Dillon was all set to chuck himself over that crag, why had he troubled to put on the rucksack? Why not just dump the bally thing in the back of the car? And it's all the more crazy because I just don't see how it could have been the *same* rucksack. Dammit all! that Thermos couldn't have changed colour in mid-air. No—for some reason or other, when he walked over to the car he must have swapped the original rucksack for the one we found on the body. Kitty didn't notice that they were different?" Dilys shook her head. "Then we can only assume that the two rucksacks were identical, eh? But why? That's the point. Why *two* rucksacks?"

"Well, don't look at me," smiled Dilys. "I'm as mystified as you are."

"What about Dillon's car—is it still round in the garage?" Dilys nodded. "Good! Suppose we nip round and take a dekko at the old bus."

It took Freddy exactly four and a half minutes to prove that his theory about the two identical rucksacks was a winner! He found the second one rammed away under the detachable leather cushion of the driving-seat. When the cushion was lifted out of its metal frame, there was a hollow space between the underside of the seat and the floor-boards large enough to accommodate the object in question. Inside the rucksack was a *blue* quart Thermos-flask, several screws of greaseproof paper, a crumpled carton bearing the imprint of a well-known Menton *pâtissier* and *no* orange peel!

III

Meredith was already seated in the gay little courtyard of *Le Poisson D'Or* when Strang showed up for lunch. There was a glum, preoccupied expression on the Inspector's sun-browned features as he sprawled back in his chair with his legs thrust out and his hands deep in his pockets. On seeing the Sergeant he glanced at his watch and shot out:

"Ten minutes late! Couldn't drag yourself away from that young woman, I suppose. Quite happy to let me sit here kicking my heels until—"

"Sorry, sir," cut in Strang, as he sidled somewhat apprehensively on to his chair. "But I promise you I haven't wasted a minute. Fact is, sir, I've picked up some pretty puzzling information."

"You mean Dillon *was* heard sneaking out of the villa during the small hours of yesterday morning?"

"No, sir. I drew a blank there. If he did creep out then it's a dead cert nobody heard him."

"Then what's this 'puzzling information' you've been yammering about?"

"Well, sir, it's this way..."

And Freddy handed on the mystifying evidence that he'd gleaned during the course of the morning's investigation. As he proceeded, Meredith's dour expression gave way to one of ever-increasing interest. His hands came out of his pockets. He straightened up in his chair. He leaned forward eagerly across the table, utterly absorbed by his subordinate's quick-fire narrative.

"But, good heavens!" he exclaimed when Strang had finally rounded off his report, "the whole thing's ridiculous. What was the point of substituting one rucksack for another about a couple of minutes before he flung himself off that crag?"

"I've been worrying that bone, sir, ever since I left the villa. I suppose it couldn't have been a mistake?"

"How do you mean?"

"Well, Dillon was probably in a pretty keyed-up sort of mood. When he walked over to the car he might have dumped the first rucksack and, a bit later, picked up the second rucksack and strapped it—"

"Balderdash!" broke in Meredith, crushingly. "Rucksack Number One wasn't just slung in the back of the car. It was carefully concealed under the driving-seat. So that theory's out for a start." Meredith reached for the menu-card. "Now suppose we order lunch and start analysing the evidence bit by bit. No good rushing to conclusions. We want a logical answer to the mystery, not a high-faluting possibility."

Although during lunch they did to a certain extent discuss the problem before them, Meredith for the most part remained silent. He had a feeling that somewhere within the framework of this fresh evidence lay the final answer to the enigma of Shenton's disappearance. Two questions above all others hammered away in his mind. Why had Dillon troubled to conceal the first rucksack and substitute the second? And why had he troubled, in any case, to strap it on his back? Time and again he came back to these two puzzling factors in the set-up. But when at length they rose from the table, Meredith had to admit that he was still completely flummoxed.

IV

Dropping Strang at the hotel, where the Sergeant was to write up an official report of his morning's enquiries at the villa, Meredith set off on a leisurely drive along the promenade towards Cap Martin. It was his intention to find some shady, isolated spot out on the headland and settle down for a quiet pipe and a long, uninterrupted spell of concentrated speculation. In point of fact the Inspector never arrived at the cape.

Half-way along the Promenade Marechal Joffre a sudden, electrifying idea shot across the terminals of his mind. It was, in essence, not exactly a new idea. Rather was it a variation on an original theme. It stemmed, in fact, from his previous supposition that the body at the foot of the crag might well be that, not of Dillon, but of Shenton. So startling was this new conception that Meredith automatically swung the car into a quiet side road and, braking up, settled down to analyse the possibilities of his theory.

Suppose Shenton, despite the girl's denial, *had* been up in the mountains when Dillon and his wife had set out on that ill-fated drive. And suppose, for some reason or other, Dillon had strolled off on his own and encountered Shenton without the girl being aware of the fact—perhaps even by appointment. And suppose the spot where they'd met was not up on the Col de Braus but *at the foot of the precipice* over which Dillon had ostensibly plunged to his death! Well, there was a set-up that completely altered the whole aspect of the mystery.

Shenton had been murdered, perhaps, only a few yards from where the body was found—presumably battered to death by some blunt instrument so that his features should be unrecognizable. Thereafter Dillon must have rejoined his wife and driven up on to the Col de Braus, where the couple eventually had their picnic lunch. So far so good.

Now for Dillon's alibi. Suppose on his previous expeditions up in the mountains Dillon had made a careful survey of the spot where he'd leaped over the crag. Suppose he'd noticed that a few feet below the actual brink of the drop there was a ledge on to which he could safely jump and thence inch his way back on to comparatively level ground. He could bank on the girl not caring to look over the edge of the crag. What's more he could rely on her to convince the world at large that he'd deliberately taken his own life.

Admittedly this reconstruction of the crime didn't account for the bloodstained and abandoned Vedette out at Cap Martin, nor for Dillon's peculiar actions in regard to the rucksacks. But, again, there *was* a possible explanation. Once Dillon had disappeared over the lip of the rock-face he'd be a man on the run. Wasn't it possible that, anxious to avoid any idle speculation, he'd wisely decided to give all shops and cafés a wide berth and be self-supporting? In brief—hadn't that second rucksack been packed with enough provender to see him well on his way out of France? Well, it was an idea and in the circumstances—

Meredith swore under his breath. What the devil was he thinking about? The second rucksack had been removed from the body. And if it *were* Shenton's body then there must have been a *third* rucksack. But why? Well, wasn't there a perfectly logical answer? Kitty Dillon might recall that when her husband had disappeared over the crag he had a rucksack on his back. So, *ipso facto,* there had to be a rucksack on the body at the foot of the crag. Otherwise the discrepancy might arouse suspicion.

The longer Meredith ruminated on these fresh deductions, the more inclined he was to accept their feasibility. It naturally argued from Dillon's point of view the execution of a carefully laid scheme. A second set of clothes, for example, secreted in the car, in which to dress the body after the murder. Three more or less identical rucksacks. Some subtle means of persuading Shenton to meet him at a certain spot at a certain time. The evolution of a careful time-table. An excuse to rid himself of the girl's presence so that he could meet Shenton alone. True, at first sight, it seemed crazy to take the girl along at all, but she was, of course, an essential factor in the creation of his alibi. It was vitally necessary that she should be on the spot to witness the faked suicide.

So much for that. But how to check-up on his theory?

Well, thought Meredith, that at least was simple. His latest reconstruction of the crime depended on one basic feature in the set-up— *that ledge below the brink of the precipice.* If there was no ledge then all the rest of his theorizing wasn't worth a row of beans. Very well, he'd drive up to the Col de Braus and settle the point once for all.

And within the next hour the point *was* settled! Parking the car beside the low wooden fence that edged the precipice, Meredith climbed the fence, stepped cautiously to the brink of the drop and gazed down. Meticulously, without haste, his eyes raked the smooth and gleaming rock-face. Then, with a violent oath, he swung round and returned, dejected, to the car.

For three hundred feet the great wall of rock rose sheer and unbroken from the valley below. There *was* no ledge! In a split second his latest theory had, so to speak, come to pieces in his hands.

CHAPTER XXII

MOTIVE FOR MURDER

I

BACK AT THE Hotel Louis, Meredith learnt from Strang that his immediate superior, Chief Inspector Cox, had come through on the telephone from the Yard. Would Meredith ring back the moment he came in?

"Any idea what it's about, Sergeant?"

"Yes, sir. It's that information you wanted about Dillon. The Chief's evidently been in touch with the Hawland Aircraft people."

"Good," nodded Meredith. "I'll get on to him at once."

For a long-distance call it was remarkable how quickly Meredith got through to Whitehall 1212. In less than ten minutes the Chief Inspector's familiar bark was winging to him over the wires. According to Meredith's request he'd made contact with the head of the research department of the Hawland Aircraft Company and picked up quite a lot of information about Dillon. If the Inspector had his notebook at the "ready" then he'd read the details of his report at dictation speed. Five minutes sufficed for Meredith to scribble down in his own private shorthand the salient points of Cox's streamlined statement, and, after the exchange of a few pleasantries, Meredith rang off and went up to his room.

There, still profoundly depressed by the result of his visit to the Col de Braus, he settled down to study the Chief's report. Apart from a brief assessment of Dillon's character and abilities, it dealt mainly with his recent work in the firm's laboratories, covering both the technical and scientific aspects of his particular line of research—i.e. aerodynamics. It appeared that Dillon, although still a comparatively young man, had already displayed considerable originality in his approach to the subject. He was rated one of their most reliable and promising young scientists. So much for that.

His employers were able to sketch in only the barest outline of his private life—the sort of details that are normally incorporated in the official form filled in by an employee on entering a firm—education, war service, domestic background and so forth. His next-of-kin, however, was given as Charles K. Dillon, Mullion House, Sealand Road, Douglas, Isle of Man.

From a perusal of this somewhat meagre report, Meredith turned once more to the rest of the data connected with the case. For over an hour he sat at the table, struggling to isolate from the mass of irrelevant evidence the clues that really mattered. Then, coming to a sudden decision, he reached for his hat and set off through the town towards the *Commissariat de Police*.

There, after a word with Gibaud, he learnt that the results of the tests had come in from Lyons and that the stains on the Vedette were unquestionably those of human blood. From Gibaud's office he crossed to the mortuary where he made another prolonged and detailed examination of the body. It was here, he felt, that the real problem lay. Despite all the evidence to the contrary he was still plagued by a persistent doubt that gnawed away at the back of his mind. Was this Dillon's body or Shenton's? On the face of it there was only one logical answer to the query. Dillon was seen by a disinterested witness (Hamel) to plunge over a sheer three-hundred-foot drop, so, *ipso facto,* the body below the crag *must* have been that of Dillon. But for the sake of argument suppose he persuaded himself that it was Shenton's. Who would be best placed to identify his remains? First and foremost Dillon's wife and then, presumably, Mrs. Hedderwick. Mightn't it be essential after all to drag these two unfortunates down to the mortuary in the hope that this nagging doubt could be scotched once for all?

Meredith had just arrived at this conclusion when he noticed a faint scar running obliquely across the inner side of the left forearm.

It was, perhaps, some two inches long—a thin white cicatrice visible only because the surrounding skin had been tanned by the sun. It was certainly a long-standing blemish, but wasn't it possible that either Kitty Dillon or Mrs. Hedderwick had noticed the scar? And if they had...? Meredith's depression lifted a little. Well, here at any rate was a line of enquiry that was well worth following up. If either of the women recalled the scar then he'd be in a position to identify the body without any shadow of doubt.

II

Looking back on the remainder of that memorable day, Meredith always marvelled that an investigation which had seemingly come to a dead-end could be transformed in so brief a time to a swift and progressive elucidation of the many problems confronting him.

It was Mrs. Hedderwick who supplied the initial impetus— a distracted, hysterical Mrs. Hedderwick, frantic with worry and apprehension, whom Meredith was forced to interview in bed. As she lolled back limply against the pillows, drained of all her vigour and self-assurance, it was hard to believe that this was the same woman who had swept into the Chinese room with such devastating authority only a few days back. Meredith found her ready, even eager, to talk—clearly anxious to do all in her power to put an end to the suspense that was driving her out of her senses. It was obvious that Dillon's suicide, though naturally upsetting, hadn't deeply affected her. It was the ominous and inexplicable disappearance of Tony Shenton that had brought about her collapse. And about Tony she was prepared to talk freely, lengthily and, above all, with startling and revealing frankness.

When eventually Meredith left the villa, he set off through the town like a man in a daze. For although Mrs. Hedderwick's surprising evidence had finally disposed of one important question, it had resurrected a score of equally vital problems that he'd already endeavoured to solve without a glimmer of success. Now, like a hen scratching over the same well-worn patch of earth, Meredith began for the umpteenth time to analyse the evidence in hand.

Ignoring the fact that it was well past his customary dinner hour, the Inspector lit his pipe and, with long easy strides, set off on a protracted walk along the sea-front. And it was then that he was visited by one of those revealing flashes of deduction that spring, not from any inspirational source, but from a clearly realized and logical appreciation of the facts. And, as was so often the case, the moment he grasped the full significance of this infinitesimal scrap of evidence all the other mysteries surrounding the case were abruptly clarified. Now the sequence of events that must have occurred on Thursday night became obvious. He realized with an inaudible whoop of triumph that, apart from following up a few conclusive lines of enquiry, the problem of Shenton's disappearance was virtually solved! By midday tomorrow he should be in a position to put in a full and final report to his good friend Blampignon.

His immediate concern, however, was to get in touch with Gibaud and see that the official machinery for the apprehension of the murderer was immediately set in motion. With any luck the criminal was still at large "somewhere in France". And since a detailed description of the wanted man could be broadcast to every policeman and *gendarme* in the country there was reasonable hope that within the next twenty-four hours an arrest would follow!

III

It was precisely twelve o'clock the following day when Blampignon, Gibaud, Strang and Meredith gathered for their last conference in the local Inspector's office. Although Meredith had been forced to reveal to Gibaud the identity of the murderer, he'd deliberately kept Blampignon in the dark concerning the ultimate phase of his investigations. Blampignon, as a matter of fact, had been out all night on a burglary case at Fréjus and had driven over direct from Fréjus to Menton. He was, therefore, unaware that a general call had already been sent out for the arrest of the wanted man. In fact he'd no inkling of the real significance of Meredith's urgent request for this meeting. Even Gibaud was still ignorant of the details that had finally led Meredith to a solution of the puzzle.

"*Eh bien,*" demanded Blampignon once the little group was comfortably settled about Gibaud's imposing desk, "what is the reason you call me over here? You say, *mon ami,* it is necessary we should talk together at once. You have made, perhaps, some progress in your investigations?"

Meredith exchanged a twinkling glance with Gibaud and said with a malicious little smile:

"Well, it all depends on what you call progress, my dear fellow. I've solved the mystery surrounding Shenton's disappearance, if that's what you mean."

"*Qu'est-ce-que vous dites?*" thundered Blampignon, springing to his feet and staring at Meredith dumbfounded. "You know what happen to Shenton? You know where he is?"

"I do," nodded Meredith.

"Then, *mon Dieu!*" pleaded Blampignon, almost tearful in his impatience, "why do you not tell me? Where is he—this M'sieur Shenton? Where can we discover him?"

Meredith smiled.

"He's not far away."

"Not far away?" gasped Blampignon. "Then where? Where?"

Underlining the effect of his sensational announcement with deliberate under-emphasis, Meredith said:

"Stretched out stiff and cold on the mortuary slab only a stone's throw from this window!"

"Shenton!" cried Blampignon incredulously. "So the body you find at the foot of the crag was not that of Dillon? But how can this be, *mon vieux?* How did you come to make the identification?"

"An almost invisible scar on the inner side of his left forearm," explained Meredith. "It was Mrs. Hedderwick who finally settled the point. She recalled the scar at once. She actually remembered the occasion when Shenton had cut his arm on a sliver of broken glass."

"You mean it happened recently?" asked Gibaud.

"Recently?" Meredith laughed. "According to Mrs. Hedderwick's calculations it must have happened when Shenton was just seven years old. He shoved his arm through a cucumber-frame."

"But... but how should she know this?" asked Blampignon, dropping again into his chair. "I did not think that Madame Hedderwick—"

"Neither did I," cut in Meredith incisively. "I was under the impression that they'd only known each other for the last three or four years. Well, that's just one of the many illusions under which I've been suffering. Mrs. Hedderwick knew all about the accident for the very simple reason that she was there at the time."

"But how?... why?" demanded Gibaud.

"*Tony Shenton happens to be her son.*"

"Her son!" gasped Blampignon.

"By her first marriage. Obvious now, isn't it? why she was so concerned about his sudden disappearance. A very natural maternal solicitude for the welfare of an only child, eh? When she married Hedderwick, Tony was about eighteen and since he and his step-father hated each other on sight, Tony kept out of his way. Well, to cut a long story short, Shenton got into trouble with the police. You may recall that, thinking his face familiar, I got in touch with the Yard to see if they knew anything about his past record. You recollect their reply. A six months' sentence in 1939 for theft. Charged under the name of Anthony Shenton, though this was suspected to be an alias."

"And it was?" asked Gibaud.

"Yes—about the one decent thing the lad ever did, I imagine. His mother's name by her first marriage was Fenman-Smith. An easy name to remember. So when he was pulled in, he gave his name as Shenton—a moniker that he's stuck to ever since."

"But look here, sir," put in Freddy. "Didn't Miss Westmacott realize that Shenton was her aunt's son by her first marriage?"

"Not a bit of it. Mrs. Hedderwick led her to believe that the boy had been killed in the War. He and the girl had never met, so when he turned up at the villa as Tony Shenton... you follow?"

Blampignon burst out explosively:

"Yes, yes... this is all very interesting, *mon ami*. But it is really of little account. What I demand to know is—"

"Who murdered Shenton, eh? Well, that's obvious, isn't it?"

"You mean it was Dillon?"

"Of course," nodded Meredith. "Who else?"

"And the motive?" put in Gibaud.

"An exceptionally strong one as you probably realize. Dillon was desperately in love with his wife. Shenton not only came between them and whisked the girl down here to his mother's villa, but got the poor kid into trouble. I mean, of course, this baby that's on the way. Dillon realized that Kitty was infatuated with Shenton, that he was the father of the child. Much as he loathed Shenton, even then, I reckon, Dillon would have done nothing really violent. His one thought was for his wife. If Shenton was prepared to marry Kitty then Dillon was prepared to agree to a divorce. The whole point was that Shenton *refused* to marry the girl. And that, so to speak, put the lid on it. From that moment onward Dillon settled down with malice, aforethought, to plan what might well have been the perfect murder. And if you ask me he all but succeeded in pulling it off."

"But what first made you suspect that Dillon was the wanted man?" asked Blampignon eagerly. "How did you arrive at the *modus operandi* of the murder? What made you first to think, *mon ami*, that the body below the Col de Braus might not be that of Dillon?"

"Whoa! Whoa! One at a time, my dear chap," chuckled Meredith. "Suppose I deal with your last question first. Let me put it this way. If Dillon had been short and dark there would have been no question as to the identity of the body, even if the features were completely unrecognizable. The point is Dillon and Shenton were remarkably alike in their general physical appearance. Both broad, well-built fellows with fair hair and blue eyes. And with facial recognition impossible, there naturally entered in some element of doubt. Don't forget, until Hamel put in his report, there was only one witness who actually saw Dillon go over that precipice—namely his wife. And it struck me at once that the couple *might* have collaborated in Shenton's murder—the girl, of course, having suffered a sudden change of heart after Shenton's refusal to marry her. And that, more or less, explains how I first came to suspect that it might be Shenton's body at the foot of the crag." Meredith paused for a moment to draw frantically at his expiring pipe; then went on: "Now for your first question. Why did I place Dillon at the top of my suspect list? Answer—A—because he had a thumping good motive for the murder. B—because he was the last person to see Shenton alive."

"But how do you know that?"

"This somewhat unexpected and secretive meeting on Thursday night at the Bar St. Raphael," pointed out Meredith. "You see, from the moment Shenton walked out of the place he wasn't seen again until we discovered his corpse under the Col de Braus. Though at the time, of course, we didn't realize it was his body."

"But wait a minute!" sang out Gibaud. "What about M'sieur Picard? He saw him sitting in the parked Vedette later that evening on the corner of the Avenue St. Michel."

"But did he?" asked Meredith bluntly. "Admittedly he claimed there was somebody sitting in the car, but he didn't actually identify that 'somebody' as Shenton. In fact, my dear chap, Picard wasn't even certain that the car *was* occupied."

"*Eh bien*," put in Blampignon, "do you have the answer to this little question yourself?"

"I have it *now*," said Meredith promptly. "As a matter of fact, Picard wasn't deceived. The car *was* occupied and the man sitting inside it *was* Shenton."

"And it was Shenton, of course, who drove down through Monti about 2 a.m. on Friday morning," observed Gibaud.

Meredith winked and said with tantalizing vagueness:

"Was it? I wonder..."

"Oh for heaven's sake, man!" cried Gibaud. "You might—"

"No, no," broke in Blampignon. "Let him tell his story in his own way. Let him amuse himself at our expense, *mon cher* Gibaud. All in good time, no doubt, he will satisfy our curiosity. Allow him to enjoy his little hour of triumph, even if, in my heart, I could choke the life out of him!"

Meredith grinned amiably.

"O.K. O.K. I'll cut the cackle and come to the goose. The *modus operandi,* eh, gentlemen? That's what's got you guessing. Just as it had me guessing until I stumbled on the clue that suddenly clarified the whole mystery. But being an obstinate fellow with a perverse sense of humour, I'm going to leave this tit-bit to last. I'm going to start my reconstruction of the crime with Bill Dillon walking into the Bar St. Raphael about twenty to ten on Thursday night..."

CHAPTER XXIII

CASE CLOSED

I

"Why had he gone there? By chance or by appointment? Well, it's pretty obvious he didn't show up there by chance. I felt certain that he'd gone to meet Shenton for a final showdown about the girl. Either Shenton promised to do the right thing by Kitty or else... you get the set-up?" Meredith turned to Blampignon. "Last night I dropped into the Bar St. Raphael and had a word with the proprietor myself. Gibaud here kindly came along as interpreter. The result was we picked up a very significant clue. Hivert, the proprietor, noticed that when Shenton left the bar with Dillon about ten-thirty he was scarcely able to drag one foot after the other. Dillon, in fact, had to more or less haul the poor devil out to the car. Admittedly Shenton had knocked back a few brandies, but as Hivert pointed out he'd often seen Shenton drink twice as much without really being affected. In Hivert's opinion he had the look of a man, not under the influence of drink, but drugs!"

"Drugs!" exclaimed Blampignon, suddenly stabbing a finger at Meredith. "You say drugs? Then is it not possible, *mon ami...?*"

Meredith laughed.

"Just as I anticipated. You reacted to that observation exactly as we did. Shenton *was* drugged. And it was Dillon who'd slipped what was evidently a pretty potent dose of morphia into his brandy."

"Morphia?" demanded Blampignon. "But how do you know that? Is it that M'sieur Hivert actually see—?"

Meredith shook his head.

"No, it wasn't as simple as that. Hivert hadn't spotted anything suspicious in Dillon's actions. But the moment Gibaud and I suspected Shenton had been drugged, we arranged for an autopsy to be performed on the body in the mortuary. We had the doctor's report about an hour ago. He'd been on the job all night. It was the result of the P.M. that proved our hunch was correct and that the drug employed was morphia."

"*Eh bien!*" said Blampignon with a gesture of impatience. "Please to go on."

"Well, once Dillon had got the fellow into the car—Shenton's car, remember—he drove all out to the corner of the Avenue St. Michel. By that time, I imagine, Shenton had passed out completely. Dillon then returned on foot to the villa and joined Miss Westmacott and his wife in the lounge."

"Time," put in Gibaud helpfully, "ten-forty."

"Precisely," nodded Meredith. "Giving him roughly ten minutes to get from the Bar St. Raphael to the villa. Which, in Gibaud's opinion, is just about what we should expect. After a chat and a drink, Dillon, as we know from the girls' evidence, went up to bed. And shortly after the young women also retired for the night. It was then just after eleven o'clock. And that's more or less all the *definite* information we have concerning Dillon's movements on the night of Thursday-Friday. The rest, I admit, must be in the nature of surmise, though based, of course, on a series of reasonable suppositions. But this, at any rate, is my reconstruction of the events that must have followed on Dillon's retirement to his room." Meredith paused a moment to relight his pipe, cleared his throat, and went on with undiminished energy: "Waiting until all was quiet in the villa, Dillon sneaked downstairs, let himself out of the house and returned to the parked Vedette. From the Avenue St. Michel he drove direct to the foot of the Col de Braus."

"To the place where you discover the body, eh?" asked Blampignon.

"Exactly. To the point where that mule-track joined the road down to Escarene. The Sergeant and I noticed that the track, at any rate as far as we followed it, was quite wide enough to accommodate a car. As I see it, Dillon *backed* the car along the track until he reached a spot directly below the rock-face."

"Shenton still in a drugged sleep, eh?" put in Gibaud, who was hearing for the first time this particular part of Meredith's reconstruction.

The Inspector nodded.

"Well, what followed must have been a pretty grim and ghastly business. Dillon, I imagine, dragged Shenton from the car, stripped off his clothes and redressed him in the bush-shirt and shorts etc., which he'd brought along for this specific purpose. A set of clothes, mark you, that was an exact replica of those he wore himself the following morning. Nor did he forget to strap a rucksack on the poor devil's back—the rucksack, of course, that contained the *scarlet* Thermos-flask. This done, *he deliberately battered the fellow to death, executing the gruesome job in such a way that Shenton's features should be unrecognizable!*"

"*Mon Dieu!*" murmured Blampignon with a shudder.

"Not exactly a bed-time story, eh? But I'm pretty certain that's what happened. A moment ago I suggested Dillon must have *backed* the car along the mule-track. This isn't just guesswork. I was thinking of those bloodstains on the bodywork and running-board of the Vedette. On the side opposite the steering-wheel, remember. That's to say on the right of the car since the Vedette naturally had a left-hand drive. Well, there's no doubt now how those bloodstains came to be there. When Dillon got to work with that blunt instrument the body must have been lying on the ground right beside the car. And that," said Meredith, pausing a moment to mop his brow, "more or less covers the first part of my reconstruction. Any questions, gentlemen?"

"Just one," put in Gibaud promptly.

"And that?"

"What do you say to an *apéritif* and a bit of a breather before you ring in the second half of your report?"

Meredith swung round on Strang and grinned broadly.

"To employ one of the Sergeant's favourite colloquialisms—bang on, m'lad!"

II

"And now, gentlemen," went on Meredith, considerably refreshed by the ten-minute interval, "we come to the brilliant idea that formed the real basis of Dillon's alibi. But before I deal with that we'd better consider the rest of Dillon's movements on that fateful night." He turned to Gibaud. "You asked me a moment ago if the man seen at the wheel of the Vedette as it shot through Monti was Shenton. Of course it wasn't. It was Dillon. The fellow was obviously driving down hell-for-leather off the Col de Braus in the direction of Cap Martin. Time—about two ack emma on Friday morning. At Cap Martin, as we know, he abandoned the Vedette, planted the dead man's black béret out on the rocks as a red-herring, and hoofed it back to the villa. At a rough estimate I should say he arrived there about four a.m."

"One little point, *mon ami*," put in Blampignon. "What of the clothes he remove from the body of Shenton? You think he conceal them somewhere up on the mountain?"

Meredith exchanged a meaning glance with Gibaud.

"As a matter of fact we'd already thought of that one. Gibaud's detailed a couple of fellows to make a thorough search around the spot where we found the body. They're on the job now."

"*Bon!*" ejaculated Blampignon, with a nod of approval. "That is good sense. Please to continue."

"Well, we come now to the Friday morning expedition that Dillon and his wife made up into the mountains. As the young woman told us, he persuaded her to accompany him so that they could have a final discussion about the damnably unhappy situation in which they found themselves. It was absolutely vital to his plans that his wife should agree to the outing. The reason, of course, is clear. He wanted her to witness his 'suicidal' leap over that precipice."

"But why?" demanded Blampignon with a bewildered expression. "Since you find only the body of Shenton, it is evident now that he did *not* throw himself off the crag."

"But he did!" contested Meredith emphatically. "Every detail of the girl's statement was true. He did cross the road, climb the fence and chuck himself over the edge. Don't forget we've got corroborative evidence of this fact."

"Hamel, eh?" said Gibaud. "His identification of that portrait?"

"Exactly. You see where that left me when I discovered, without any shadow of doubt, that it was Shenton's body in the mortuary. Here were two independent witnesses who *saw* Dillon plunge into space off the Col. There should, of course, have been two bodies in the valley below. But there weren't!"

"But *mon Dieu!*" spluttered Blampignon, "how do you explain? A... a... now how do you say?—*un corniche,* perhaps?"

"A ledge," chuckled Meredith. "No—I thought of that. I drove out and carefully examined the rock-face. Smooth as a baby's *derrière,* my dear fellow."

Blampignon threw wide his hands in a gesture of despair.

"*Sacré nom!* Then what is the answer?"

"Remember what I told you about the mystery of the three ruck-sacks? One on Shenton's body containing a scarlet Thermos. One containing the picnic meal put up by the cook at the villa, including the blue Thermos. Later found by the Sergeant stuck away under the driving-seat of Dillon's car. And the third attached to Dillon's back when he went over the crag." Meredith paused and gazed round expectantly at the blank, puzzled faces of his colleagues. "Great Scott, don't you get it now? *That third rucksack contained a parachute!*"

"A parachute!" exclaimed the three men in unison.

Meredith nodded.

"A specially designed short-drop parachute. You see, Dillon had been working on the evolution of this particular type of parachute in his spare time. The Yard forwarded me the information which they'd picked up from the Hawland Aircraft Company, the firm in which Dillon was employed. Aerodynamics—that was his pet line. And what that fellow didn't know about aerodynamics you could write on a pin's head. At least that seemed to be the opinion of his boss in the research department. Dillon had spoken to the chap about his spare-time experiments with short-drop parachutes. He'd evidently thought up an entirely new principle and was hoping to patent it. It was this that first put me on to the *modus operandi* of his alibi—plus the fact that he'd been in the Airborne during the War. No question that his recent jaunts up in the mountains were connected with these experiments. Heaven knows! Dillon's got guts."

"You mean he's been trying out experimental jumps ever since he arrived in Menton?" asked Gibaud.

"Yes—acting as his own guinea-pig. And, if you ask me, the place he finally selected for these tests was the rock-face up on the Col de Braus. That's why he was familiar with the lie of the land. Daresay that is how he came to hit on the amazing idea behind his alibi. Simple, eh? But devilish subtle." Meredith shrugged. "Well, that, gentlemen, more or less covers my reconstruction of the crime. I may be mistaken about some of the details, but I'm certain that—"

There was a knock on the door.

"*Entrez!*" sang out Gibaud.

A constable entered and, crossing to the Inspector's desk, dumped on it a dusty bundle of clothes.

"*Voilà, M'sieur!*"

"Well, I'll be darned!" breathed Meredith. "A perfect piece of timing, eh?" He turned to Gibaud. "Ask him where he found the confounded things."

After a brief catechism in French, Gibaud congratulated the constable, dismissed him and turned back to Meredith.

"Pushed in under a thick clump of scrub near the roadside, about half-way between the mule-track and the Col itself. He says there's a few oddments in the pockets, including a wallet." As the others crowded round the desk, Gibaud examined the clothes in silence— cream silk shirt, American lumber-jacket, fawn worsted trousers, chequered silk socks, white-and-tan shoes. From the hip pocket of the trousers he pulled out the wallet and extracted from it a thick wad of notes, several visiting-cards and an international driving-licence. "Well," he announced, holding up the licence and pointing to the attached photo of the dead man, "this settles the question of identification. They're Shenton's clothes right enough."

"Here, wait a minute!" snapped Meredith, making a grab at the notes. "Let's take a dekko at—" A smile spread over his aquiline features—a smile that broadened to a grin, and finally resolved itself into a prolonged and unchecked roar of laughter. "Well, of all the...!" he spluttered. "What do you know about that? I reckon M'sieur Hivert of the Bar St. Raphael's all set for a pretty nasty jolt."

"What do you mean, *mon ami?*" asked Blampignon.

Meredith held up the notes and flicked through them with a forefinger.

"These notes, gentlemen. All guaranteed original works of the master! Perfect examples of Cobbett's later period! Any bids, gentlemen?"

CHAPTER XIV

AU REVOIR

I

"Well," said Freddy with a melancholic sigh, "I suppose this is it! No good kicking against the pricks. It's been fun while it lasted. We're off tomorrow as soon as it's light."

He and Dilys, cosily intertwined, were leaning over the terrace of Le Rocher de Monaco gazing out across the placid waters of the harbour towards the lights of Monte Carlo.

Dilys asked with a faint hint of apprehension:

"But surely you'll... you'll be glad to get home again?"

"What!... to Willesden, N.W.2? After this?" He gestured toward the insubstantial fairyland that seemed to be suspended between sea and sky like some spangled and impossibly romantic backcloth. "Have a heart, darling!" Freddy sighed again. "I suppose you realize you've just about knocked me for a six? I came down here a carefree, uncomplicated sort of chap. And now look at me! Befogged, bewitched and bewildered. You've got a heck of a lot to answer for, Miss Westmacott."

"I'm sorry."

"Well, you don't look it!" snorted Freddy, gazing down at her upturned face with an expression of agonized approval.

"Really? Then how *do* I look?"

"Unbelievable," breathed Freddy. "Out-of-this-world."

Dilys laughed.

"A week from now you'll remember saying that and blush to the roots of your hair."

"A week from now," contested Freddy, "I shall be sitting in my lonely bachelor room writing you a ten-page letter."

Her hand tightened over his. She demanded earnestly:

"You *will* write, won't you?"

"Every dreary day until we meet again. Though heaven alone knows," he added glumly, "when that will be."

"Why not when I come to London?"

"What!" whooped Freddy, twisting her round and almost whirling her off her feet. "You're coming to London? Why the deuce didn't you tell me? Why? When? How long for?"

"Well, I don't know exactly. But Aunt Nesta wants to let the villa for at least six months. We'll probably be coming over to England in a few weeks. You can imagine how dreadful she feels about poor Tony."

Freddy nodded and went on in more sober tones:

"Yes—a rotten show. I didn't mean to talk about all this—but now that it's cropped up... well, I may as well tell you."

"What?"

"They arrested that poor devil Dillon this morning at the Gare du Nord in Paris. I suppose he was trying to edge his way back across the Channel. You know, darling, I can't help feeling sorry for the fellow. Take it all round he's had a pretty raw deal. More sinned against than sinning, eh?"

"And now..." asked Dilys unhappily, "now that they *have* arrested him...?"

Freddy shrugged.

"Difficult to say. Heaven knows he had plenty of provocation for what he did. It's what they call a *crime passionel* over here, isn't it? So perhaps they won't hand out too stiff a sentence." For the third time Freddy sighed. "Funny how some blokes get all the hard knocks, whilst others..." He broke off and slowly shook his head. "No—maybe I'm being a bit too optimistic."

"Over what?"

"You, darling. You see, when you come to London..."

"Well?"

"Well, I was wondering if we could sort of... well, knock around together—see the sights, do a few shows and all that."

"But why not? I'd get lost in London on my own."

"Yes, but I mean... er... officially. You see, I was wondering if you and I..." Freddy gulped, took a firm grip on himself and blurted out: "Good heavens, darling, you know I'm absolutely crazy about you! Do you think we could make a go of it? Do you? I mean, sort of... er... together."

"Is this a proposal of marriage? It sounds ominously like it."

"Well, it *is*... actually," mumbled Freddy with a hangdog look.

"I rather thought it was," murmured Dilys.

"And your... er... reaction to the idea?"

She threw him a provocative, sidelong glance.

"As a detective I must naturally leave you to find that out for yourself."

"Find out? How?"

"By exercising your well-trained powers of observation and deduction."

Freddy took a single, infatuated look at her smiling, upturned face and scooped her unceremoniously into his arms.

"O.K.," he murmured. "O.K.! Good enough, my girl. Case closed!"

ALSO AVAILABLE

Murder of a Lady
A Scottish Crime Story

Duchlan Castle is a gloomy, forbidding place in the Scottish Highlands. Late one night the body of Mary Gregor, sister of the laird of Duchlan, is found in the castle. She has been stabbed to death in her bedroom – but the room is locked from within and the windows are barred. The only tiny clue to the culprit is a silver fish's scale, left on the floor next to Mary's body.

Inspector Dundas is dispatched to Duchlan to investigate the case. The Gregor family and their servants are quick – perhaps too quick – to explain that Mary was a kind and charitable woman. Dundas uncovers a more complex truth, and the cruel character of the dead woman continues to pervade the house after her death. Soon further deaths, equally impossible, occur, and the atmosphere grows ever darker. Superstitious locals believe that fish creatures from the nearby waters are responsible; but luckily for Inspector Dundas, the gifted amateur sleuth Eustace Hailey is on the scene, and unravels a more logical solution to this most fiendish of plots.

Anthony Wynne wrote some of the best locked-room mysteries from the golden age of British crime fiction. This cunningly plotted novel – one of Wynne's finest – has never been reprinted since 1931, and is long overdue for rediscovery.

ANTHONY WYNNE is a pseudonym of Robert McNair-Wilson (1882–1963), who wrote twenty-seven detective novels featuring Eustace Hailey, a physician and amateur sleuth. He also published on economics and history, notably a biography of Napoleon.